AN **AMERICAN GHOST** THRILLER

RECKONING

J. B. TURNER

AN **AMERICAN GHOST** THRILLER

RECKONING

THOMAS & MERCER

Text copyright © 2018 by J. B. Turner
All rights reserved.

Published by Thomas & Mercer, Seattle

www.apub.com

Amazon, the Amazon logo, and Thomas & Mercer are trademarks of Amazon.com, Inc., or its affiliates.

ISBN-13: 9781503947979
ISBN-10: 1503947971

Cover design by @blacksheep-uk.com

Printed in the United States of America

For my late father

One

The Florida sky had begun to darken.

Nathan Stone was sitting on the balcony of his fleabag motel, dragging hard on a cigarette. He kept the military-grade binoculars trained on the relaxation area of the psychiatric hospital in the distance. The last remnants of the morning sun glinted off the razor wire that topped the chain-link fence as storm clouds rolled in from the Everglades.

Nathan scanned the area again. He still couldn't see his sister. She was usually seated on one of the benches, her art materials spread out. But today her usual place was empty.

Nathan checked his watch. It was 1009 hours. She was now nine minutes late. It wasn't like her. She loved her time outside.

He put down the binoculars on the small table and crushed his cigarette in the ashtray.

Nathan yawned. He had just returned to the motel room after a short vacation in the Keys.

It had felt good to kick back. Fishing out in Florida Bay, drinking a beer, enjoying the bloodred sunsets. Hauling in the marlin. Building campfires on beaches. The silence. The stillness. The solitude. The smell of the fresh salty air on his face as his boat sped through the waves. He was free again. The tension had begun to lift. He had even managed to spend a couple days down in Cudjoe Key. Shades on all the time, baseball cap pulled low.

The sound of rattling from the faulty air-conditioning unit in his room snapped him out of his reverie.

Nathan knew the motel room was crummy. It had, however, served a crucial purpose. It had been his hideaway since he had returned to the States six weeks earlier using a fake ID and passport. The motel's location meant he was close to his sister. And the fake ID meant he wouldn't be found.

Nathan knew they would be after him. The operation in Scotland had gone south big-time. What had started off as a straightforward hit on a senator had turned into a full-blown shitstorm where he had become the hunted rather than the hunter. He learned that the shadowy organization that hired him, the Commission, had compiled a kill list of leading politicians and business people they deemed to be working against America's national interest. And he had passed that list on to a leading journalist, Mark Mahoney, at the *New York Times*. But he had no idea what had come of that information. He hadn't kept a copy of the list. He'd just passed on the encrypted details.

Nathan's thoughts again returned to his sister's whereabouts. A sense of foreboding washed over him. Had something happened to her? Had she been moved while he was away? It was possible, he supposed. The thought alarmed him. He loved his sister. She was all he had. His mind flashed back to his childhood. When they were growing up on the Bowery, on the Lower East Side, their alcoholic father had beaten them till they were black and blue. That was until his sister stabbed him to death.

Nathan was still haunted by his death. Even after all these years: the look in his father's eyes as she plunged the scissors in time and time again.

But Helen had saved him. He owed her. She had been incarcerated in the psychiatric hospital for decades. He made sure she got moved to the state-of-the-art facility in Florida City, on the outskirts of Homestead.

He could rest easy knowing she was in a safe, nurturing environment, unlike the hell they'd endured as kids.

The minutes dragged, and still no sign of Helen. "Fuck," he said.

It was perfectly possible his sister had just been transferred. But he knew any change wasn't good for her.

She liked certainty. Routine. The same private room. The same sense of familiar surroundings. The same smells. The same sounds from the games room. But most of all, her room. Her space. Her sanctuary.

His cell phone rang, jolting Nathan out of his contemplation. "Yeah."

He was met with silence. But he could sense someone on the other end. Eventually, a familiar voice spoke. "It's been quite some time. We've been watching you."

They'd found him. The people he'd done *wet* jobs for. And then he'd turned on them. Somehow they'd found him. Not good.

"We're watching you now, Nathan. That *is* your real name, isn't it, Nathan?"

Nathan picked up the binoculars again and looked over toward the hospital. Where exactly were they watching him from?

"Does that surprise you? You see, we could delete you anytime we want, Nathan. You know that, don't you?"

Nathan said nothing.

"I'm going to be frank, Nathan. I like you. Always have. Admire you even. And your work. But you've got to look at things from our side. Have you considered the cost of the loss of that carefully constructed facility in Scotland you burned to the ground? Do you know the cost of giving you a new face? A new identity? I'll give you a clue . . . millions. Tens of millions. A lot of money, right? That's a big investment. And the money men want their pound of flesh."

Nathan stared through the binoculars at the sun-scorched yard.

The man sighed. "You're not saying much, Nathan. Why is that, I wonder?"

"Where's my sister?"

"Ah . . . I was wondering when you were going to ask about that. Yeah, your sister. Very trusting. Very sweet."

"What do you want?"

A long sigh. "What do I want? I want a lot of things, Nathan. I want us to get back to the way things were before. Before everything got so fucked up."

"You don't know anything about me. You don't know what happened."

"That's where you're wrong. I know what happened. And I know you thought we double-crossed you."

"You sent out a team to kill me."

"But they never—"

"Only because I killed them first."

"I think we need to build up some trust, don't you?"

"What trust?"

"Well, I know where your sister is. And I know where she's being held. And I give you my word she won't be harmed . . . That is unless . . ." The man let the words hang in the air.

"Unless what?"

"Unless you don't do exactly what we ask you to do."

Nathan felt his stomach tighten. They had all the cards.

"So now we've established some ground rules, I think we're making progress already, don't you?"

"Go to hell!"

"Not yet. Plenty of time for that. Nathan, you know what we can do. We know where you live. We know what you are. We know you kill people."

"You wanna get to the point?"

"This is how it's going to work. You need to get on the expressway and drive to Miami Homestead airport, nice and close. Four miles northwest of downtown Homestead."

"Why?"

"Love that curiosity, Nathan. Why? You'll see."

Two

The Gulfstream's engine was turning as Nathan climbed the steps, shirt sticking to his back. He boarded the plane. The cool air of the cabin was a welcome relief. He was shown to a leather seat by the rear left window. A stewardess handed him a bottle of Evian water and some sandwiches. He strapped himself in, and the plane took off into the pale-blue sky. Down below, the lush expanse of the Everglades stretched out as far as the eye could see.

The plane climbed high through the storm clouds over Florida until they were at cruising speed. He wondered what the hell awaited him. Where exactly were they taking him?

His thoughts turned to his sister. He felt sick that she was at someone else's mercy. She needed him. And he wasn't there for her.

Nathan's mind raced ahead, imagining the worst possible scenarios for his sister. She was gentle and kind, despite her one act of extreme violence as a frightened child. She'd pay the price for that psychotic episode for the rest of her natural life.

He thought of his own situation. The one crumb of comfort was that if they wanted him dead, they could easily have him killed. So they obviously needed him. But for what exactly?

He didn't have to wait long to find out.

Twenty minutes after takeoff, the phone on his armrest rang.

"Are we comfortable, Nathan?" The voice of the same man.

"Why are you doing this?"

"I thought I made myself clear."

Nathan said nothing.

"Payback. Pure and simple. You destroyed all our work, so now you owe us. And what better way to pay back that significant debt than to come work for us? At least for a time."

"What do you want?"

"You're going to do a job. And everyone's gonna be happy."

"What about my sister? How do I know she's still alive?"

"You don't."

Nathan said nothing.

"You've got to trust us. Do you understand?"

"I need to know Helen's still alive."

"You will."

Nathan stared at the bottle of water and the sandwich.

"See, we're not so bad."

The guy was obviously watching him from a remote location via onboard surveillance cameras. In real time.

"We've always liked you, Stone. Even after you underwent that major surgery and came back a different person. No one knows you like we do. We know what triggers you. We know what infuriates you. And sure, we know this whole thing will be maddening to you, but you have to look at it from our point of view."

"And what exactly is your point of view?"

"You went rogue in Scotland. Killed several highly valued operatives. People who understood the meaning of sacrifice. But you decided to wipe them all out. Destroy all their work."

Nathan sighed.

"That's not how it fucking works. But you know that, don't you? You know the rules of this game. This business we're in. You kill people as and when required. And I respect that. But we all work within set rules. We have to, don't we?"

Nathan closed his eyes for a few moments.

"Relax. I appreciate this must be a lot to take in."

"Where are we headed?"

Silence.

"I said, Where are we headed?"

"I heard you, Stone."

"Is it somewhere on American soil?"

"Maybe."

Nathan didn't respond to the man teasing him.

"You've shown us how devastating you can be, Nathan. And you've got me to thank for saving your life. You owe me."

"I don't owe you anything."

"But that's where you're wrong, Nathan. I spoke up for you when some other people—people who run the show—wanted you neutralized for what you did in Scotland. They haven't forgotten. And they sure as hell haven't forgiven. But I persuaded them to give you one last chance. I said, 'Stone is the best there is. And we'd be idiots to throw him to the wolves, and for what?' I told them, 'Stone can do a job for us. He's useful.'"

Nathan cleared his throat. "Are you finished?"

"Yes, I am. Take it easy, Stone. Eat up. And try and get some sleep. We'll speak again in a few hours."

Three

Mark Mahoney looked up from his laptop. He stared out the window and across the downtown Toronto skyline, far from home. He was working out of the *New York Times*'s Canadian bureau. He loved his job. But he sorely missed his family and Manhattan. He longed to see them. It was months since he'd been home.

He missed his apartment in Chelsea. He missed the walks in Central Park. The High Line. He missed the energy. He missed everything about his hometown.

Mahoney had been in Canada for nearly three months, working on a secret investigation known only to the paper's editor and the publisher. Even the journalists in the Toronto bureau didn't know what he was investigating. They'd been told he just wanted a change of scene. He enjoyed Toronto. It was a nice city. But it wasn't home. He missed the familiarity of New York like crazy. He missed Bryant Park. He missed Mets games. He missed drinks with colleagues after work. He missed going to concerts at Madison Square Garden. He missed the Village. And the general craziness and unexpectedness of Manhattan.

The one saving grace was that his investigation was making progress. He'd made a few crucial contacts in Canada. It was taking time. It was a slow-burn job, the kind the *Times* did so well. Getting underneath a story. Peeling back the layers to reveal something else. Something more important.

His cell phone rang, interrupting his thoughts.

Mahoney picked up. "Yeah."

"Is this Mark Mahoney, of the *New York Times?*"

"Yes, who's this?"

"I was given your number, Mr. Mahoney."

Mahoney leaned back in his seat. He wondered if it was a new source for the story he was working on. "Call me Mark."

"Very well, Mark."

"So how can I help?"

"A friend of mine spoke to me about a week ago, told me you were asking a few questions."

Mahoney nodded. "Can you be a little bit more specific?"

A beat. "He works for the Canadian Security Intelligence Service."

Mahoney sat up and scribbled the words down in shorthand. "Sir, I know and speak regularly to numerous sources across North America and Europe. What do you want to discuss?"

"I work for the same organization. And I believe I might have something you were asking about."

Mahoney sensed the guy wanted to open up. "Can you be more specific?"

A silence stretched between them for a few moments. "My job covers foreign intelligence and security intelligence. More and more of my time is taken up with security intelligence."

"So we're talking potential terrorism and espionage going on within Canada."

"Correct. But what I think might interest you covers both these areas of responsibility."

"That's interesting."

"I think so."

"Would you be willing to meet with me?"

A beat. "That shouldn't be a problem."
"When and where?"
"Let's take this one step at a time."
"When and where?"
"Within the next forty-eight hours."
The line went dead.

Four

Nathan was blindfolded just before the Gulfstream landed. When he was finally told to remove it, he looked out and saw a small airstrip in the middle of what looked like a forest.

Nathan stepped down off the plane, breathed in the cold air. He was met by two guys dressed in thick coats, jeans, and sneakers. Then he was shown inside a modern facility, where his fingerprints were taken and retina scanned and photographed, side, front, and rear.

He was shown down to a basement area, down a corridor, and through some secure doors. Then he was shown into a huge room with a desk and a chair.

The door was shut behind him.

Nathan slumped in the seat and put his feet on the table.

The familiar voice spoke through speakers in the ceiling: "Nice to see you're making yourself at home, Nathan."

Nathan shifted in his seat.

"You must be wondering what this is all about, right?"

"It had crossed my mind."

The lights went out and a photograph of a man appeared on the wall. "You know this guy?"

Nathan stared at the image. He knew who it was alright. "I believe he's a journalist."

"Can you identify him by name?"

"Mark Mahoney."

"That's right. Mark Mahoney. A *New York Times* investigative reporter hotshot. He was embedded with you guys when you were in Iraq, I believe."

"That's going way back, but yeah, that's right."

"Nice man by all accounts. Highly thought of at the *Times*. Nothing flashy. Does his job. Does it right. Does it good. He's very, very thorough. Uses numerous sources to copperbottom a story."

Nathan stared at the photo long and hard.

"This is also the man to whom you sent sensitive information about the operation you were involved in, to kill Senator Brad Crichton, isn't it?"

Nathan said nothing.

"And this resulted, not surprisingly, in setting this guy to work. He's been very busy since our facility in Scotland was compromised and destroyed. Recently, we've been hearing stories about Mr. Mahoney. And he's been getting around. Paid a visit to the Outer Hebrides. He was seen with a *Times* photographer near the ruins of the facility. And they've been asking a lot of questions. We have it on good authority that Mark Mahoney is close, maybe a week away, from taking his story to the editor, who's been kept abreast of developments. He's taking a keen interest."

"Do you want to get to the point?"

The man sighed. "Let's establish where we are. You sent this journalist documents about the assassination, about how you didn't really die a few years back on a mission, and that you had a new identity and a new look. Do you accept that?"

Nathan nodded. "Yes, I do."

"Thank you. You did it out of anger. And we understand that. So you're going to have to put this right. Look in the desk drawer."

Nathan took his feet off the desk and opened the drawer. Inside was a buff-colored file marked *Highly Classified*. He opened it up and saw pictures of Mahoney and details of his life: blood group, interests, friends, and family. "Very comprehensive."

"It's a start. Study this. Learn about his haunts. His habits. His friends. You're going to get into his life. Find out his routines."

"And then?"

"Then . . . you're going to figure out the best way to kill him."

Five

Five security personnel escorted Nathan back to the plane. Once he was safely in his seat, he was blindfolded again before the plane took off. He was thinking ahead to the operation. The instructions. A lot of preparations had gone into this. Identifying the target. Taking his sister.

A short while later, once they were clear of the facility, the plane still climbing, he was allowed to take off the blindfold.

In no time at all, the plane was descending.

The Toronto skyline loomed in the distance. The plane landed at the city's island airport, not far from downtown. He disembarked and headed through a pedestrian tunnel, where a car was waiting for him.

It was a short drive to a duplex apartment in downtown Toronto.

Nathan looked around his "base," as the man had described it. Bright, airy, with pale-orange sunlight glinting through the floor-to-ceiling glass and stunning views of the city's skyscrapers.

He locked the door, checked out every room. Inside the freestanding closets were new clothes his size: shoes, accessories, you name it.

Nathan went into the bathroom and splashed cold water on his face. He stared at his new face, puffier with the filler, Botox around the forehead. Younger, stranger, eyes still cold. The same expression his father had. He had changed from a frightened boy to a man with a dead look in his eyes.

His thoughts turned to his sister. Where had they taken her? How had they gotten access to her? Was it an inside job at the psychiatric hospital? Was she at the same secret facility he'd been taken to in the middle of nowhere?

The questions wouldn't go away. Why hadn't he seen this coming? What was the endgame? Were they really going to leave his sister alone if he killed Mark Mahoney? Was that really plausible? And if not, what the fuck was he going to do?

More and more doubts began to encroach on his thoughts.

He wondered if the apartment was bugged. Were they watching him now? He was struggling to contain his anger. He felt sick at the thought of Helen being taken out of her comfort zone, being used as a pawn. But as it was, Nathan would have to go along with this hit. He had no choice. He was at their mercy. As was his sister. He would have to do as they said. It was a grave situation, but it was the only way.

Nathan realized he needed to keep up a front. He couldn't let them know the true anguish that was devouring him. They might imagine what he was feeling. But he wouldn't show it. Ever.

Instead, he needed to focus on the task at hand and deal with things like getting his sister back later, as the situation became clearer.

He sat down and began to read the file on Mahoney.

It soon became clear that this guy had been born with a silver spoon in his mouth. An impressive career had followed. New England prep schools followed by the Ivy League, graduate entry-level job at the *New York Times*, and then he began to make a name for himself. Year after year, he was knocking it out of the park. Black Lives Matter, police corruption, Wall Street corruption. Then he moved on to bigger issues. Geopolitical in nature. He exposed corrupt politicians. Senators who took kickbacks from union bosses, Republican congressmen with links to the military-industrial-complex arms industry—on and on, solid stuff.

Nathan immersed himself in the file for another hour until his cell phone rang. "Yeah?"

"Settling in, Nathan?"

"Yeah, yeah, it's great. Listen, if we're going to do this, I think we've got to establish some trust."

"I couldn't agree more. So . . . what are you thinking?"

"I need to know my sister is alive."

"I can categorically assure you, Nathan, your sister is alive. I was just talking to her fifteen minutes ago. She's fine."

"I want to speak to her."

There was a pause. "We can do that. I'll put her on now."

"I appreciate that."

"Hey, Nathan!"

The sweet voice of his sister overwhelmed him. Nathan closed his eyes—it was such a relief to hear her again. "Helen, just a superquick call. How are you being treated?"

"Your friends are great. So, so friendly."

"That's good to hear."

"Nathan, when will I see you again?"

Nathan sighed. "I'm kinda busy. But real soon. I just wanted to make sure you're safe and doing well. So everything's good for you?"

"They're real nice. They said you'd asked them to look after me for a while . . . I liked where I was, Nathan."

"I know you did. That's good to know. And I'm sure we can get you back in good time."

A few moments later, the man came back on the line. "She says we're lovely. And we are. But Nathan, make no mistake, that will change if you don't make this right."

Six

Nathan was wearing flesh-colored surgical gloves as he watched through binoculars from the back of the Dodge Charger. He saw Mark Mahoney leave his apartment and felt a jolt of adrenaline run through his body. The journalist was speaking into his cell phone as he headed down the street, oblivious to Nathan's presence nearby. Mahoney walked straight past his metallic-blue Audi A3 with New York license plates, parked twenty yards down the road.

Nathan began to consider suitable options. He wondered if Mahoney could be killed in a car accident. He had been taught the Boston Brakes method. The method of assassination relied on a microchip transceiver being inserted into a car's onboard computer, which then took over the steering and brakes. The result would be a high-speed car crash, the driver unable to control his car as it careered into oncoming traffic. Maybe a house. Then again, maybe when Mahoney was walking to work Nathan could hack another vehicle, which would plow into the journalist on a sidewalk, again at high speed. The beauty of such fatal "accidents" was that they would be blamed on the innocent driver or a technical malfunction.

The more Nathan thought of it, the more he liked the sound of such an accident. It needed serious consideration. Would that be the best way to kill Mahoney? The journalist lived alone in the rental apartment. So, theoretically, no one else would be driving the car. He could take the car while Mahoney was at work, carry out the modifications, and then return it as if it hadn't moved all day.

Nathan's mind was racing as his thoughts turned to another scenario. What if Mahoney was stabbed with a syringe or modified umbrella containing a paralyzing anesthetic agent? In the middle of a crowded downtown Toronto street. Maybe that would be a better option. Mahoney wouldn't know what had happened. But within a few seconds he would collapse to the ground, unable to breathe, clutching his chest, having a massive heart attack.

It was a classic hit technique: suxamethonium chloride. It was colloquially known as sux, a paralyzing agent that brought on a heart attack. It ordinarily left no trace during a routine autopsy. Only a highly experienced medical examiner testing the brain through toxicology procedures could determine if there was a trace of the drug. The drug was used in hospitals all over the world for operations.

Nathan would need to wear a disguise. But that wasn't a problem. He knew the drug was a tried and tested way of assassinating people. Passersby would think the guy writhing on the ground turning red in the face was just having a massive heart attack. And he would be.

A medical examiner would do an autopsy, cutting open the chest, examining the heart. They would find nothing amiss. No one would be any the wiser.

A few minutes later, a voice in his earpiece. "The subject has arrived at his workplace. Do you copy that?"

"Yeah, got it."

Nathan waited a few moments before he got out of the vehicle. He pulled on a backpack and headed over to the tower. He knew the security cameras had already been remotely deactivated. It was apartment 624. He rode the elevator to the top floor and punched in the code, 0911. Then he opened the apartment's front door and headed in, quietly locking the door behind him.

He took off the backpack, unzipped a side pocket, and took out a screwdriver. He reached up and unscrewed the smoke alarm above him, replacing it with an identical model with a hidden camera and microphone inside. He did the same with the carbon monoxide detector in the bedroom.

Nathan tested both alarms, which emitted piercing sounds for a few seconds. He clicked on a phone app. It showed real-time footage from inside the apartment. Then he replaced a room-freshener plug in the living room with one that contained another hidden camera and microphone.

He did a few more checks as he looked around the apartment. He knew Mahoney's cell phone was already bugged.

Fifteen minutes later, he let himself out, backpack over his shoulder, and locked the door. He headed down to the Audi outside. He kneeled down as if tying his laces and reached under the car, attaching a tiny magnetic GPS tracking device.

Nathan stood up, brushed himself down, and got back in the Charger and pulled away.

It was nearly dark when Nathan finally finished rereading Mahoney's file. Time had dragged throughout the day; he was preoccupied with his sister. But he knew he didn't have the luxury of wallowing in self-pity. He needed to focus.

Over the next hour, Nathan watched remotely from his own apartment as Mahoney returned home. His experience told him it was good to get in close to see the true picture. Besides, what if Mahoney left his home suddenly? What then? But the downside was that getting too close brought its own risks.

The setting sun was glistening off the top floors of the downtown glass tower as he hunkered down in the surveillance space in the back. He put the wireless Bose headphones on and switched on the laptop showing the journalist sitting back on his sofa, calling his wife in New York.

Nathan sat in silence and listened to the conversation. He detected a tension in the wife's voice. She wondered when he was going to return to Manhattan. But Mahoney reassured her he was making real progress. He hoped the investigation would firm up the story in the next couple of weeks and was planning to be back home in time for his youngest daughter's birthday.

The sound of his cell phone ringing made Mahoney end the call early. Then he answered his cell.

Nathan watched and listened as the new conversation began.

The caller sounded Canadian. *Sorry I haven't managed to get that message to you. I've been busy. Will contact you with details in the next twenty-four hours.*

Nathan reflected on the quick exchange. He called his handler, a man he'd worked with in the past, and relayed the information. "So what do you think?" he said.

The handler drawled, "So you're back in the saddle, bro?"

"Something like that. What now?"

"Do you think the next contact will be by landline or cell phone?"

"Not sure." Nathan pondered that for a few moments. "If it was me, I'd be doing a dead drop. Or maybe getting someone to drop a letter through his door."

The handler went quiet.

"Yeah, that's how I'd do it," Nathan said. "Have we got the outside of the apartment covered?"

"Yeah, we already have a device fitted in the stairwell lights."

"So we should have sight of whoever visits, if that's how they play it," Nathan said.

"Exactly. Stone, while we're talking, I've been told you're required to see the operation's psychologist."

21

Nathan reflected that it was the same setup they'd had for him in Scotland. He'd been monitored and analyzed to ensure he was up to the task.

"Look, they just want to check how you're doing. That kind of thing. You OK with that?"

"My sister's been kidnapped. How do you think I'm doing?"

"Sure. But—well, you're required to see the psychologist anyway."

"Where?"

"I'll message the address."

"Do I know him?"

"Oh yeah, you know him."

Seven

The first tinge of a tangerine dawn peeked over the horizon as Dr. Mark Berenger pulled up at the remote house, fifteen miles from downtown Toronto.

He picked up his briefcase and walked up to the front door, cameras watching his every move. He pressed his thumb against the scanner and the door clicked open. As he pushed it open and went inside, the door shut automatically behind him. Inside was an inner door with another scanner. He pressed his face close and stood still as the retina scanner processed his details. The door clicked open. He headed up a flight of stairs till he got to his office, on the first floor.

Berenger took off his coat and hung it up. He sat down, turned on his laptop, and scanned his emails. Nothing important. He took his notes from the briefcase. He felt his stomach tighten as he thought of the meeting coming up. Face-to-face with a man he'd spoken to before. A man he knew very well. A man who fascinated him. A man who unnerved him at the mere mention of his name. He hadn't shared his deepest, darkest thoughts and fears with those who employed him. They would have thought him weak. Soft. So he decided to move forward, ignoring the disturbing thoughts inside his mind.

Berenger leaned back in his seat and reflected on Nathan's profile.

He'd seen numerous Special Forces soldiers over the years. But there was something about Nathan that intrigued him. It might have been Nathan's advanced technical killer skills, aligned with his surgically changed face, before he was resurrected by a private company loosely aligned to elements within the CIA. Some might dub it the "deep state," and there was more than a grain of truth to that.

Berenger knew Nathan had an interesting skill set. The assassin's forte was patience. He took it slow. He was methodical. There was an attention to detail. Nathan was never put off by difficult hits. If the target was to be deleted, Nathan would rather assess and evaluate the target, take his time. Monitor the target's movements and home environment, and listen in on their conversations as he built the big picture before deciding how the target was to be killed. But perhaps more than anything, Nathan adapted to changes in circumstances. He wasn't fazed.

Berenger hadn't seen Nathan for a while. He stifled a yawn, not having slept well the previous night in anticipation.

The buzzer downstairs rang just after 8 a.m., snapping him out of his musings.

Nathan had arrived. Berenger got up from his seat and checked the video intercom to allow him in. He saw the familiar shape of the reworked face. Eyes deeper set. He buzzed him up.

Once again he was going to get acquainted with the deeply fascinating Nathan Stone.

A couple of knocks at the door.

"Yes, come in."

The door opened, and Stone sauntered in. He looked around the room as if looking for cameras. "Nice place you've got here, Doc."

Berenger smiled and sat back down. "Been in worse, trust me."

Nathan went over to the window and stared out toward Toronto in the far distance. "What's the purpose of this little chat?"

"We think it's important we evaluate how you're feeling."

Stone turned around and looked at him. "Do you know about my sister?"

"It was brought to my attention, yes."

"How do you feel about that, Doc?"

"How do I feel about that? I don't have any views on that, Nathan."

"Really?"

"I'm here to talk to you. To see if you're going to proceed with the mission."

Nathan pulled up a seat and put his feet on the desk. "You're going to analyze what exactly it means when I put my feet here?"

Berenger stared back at Stone. "If you wish."

"So what does it mean, Doc?"

Berenger felt his throat tighten as the tension rose. "I'm thinking it probably means you're annoyed, wanting to dominate the territory, right?"

"You don't have any fucking idea, do you? So, since you've got me here, what are your views on whether my sister should have been kidnapped from the hospital in Florida?"

Berenger took a few moments to contemplate before he answered. He felt himself breathing quicker. "I don't believe she was kidnapped. I believe she went voluntarily with a specially selected team."

"Is that what they told you? How did they get her out?"

"No idea. Nathan, you need to start to focus. Because if you don't focus, you and your sister will be in real danger."

"I gathered that, Doc," Nathan said. "But thanks for reminding me."

"It's not up to me how other elements of the operation unfold, but we are where we are. I'm not responsible for what happened to your sister, am I?"

"I don't know, are you?"

Berenger forced a smile. "You know as well as I do this has nothing to do with me. I've been brought in to do a job. My job is to focus on the challenges you're facing and determine if you're ready. Because if you're not ready, Nathan, you'll be killed, as will your sister, at a time and place not of your choosing. Am I making myself clear?"

Stone went quiet.

"So it's in your interests to push aside those feelings about your sister and convince us you have this under control."

Stone remained silent.

"OK, I'll kick things off. And I'll start from when things went seriously wrong, just after our last encounter. We need to understand what you were thinking."

Nathan's gaze wandered around the room.

"When things went south at the facility in Scotland after you killed the senator, why did you return to the facility and do what you did?"

"Retribution."

"Retribution for what?"

"Don't be a smart-ass. You know what. The shadow operation. They double-crossed me after the senator's girlfriend decided to push me off a ledge up a goddamn mountain, that's what."

Berenger wrote down the salient points. "Tell me more about this shadow operation in Scotland, as you allege."

"They sent a team of operatives. And they were good. But they were so focused on killing the senator's girlfriend, they forgot I was back in the game. And they'd clearly been tasked to kill me too."

Berenger nodded as he allowed some space for Nathan to open up.

"Am I making myself clear, Doc?"

Berenger sighed. "I detect some palpable anger."

Stone stared at him.

"Do you want to end this current operation, Nathan? Because if you do, you need to say so, and there will be consequences for your sister."

"I know how this shit works. I know it all too well."

"So do you wish to proceed with the operation?"

"Yes, affirmative."

Berenger nodded and scribbled a few points about Stone's abrasive and combative attitude. He thought Nathan's belligerence was a major plus ahead of any operation. He was wired. Wound up so tight he was ready to go off. "Are you sleeping?"

"Two hours a night. Usually enough."

"That's not enough for most people, Nathan."

"I'm not most people."

"No, Nathan . . . No, you're not."

"I'm far from most people. So if I say two hours is enough, trust me, it's enough."

"How do you like Canada? Does it suit you?"

"I could just as well be in Belize. Makes no difference."

"Nathan, you talked about your sister. And I appreciate this is a very tough situation you've been put in. But what outcome are you looking for when this is all over?"

"I want her to be returned unharmed, safe, and happy back to the facility in Florida."

"What if that request isn't met?"

"Then I guess you'll just have to wait and see what happens."

Berenger shifted in his seat. "What exactly do you mean by that?"

"What I said. You'll just have to wait and see what happens."

Berenger sighed. "I detect a sense—correct me if I'm wrong—that you are saying to those who have your sister that if your demands for her aren't met, there might be some retribution. Would that be a fair assessment?"

"Not really. I said what I said. Think what you want about that. But the least—the absolute least—I expect when this is over is that my sister is unharmed, happy, and back in her hospital in Florida."

"Well, that's good to know. I'm assured that if the mission is completed as required, what you've indicated is exactly what will happen."

"The problem is," Nathan said, "how can I ever guarantee that *they* won't just do this all over again whenever they want me to do a job?"

"I'm assured that this is a one-off scenario."

"Why should I trust them?"

"I believe they're men of their word. And I accept that. The question is, do you?"

Stone nodded. "I guess I'll have to."

"That's good," Berenger said. "That's progress."

"What else do you need to know?"

"You were the one who sent encrypted details to Mahoney. Do you accept that?"

"Sure."

Berenger put down his pen and leaned back in his seat. "And I believe he was with you, embedded in your unit in Iraq."

"Correct again."

"So you've been around him at close quarters. And you trusted him enough to want to send him details of the highly classified operation in Scotland."

Stone stared at him. He didn't answer.

"So how do you feel about neutralizing Mark Mahoney here in Canada? A guy you've been in the trenches with."

"It is what it is."

Berenger nodded. "Do you feel guilt? Remorse that you're having to do this to someone you know?"

"I feel nothing for him."

"Nothing at all?"

"You know me better than anyone else, Doc. If I'm required to kill someone, that can be done. For example, I might be asked to kill you."

Berenger felt his stomach tighten again. He was already feeling very uncomfortable. "And how would that make you feel?"

"I wouldn't know until I was asked to kill you."

Berenger was keen to change the subject. "Nathan, let's get back to your time at the facility in Scotland. Would you like to reflect on your time there?"

"I thought it was a blast."

"In what way?"

"You guys told me to kill someone in the basement, and I did. I had my own room. Didn't have to share with no one. I liked that. I liked it a lot. And then being set free. That was nice too."

"You said you had your own room. I find that interesting."

"How so?"

"Well, some others might have viewed it as solitary confinement."

Stone shrugged.

"Do you know it was the Quakers that introduced the idea of solitary confinement to America for those who didn't behave? Thinking it would give them time to find themselves and God when alone."

"Interesting."

"What I'm getting at is, solitary confinement is a punishment, isn't it?"

"I don't see it like that."

"How do you see it?"

"I found it liberating. I love being by myself. Yeah, it gives me time to think. Space to breathe."

"You didn't have that when you were growing up, did you, Nathan?"

Nathan grinned. "Are you getting all Freudian on me, Doc?"

Berenger felt himself blush. "Can you answer the question? You didn't have space when you were growing up, did you?"

"No, I didn't. And that's why I like it. Actually, I love it."

"You embrace it?"

"Damn right. Can't get enough of it."

"It drives some people out of their minds. Not you."

Stone shook his head.

"Nathan, I'm done for now. I'd like to arrange another appointment shortly before the operation begins."

Stone got to his feet and smiled. "Don't try and understand me, Doc. It won't work. You'll never understand me. Ever."

29

Berenger nodded as Nathan turned and walked out of the room. He watched from the window as Nathan got in his car, then drove away, back to Toronto.

Berenger felt relieved that Stone was no longer in the same room. Breathing the same air. He picked up his cell phone and called Clayton Wilson. It rang twice before he answered.

"Morning, Mark."

"Sir."

"So how's our guy today?" Wilson asked.

Berenger sat on the edge of the desk. "It was just a preliminary chat."

"And how was he?"

"He's extraordinary. Remarkable. And fascinating."

"Can he do this? Is he ready to do this?"

"He's more than ready. He's so dangerous it's unreal. He's unfathomable. He really is something else."

"That's what I like to hear. So, within the next week—would that be realistic?"

"That's not a problem. He's primed, ready to go off."

Eight

After the consultation, Nathan headed back to his apartment in Toronto, made himself a coffee, and flopped down on the sofa. He was pleased to get away from the psychobabble bullshit of Berenger. It was 8:59 a.m.

Then he put on his wireless Bose headphones and switched on the huge TV to see inside Mark Mahoney's apartment. Nathan took a couple of gulps of strong coffee. Mahoney was eating a bowl of cereal at a breakfast bar in his kitchen, watching Fox News.

Nathan began to focus on the task at hand. He knew that Mahoney's phones, iPad, and emails, not to mention the bugs in the apartment, would be monitored by his handler and the backup team. But he always liked to get a feel for the mood of the target.

The more he got to know the target ahead of that person being neutralized, the more relaxed he felt. He loved seeing their movements. Their foibles. The humdrum existence. But also he wanted to know he could physically overpower them.

Nathan watched. Mahoney put on his tie as he glanced at the news. He appeared to be in very good shape. He clearly worked out. Nathan didn't know if Mahoney did any martial arts. He hadn't seen any reference to that in the dossier he'd studied. He looked like he did lots of running, jogging, gym work. But he didn't think he'd pose too much of a problem training-wise.

Besides, Mahoney's death would be achieved by a method that would surprise Mahoney. It could be drugging him. An accident.

Nathan had begun to think up some scenarios. It was always smart to plan the best strategies. But in his experience, it often came down to whatever opportunity presented itself.

He needed to get into this guy's life, or close enough, to do what had to be done. But not be noticed.

Which was easier said than done.

Nathan watched the screen as Mahoney put on his black shoes. He saw the attention to detail of the clothes. The way the pants sat perfectly on the shoes. Perhaps he had a bespoke tailor. Then again maybe not.

His mind began to conceive new scenarios.

He adjusted the headphones. Mahoney's cell phone was ringing.

Mark, it's you know who.

Hey, you free to meet up yet?

We can't meet in town. I think I was being followed yesterday.

Are you sure?

Yeah.

OK, where do you want to meet?

I'll let you know.

But how?

You'll find out.

The call ended.

Nathan took the Dodge Charger downtown and parked a block from Mahoney's office. He waited until ten, when he saw Mahoney walking into the *New York Times*'s Toronto bureau, cell phone pressed to his ear. He poured himself some good, strong coffee from a flask and drank. He climbed into the back of the vehicle, popped on the headphones, and sat down and watched the monitor, which showed real-time feeds from inside the bureau.

They now had all bases covered.

Reporters sitting around discussing Iraq, Mosul, Syria, and a whole plethora of geopolitical topics.

Nathan spent the rest of the day listening as the journalists talked earnestly about whether Hillary would make a comeback.

The hours dragged, but Nathan didn't mind that. He was good at killing time. It was in the job description. Waiting, watching—it was just the way it was.

Nine

It was nearly eight at night when Mahoney returned home, stopping off for a pizza after work. Locking his door, he noticed a white envelope on his mat. Picked it up. Written in black ink was his name, *Mark*, and *Do not tell a soul.* He opened it up. Inside was a folded piece of paper. It gave directions to a parking garage across town. He was to meet his contact at ten on Level C.

Mahoney showered and changed into fresh clothes. He began to feel the first twinges of excitement. He always thought these moments were one of the best parts of being an investigative journalist. The thrill of piecing together small fragments of the story. The big picture emerging, but only after he'd painstakingly put it all together, the jigsaw only then complete.

He felt good. He sensed the story was beginning to take shape. And hopefully this new source would give him some new avenue to pursue. He was optimistic. He'd often found that a meeting face-to-face with a source produced exciting results. Then again, maybe he'd just been lucky so far.

After tidying up his apartment, loading the dishwasher, and watching TV, he headed down to his car that was parked outside. He entered the details into the GPS and drove off. Through the near-deserted downtown streets of Toronto. And then out to the suburbs.

Twenty minutes later, he pulled up at a virtually deserted parking garage adjacent to a mall. He headed up to Level C and pulled into a spot.

Mahoney switched on some Bach arias on his iPhone and the music began to fill his car. He hadn't been told anything apart from how to reach the parking garage and which level to park on.

He began to wonder about this new source. Usually it took months to build up trust with sources. This fit that pattern. It was a slow burn. But he sensed the meeting was going to yield something significant.

The minutes dragged. He checked his watch numerous times. He wondered if he'd been sent on a wild-goose chase. It wouldn't be the first time.

Forty minutes after he arrived, Mahoney spotted a Jeep in his rear-view mirror. The vehicle drove slowly around the parking garage as if looking for the best space, though every spot was available. Then it reversed into the bay right beside him.

Mahoney wound down the window and looked into the Jeep's window. A sixtysomething man with short silver hair was staring back at him. Dark-brown eyes, clean shaven.

"Tell me your date of birth," the man said.

Mahoney gave the details.

"Your father's middle name."

Mahoney told him.

"Give me the last four numbers of the checking account your salary goes into."

Mahoney complied.

The man nodded and smiled. "Very good. There needs to be trust. We're going to take this step-by-step, like we've been doing. But as of now, I believe you can be trusted to know a little bit about what we, in the Canadian intelligence community, know."

"Can I record what you're saying? I need verification."

"All your software up-to-date on your cell phone?"

"Absolutely."

The guy nodded. "Here's what I know. The cold-blooded killing—and make no mistake, it was a cold-blooded killing—of Senator Brad Crichton was an operation sanctioned and executed by the dark state in America."

"Dark state? How would you define 'dark state' in these circumstances?"

"An element outside the day-to-day control of the intelligence agencies but loosely aligned with them. Private money funded it."

"You got any further details on that?"

"Not so fast. We haven't even gotten to first base. So what you've got is the classic shadow government. Plausible deniability for those in government. But agencies like the CIA can know there's an operation under way that aligns with what they perceive the nation's interests to be."

Mahoney thought the man was using language more akin to the libertarian/isolationist wing in the US. "Which is?"

"Politicians who know the game, understand the need for intervention, regime change . . ."

"Globalists?"

"Precisely. Well, this Crichton, he wasn't buying the bullshit that the Pentagon, Washington, and corporate interests have been pushing. Permanent war, permanent regime change, complicit poodles in the media."

Mahoney felt compelled to speak up for his trade. "I'm no poodle. And I don't know any poodles at the *New York Times*."

"Whatever."

"I've heard this sort of talk before from a former CIA contractor."

"Let's be clear what we're talking about. Instead of upholding the genuine national interests of America—and trust me, we Canadians don't want to get involved in your ambitions to be the world's policeman—it's clear there's a virulent strain of opinion, some call them neocons, who believe in toppling regimes that oppose American hegemony, namely

Libya, Iraq, and Syria, and bombing them back to the Stone Age. But some of us within the intelligence community in Canada don't believe it's in our long-term interests to go along with that."

"Tell me about this facility in Scotland. How did you hear about it? What exactly do you know?"

"Very interesting place. We heard about it six years ago. Then a year after that we had an observation team assigned to get near the facility. And then we heard it was being used as a dark site, run by a quasi-CIA organization made up of former directors of the CIA and handpicked guys from the Pentagon. It was used to train, house, and monitor a team of assassins."

"When you say *we* heard, how did *you* hear?"

"I'm not divulging how we got this information."

"Was it electronic surveillance?"

"I'm not going there."

Mahoney sighed as his gaze wandered across the parking lot. "I'm going to give you a name. And you can confirm or deny that this guy was involved. An operative."

The man nodded.

"Does the name Nathan Stone mean anything to you?"

The man nodded. "Yes. It most certainly does."

Mahoney had heard that now from three separate sources. "Officially, he doesn't exist."

"Neat trick, isn't it?"

"How did you hear about all this?"

"As I said before, I'm not going there."

Mahoney went quiet.

"Look, we heard whispers on the grapevine. That's how it usually starts."

"How exactly?"

The man sighed. "Can't say any more."

"Why?"

"It may inadvertently reveal a source."

"So how did you go about verifying that there was indeed a facility off the coast of mainland Scotland?"

"Canadian and Scottish links run deep."

"Sure."

"So we had a fishing boat with a couple of our guys on board taking long-range photos. Then we hired a chopper and got within five hundred yards before it was fired at. We also had a drone used for aerial photography. But we got photos of a former CIA operative who'd trained Stone. We also intercepted encrypted messages that mentioned his name."

"You've got all that?"

"Yes. And we're quite sure about all of it."

"What else?"

"OK, so this secret facility is run by a private company."

"Details?"

The man shook his head. "Not at this stage."

"When can I get that?"

"When we're ready to give it to you. There's something else I want to let you in on."

"What?"

"This secret facility in Scotland was effectively burned to the ground, destroyed, in a series of fires and explosions."

"Jesus Christ."

"The work of Nathan Stone."

Mahoney cleared his throat, mind racing.

"There's something else you might want to know."

Mahoney leaned a bit closer as the man lowered his voice.

"We've now uncovered a second facility."

"A second facility?"

The man nodded.

"Where?"

The man looked around, as if sensing he was being watched. He turned back to face Mahoney. "Here in Canada."

Mahoney's heart was beating fast. He had heard similar rumors from an intelligence source in DC, which was what had prompted his move to Canada. "Where exactly?"

"Can't reveal that just now."

"And the Canadian government knows about this?"

"Yes, they do. But there's nothing they can do."

"Why not?"

"Think about it. Are they going to get their powerful neighbor riled up? Best to watch and wait."

"What else?"

The man's eyes were hooded. "I believe you're at grave risk."

"In what way?"

The man didn't answer. His window went up, and he calmly reversed out of the space. He pulled away, disappearing into the night.

Ten

Nathan was tailing the Jeep from the parking garage after watching the surreptitious meeting with Mahoney.

He followed the vehicle with a new GPS tracking app to the western suburbs of Toronto. The Jeep parked in the driveway of an upscale detached house.

Nathan drove on past for half a mile, then doubled back. He pulled out a telephoto lens and photographed the man getting out of his car. Then he uploaded the pictures to his handler.

He waited for a few minutes, then drove past the house and saw the number on the door and the license plate of the Jeep, and messaged those details too.

Nathan headed out of the suburbs and caught the freeway back into Toronto.

His cell phone rang and he switched to speakerphone. "Very fine work, bro," his handler said.

"What do we know about this guy?"

"He's a senior intelligence operative of the Canadian Security Intelligence Service. Matthew Blanc. Former military attaché to the UN. So he knows his way around."

"I'm wondering if this guy is being used as a conduit by the Canadian government to alert the journalist, which in turn would spook the Americans, in effect using the journalist as a proxy to get this facility out of the way, or is this guy acting alone?"

"Very good question. I suspect this guy is acting alone. It's an ideological thing with him. What they're doing doesn't sit right. That's what we believe. The smarter elements within the Canadian government, while not keen to draw attention to it, understand that America needs to keep all security options on the table."

Nathan said nothing.

"We're very pleased how you're responding to this challenge, Nathan. And the manner you've gone about your business. The report from our psychologist is most impressive. And we're hopeful we can both get what we want. Namely, us getting you to deal with this pest of a journalist, and you getting your sister back to where she should be."

Nathan wondered if the guy was fucking with him. Had the psychologist advised his handler to mess with him? To ask him questions to rile him? To tease out his anger?

"As a token of our thanks, bro, we think you've earned some gratitude."

"What sort of gratitude?"

"As a small token of our good faith, you can talk to your sister. How does that sound?"

"When?"

"When you get back to your apartment, the phone will ring five times. Then pick up."

Eleven

Half an hour later, Nathan was back in his downtown Toronto apartment. He fixed himself a coffee. He took a couple of large gulps as he sat down, awaiting the call.

The time dragged as he waited . . . and waited.

Eventually, just after one in the morning his cell phone rang. He let it ring five times as instructed and picked up.

"Nathan, is that you?" The voice of his beautiful, damaged sister.

Nathan closed his eyes. His mind flashed to images of his sister killing their father on that terrible night in their room in the Bowery. Blood splatter on her face as she drove the scissors in again and again. All these years later, the images were still there. Haunting him. "Helen, it's me. How are you?"

"I'm good, Nathan. Your friends are so cool."

"That's good to hear. They treating you nice?"

"Nice? They're treating me supernice, Nathan. One of them—I forget his name—he said his grandmother's not well, but he tries to see her as often as he can. How sweet is that?"

Nathan felt his throat tighten. Her voice was so innocent. So pure. The same singsong cadence she'd had since she was a girl. It was like she was locked into that time. While she was now a woman, her childlike qualities and mannerisms had been preserved. It was the same voice that had tried to reassure him when he wet the bed as a child. Back then he had been nervous, anxious, racked by fear and anger, which would manifest itself in rage, violence, and assassinations all these years later.

He had become a cold, soulless monster. He knew that. He understood that. And he also understood that his sister was cocooned in a parallel universe of psychiatric care, with no real contact with the outside world for decades. "That's a very nice thing, yes," he said, trying to muster some conviction. "Aren't you tired? It's way past your usual bedtime."

"It's just after ten, Nathan, it's not that late."

Nathan realized she was on Pacific time. Had they transferred her to Los Angeles, Seattle, or somewhere in between? Or had she been given a misleading time on purpose? "Sorry, my watch must've stopped. Are you eating well?"

"Eating real good. Fresh apple pie, ice cream, lots of it."

"Helen, don't overdo it. It's important we don't overeat."

"I know, Nathan, but you know how it is. I get bored, I get sad, and I feel good when I eat."

"Fair enough. So what about movies? Are you able to watch any movies?"

"Listen to this, Nathan. Your friends have a fantastic huge TV, and I've been watching everything. *Blade Runner*, *Star Wars*, amazing. And so, so kind, Nathan."

"Tell me, Helen, are you able to get out in the sun? I know you enjoy the sun in Florida, don't you?"

"It's very foggy here in the morning, but by lunch it's great. The weather's nice."

Nathan wondered if she could be in San Francisco. But then again, she could really be anywhere. "I miss you."

"I miss you too, Nathan. When will I see you again? I like when you visit."

"It won't be long, sis. And you know what? I'm looking forward to seeing you again too."

There was silence for nearly a minute before his handler came back on. "She's been well looked after, bro."

Nathan sighed.

"Soon as this is over, everything will be back to normal."

Twelve

It was the dead of night when Clayton Wilson's Gulfstream touched down at the private island off the Florida coast. The others had flown in the previous evening. The air was like glue. Lightning bugs were illuminated by the harsh exterior light. Security guards wearing dark suits escorted him from the limousine. Then into the sprawling mansion. The host shook Wilson's hand on the step.

Wilson followed the man in silence down into the bowels of the house, which contained the surveillance-proofed subbasement conference room. He, like all the other members of the Commission, had to go through an X-ray machine, and all electronic devices were left outside the room.

He sat down at the head of the oval table, with the other members along the sides.

Wilson glanced at the papers in front of him and surveyed the faces staring back at him. He sipped some water and took a few moments to compose himself before he began. "Sorry about the late hour. Couldn't be helped. OK, this is a progress report update as requested, gentlemen. I will outline our position and when I believe this mission will be accomplished."

A few nods of approval.

"We've had a long time to reflect on what happened at the facility in Scotland. The operation was far from perfect. There were problems with the mission, and for that I accept full responsibility. But what is easy to overlook is that the target, Senator Crichton, was taken out, as was his mistress. The purpose of the mission was to neutralize that threat. And this was done. So in that sense we were successful. The problem was the blowback from Stone."

Thoughtful looks crossed the table as Richard Stanton scribbled some notes.

"We thought long and hard about him," Wilson said, "and concluded, after much soul-searching, that if anyone could undertake this operation, it was him. Yes, we could have had him disappeared. But we believe that he is still an invaluable asset to our organization." Wilson cleared his throat and sipped a glass of water. "You see, Stone took years and millions—and I mean millions—of dollars in investment. His rise from the ashes—from the grave, if you will—gave him and us perfect plausible deniability. What we had not anticipated in any way, shape, or form was him turning the tables on us. And alerting a journalist— Mark Mahoney; you have his file in front of you. We have heard from numerous sources, including two people within the highest echelons of the *New York Times*—one an ex-lover of his, but also from friendly intelligence agencies, as well as the CIA, no less—that he is piecing together an investigation into our activities.

"His details are limited to what Stone knew. And the people involved were killed when Stone destroyed the facility. That said, Mahoney is clearly a risk we must shut down. And that's why we're killing two birds with one stone. We are engaging Stone to delete him, safe in the knowledge that his sister will not live if he doesn't carry out the task."

Wilson looked across at Stanton, who was peering over his half-moon specs. "Richard, I've been hogging the floor. What are your thoughts?"

"I think the nice thing about Stone again is his atonement," Stanton said. "You're right, Clayton. The rationale is sound. The costs involved in destroying what was a secret facility are tens of millions but incalculable with regards to a generation of assassins who would have been honed at the facility. But to me the smart thing about this is that it contains the threat of Stone. If we were to use another asset, perhaps in Canada, then that would mean a potential leak. But in the circumstances, I think Stone understands who runs the show."

Wilson leaned back in his seat and sighed, looking at the men around him. He could see a lot of nodding, a couple of members scribbling. "I've been informed that Nathan is making progress already. Serious progress."

Stanton said, "What sort of progress has he made?"

Wilson smiled. "Gentlemen, Stone has uncovered the identity of the intelligence operative who has begun to liaise with Mahoney. Already."

Stanton nodded. "Interesting."

"This addresses both of our problems. We keep Stone to do the wet work, and Mahoney is rubbed out of the equation. Not to mention that we have begun, after the surveillance of Mahoney's source, to understand that Canada or some elements of Canadian intelligence are aware of our presence on their soil and don't like it. But the main priority is this operation. Mahoney. We also need to consider how we push back on this Canadian operative to make sure his bosses get the message."

Stanton looked around the table. "We all know how this works. There are two possible ways to neutralize someone. You can either blackmail or threaten him into silence, or you can kill him. That's essentially it." He shrugged. "To kill a Canadian operative is just asking for trouble. It might spiral out of control, and the facility might be compromised if the media got wind, and not just the *New York Times*. I'm talking everyone and their dog would love this story. Can you imagine how that would look?"

Wilson sighed. "Not good. I agree with Richard. We can't just waltz in and kill this guy. It might suit us, but that would bring heat like you wouldn't believe. It would not end well. Best option? Richard?"

Stanton checked his briefing paper and his notes. "In my opinion, we get into this operative's private life, find out what we can—we have people that can do that, and very, very quickly. If need be, we could create a scandal . . . Having him silenced through his own misdemeanors is always a good option for everyone."

More nodding around the table.

"You know what I'm talking about, right?" Stanton asked. "Pictures of him in bed with a girl. A young girl. There are options that can be deployed to neutralize the most lily-white of people."

"Richard, pass on those thoughts to Stone's handler," Wilson said.

Stanton and those around the table nodded.

"But I'd like to task you with finding out everything there is to know about this Canadian operative," Wilson said. "I want to know his foibles. His past. Girlfriends at college. Drugs perhaps? Postings overseas. Photographed with prostitutes? What about his family? Is that a weak spot? Let's get into his life."

Thirteen

It was just after seven in the morning and Nathan was watching the feed of Mark Mahoney in his apartment. The journalist was sitting at his laptop, tapping away at the keys.

Nathan stared at the man. He was still running all the scenarios as to how the journalist could die in a way that would look like an accident or natural causes. And at that moment, his favored method was to use the assassination drug of choice, sux, that would kill Mahoney with a heart attack in a matter of minutes. How innocuous. How perfect.

Nathan's problem was getting close. He could pass Mahoney on the street. Do it that way. But that posed innumerable problems. Being seen as he jabbed him. Surveillance footage, which was all-pervasive. Cell phones everywhere. But a disguise would solve that problem.

There were so many ways to kill and make it look like a tragic death. Nathan had heard it called a contrived accident. It was an accurate description. And the sux method was a favorite for secret assassination.

Perhaps the most efficient method was a high fall onto a hard surface. Elevator shaft plunge, stairwell fall, high windows, balconies, terraces, bridges. He had read that Toronto had numerous bridges. But many were over rivers. Sometimes fast moving. That wasn't guaranteed. Not perfect. Some might drown. Perhaps have a heart attack from the shock. But some might, and almost certainly would, survive. That wasn't acceptable.

Nathan needed certainty. His handler, and those pulling the strings in the operation, would absolutely need certainty.

The conversation between Mahoney and his wife lingered in his head. It was bothering him. Her voice was soft. Gentle even. Trusting. Nathan imagined her now back home in New York, unaware of what was about to happen to her husband. Then he thought of her children.

Nathan felt strangely reflective. It was strange for him to be having such thoughts. Without fail, he got a mission and he saw it through. He didn't dwell on things. It wasn't him. But here he was thinking about the voice of Mrs. Mahoney, in New York. A woman he had never met. Blissfully going about her family life while Nathan was preparing to assassinate her husband, a brilliant American journalist.

The voice of Mahoney's wife echoed, as if in a dream. The cadence. The tone. Definite New York accent. It reminded Nathan of his beloved sister. A sweet disposition. Innocent even. Then it occurred to him why he couldn't get the woman's voice out of his head: she sounded just like his mother.

Nathan remembered the winter day as they had huddled in the one-room dump on the Bowery. A UPS driver dropped off a delivery addressed to Nathan and his sister. Inside was a cassette tape from their mother. Explaining why she'd had to leave. And telling them to take care of each other. He had listened to it over and over again. Her voice stayed with him all those years after she had left them, sustaining him in his darkest moments. Somewhere, someplace, she was there.

Nathan's thoughts quickly returned to killing Mahoney. His sister being used as leverage.

The more he thought about it, the more he began to feel the first twinges of doubt creeping in.

Nathan never used to have doubts. But now here he was, uncertainty encroaching on his thoughts. What would happen to his sister after he killed Mahoney? Could the Commission—or what was left of it—be trusted to return his sister to her rightful place?

Then it hit him like a ten-ton truck: Could he really carry out the assassination? Was that the problem?

Nathan felt cold. Shocked that these ideas were there. They'd come out of the blue. His mind was racing faster and faster. He had begun to look beyond the current mission to kill Mahoney. Nathan had tried to push any negative thoughts to the back of his mind as he tried to focus on the plot to kill the journalist. But now it was dawning on him that they would neutralize him when it was over. And his sister.

He pushed those thoughts to one side when Mahoney's cell phone rang. He turned up the volume so he could hear the conversation properly. It was a call from Mahoney's editor at the *New York Times*. After some small talk, they got down to business.

How's your story coming along?

Interesting development. I have confirmation from a source within Canadian intelligence that they're aware of the facility in Scotland. And of the kill list that had Crichton on it.

What else?

I'm hearing about a second facility. In Canada. And this lines up with what I told you I'd heard from a separate intelligence source.

Where is this facility?

I don't know yet. I'm hoping to find that out from my source very soon.

I'm going to give you seventy-two hours to send over what you've got. But only to me. The email address I gave you. You know the one?

I got it.

You've been sitting on a lot of stuff. I want to see what you've got.

Fourteen

A short while later, Nathan's cell phone rang.

"How are you this morning, bro?" The voice of his handler.

"Watching and waiting."

"This conversation with the editor—your thoughts."

Nathan sighed. "I'm assuming we're not in the business of killing the executive editor of the *New York Times*."

"Probably not."

"Do you think he could be leaned on?"

"We've got to assume the executive editor is smart. And that he's a very good journalist. But it's not unknown for him to kill stories that are unfavorable to America's national security."

"Interesting," Nathan said. He began to think ahead. "OK, let's assume that end is taken care of before publication. My concern, as the contractor on this job, is to shut down the Canadian intelligence operative. I think that's key. I can see real problems ahead if we don't deal with that. Anything else I need to know about him?"

"You think it's that important, Stone?"

"I do. Tell me more about this guy."

"Known in intelligence circles as Mr. Fox."

"Well, I think Mr. Fox needs to get out of the henhouse, right?"

"The people I've spoken to, higher up, believe this operative can't be taken out in the traditional way in any shape or form."

"Why not?"

"It'll open up a can of worms. We want to keep a lid on things."

Nathan smiled. "What've you found out about this guy?"

"Quite a lot. And like most people, he has a skeleton or two in his closet."

"What exactly?"

"He's had a couple of affairs, but they've fizzled out. But the problem with using that as leverage is that it isn't one hundred percent guaranteed to get him to stop communicating with the journalist. We could fabricate a story or two regarding financial dealings, conflicts of interest. But that's never a slam dunk."

"What about his family?" Nathan asked.

"The way to get to a man *is* through his family."

Nathan's mind flashed to images of his sister.

"Sorry, bro, I don't mean to bring this up. I'm just illustrating the point."

"Tell me about this guy's family. His blood."

"He's got a daughter. His only child. Sixteen. She's pretty wild."

"Wild? In what way?"

"She dabbles in drugs. Promiscuous. Heavy drinker."

Nathan let the words sink in. He began to think through some scenarios where he could get to the girl. Not only to silence her father, but he was also starting to consider how he could work this to his advantage. He really needed a workaround.

"Here's an idea," Nathan said. "I get a picture of this girl, preferably in a bar. She's only sixteen, and she loves to party. Find out where she likes to drink. The legal drinking age in Toronto is nineteen. I'll take it from there."

The handler went quiet for a few moments. "Should we be getting sidetracked with this?"

"I think it's essential the threat from Mr. Fox is neutralized. We can get at him through the girl. Tell me more about her."

"She's very bright and has her heart set on some fancy art college, photography nut. But I think she might find it rather difficult to gain admittance if we have pictures of her getting shit-faced."

Nathan smiled. "Precisely my point."

"You're an evil bastard, Stone, do you know that?"

"It's one of my best features. What's her name?"

"Beth Blanc. She hangs out with her fake ID at the Belmont on Bank Street. She's there seven nights a week, apparently."

"Nice."

"Let's not get too bogged down in this, Stone. And remember to send the pictures to me."

"That works."

"Then what? You deal with her first, then get to Mahoney?"

"Trust me, I've got this. Once we've put some pressure on Blanc, made sure he's out of the equation, we can focus our energies on Mark Mahoney."

"Next time we talk, Stone, I want to know what your plan is for Mahoney."

"What else?"

"Berenger wants another chat."

"When?"

"In an hour. Face-to-face."

Fifteen

Berenger was studying Nathan Stone's reconstructed face. He remembered the face as it was before. But now he looked like a completely different person. His voice was the same as ever, though, the hard New York accent still there.

And his eyes. Stone's gaze still had the same intensity. Lingering too long, as if he were trying to make you uneasy. Then again, maybe he was just sizing you up before he ate you for dinner.

Berenger shifted in his seat as he came under that imposing gaze.

"You OK, Doc?" Nathan asked, a thin smile on his face.

Berenger glanced down at his notes before making eye contact. "I'm OK, thanks. Just picking up from where we left off yesterday. So tell me: I had a little chat with your handler. He was very positive. And I believe you've spoken to your sister now. How does that make you feel?"

"I didn't feel too much."

Berenger sat silently as he contemplated Nathan's words. "Weren't you happy to talk to her?"

"Sure I was. But you know . . . the circumstances aren't the best."

"That must be tough for you."

"You wanna cut the crap, Doc?"

"OK, let's focus on what this is all about. Your operation. I believe, according to my notes, there's been a new development. This Canadian operative needs to be persuaded not to share any further information with the journalist. Right?"

Stone stared straight at him. "Right."

"And this entails a more nuanced response from you."

"I guess."

"How does that make you feel?"

"How does what make me feel?"

Berenger shrugged. "How will you remove him from the equation? Through the daughter. Are you thinking about that, Nathan?"

"I don't think much about anything usually. Trust me, that's a big advantage."

"What I mean is . . . perhaps I'm not making myself clear . . . Having a girl at your mercy. How does that make you feel, Nathan?"

"Doc, I think you need to see a shrink. This is business. I do what needs to be done. You can keep your sick little fantasies to yourself." Nathan grinned.

Berenger flushed. Nathan was playing him. Getting into his head. "You think I have dark fantasies?"

"Don't most shrinks?"

"You're fucking with me, aren't you, Nathan?"

"Am I? I don't know."

Berenger smiled. "See what you're doing there?"

"What am I doing? Do you think I'm fucking with you, Doc?"

Berenger shifted again in his seat. "I'm looking at you, Nathan, and I see something in your eyes. What is that? Your eyes are sparkling."

Nathan stared at him long and hard. "You want to know how I'm gonna deal with this girl, is that it?"

"It would be interesting to know your thought processes."

"You getting excited by this, Doc? Is this something you like to fantasize about? About me dealing with this girl?"

"Just your thought processes."

"Trust me, you don't want to know about my thought processes."

"How do you feel about the mission being changed to incorporate the girl?"

Nathan began to smile. "I'm looking forward to it. Makes it interesting. I'm also now considering something else."

"And what would that be?"

"You're really interested in this sort of stuff, aren't you, Doc?"

Berenger said nothing.

"Yeah, you really get off on this. Does your wife know about that?"

Berenger felt his blood turn cold.

"That's not a threat, Doc. Just curious, I guess."

"What do you have in mind, Nathan—for the girl, I mean?"

Nathan began to laugh. "What, and ruin the surprise?"

Sixteen

Nathan was wearing a minuscule earpiece in his right ear as he entered the bar. He felt wired. His mind thinking ahead to what would come next. The possibilities. The operation was more complex now than when it began. It would take more time. And patience. But that wouldn't be a problem. He'd already mentally mapped out what he was going to do. He was beginning to realize the enormity of the challenge ahead of him. He was going to single-handedly take it to the Commission. It was the only way. He knew he was risking his life and that of his sister. His survival instincts told him there was no other way. But he also knew that he needed to show self-control and discipline.

Now more than ever his handler, Berenger, and the Commission needed to believe he was still going ahead with the plan to kill Mahoney.

He ordered a bottle of Heineken as he stood at the bar. He gulped down the cold beer. Fast.

Easy, Nathan.

It felt almost too good. He had already popped a couple of amphetamine-and-steroid-combination pills. He began to grind his teeth as the drugs and alcohol kicked in. He was surrounded by a buzzy crowd of young urban Torontonians, talking about whatever stuff young people talked about. Mostly themselves. Their jobs. Their vacuous lives.

He sipped his beer. He felt impervious to the world. The small talk. The bullshit. The mundane lives of people who never once had to worry about where their next meal would come from. Concerned about climate change, what Father John Misty's new album really meant, if Jay-Z was a feminist, or some other bullshit.

The more he listened, the more he zoned out. This wasn't his crowd. He didn't have friends. He only had people he knew. People he worked for. And his sister.

His world was compartmentalized to the highest degree, and he preferred it that way. He liked to be alone. He adored solitary confinement. His only problem was *leaving* his cocooned existence. He was fine in the apartment they'd given him for the job. But this? This was just a drag.

His earpiece crackled to life. "She just left her father's house in a cab," the voice of his handler told him. "She's alone. But we don't know if she's meeting up with friends or what. If you copy that, clear your throat once."

Nathan complied.

"OK, good. She's certainly a pretty little thing. Real pretty. You got something in mind, Stone?"

Nathan cleared his throat once.

"Good luck, bro."

Nathan finished his beer, went to the bar, and ordered another, along with a Scotch. He got a seat as the hum of conversation around him seemed to grow louder. He observed the confident young men, the way the young women gravitated to those who exuded an effortless charm with clever conversation and witticisms. He couldn't help thinking it was all just learned mannerisms, feigned cool couched in cynical language. The whole world they inhabited was a fucking mirage.

Nathan liked uncomplicated. He liked simple things. He was a "less is more" kind of guy. He liked nothing better than sitting on a stool at a dive bar, maybe the Deuce on South Beach, beer in hand, Stones on the jukebox. Maybe some Georgia Satellites. Stevie Ray Vaughan. Raw. Loud.

Here, the sound of lo-fi music oozed through the speakers. Like ersatz Muzak. Maybe European house or trance or some such shit. He'd heard a lot of that crap one summer when he'd been hiding out in the Balearics.

White European middle-class assholes loved that shit when they were high. Or coming down. It was safe. Pleasant. And it didn't jar. If nothing else, it was good hangover music.

The bar door opened.

Nathan surreptitiously watched the stunning young woman who entered, smiling. It was her. High cheekbones, expensive clothes. Already looked like a coed. But she was just a kid behind all the lipstick, the heavy makeup.

Nathan saw her flash the fake ID and order a bottle of white wine with two glasses and sit on a stool. He wondered who she was planning to meet. A guy? If so, it might make things more complicated.

The bartender poured a glass of wine for her. The other glass remained empty. She sipped her drink, glancing around the room.

Nathan thought she looked quite a few years older than her age. Like an archetypal college girl. Maybe even a recent graduate. Midtwenties. Confident. She stared at her phone and pressed it to her right ear, finger in her left to block out the ambient noise. He heard her say, *You've got to be kidding me. No!* She ended the call, grimaced, and knocked back the rest of her glass of wine. The bartender filled her up again.

Nathan let a few moments pass before he went to the bar, standing next to the girl. He put up his finger to the bartender and ordered a large glass of an expensive Shiraz. His senses switched on. A perfect accompaniment to amphetamines and steroids. He began to feel crazy thinking about what lay ahead.

The girl smiled at him, and Nathan smiled back. He felt awkward, and his gaze wandered around the room as if he were uninterested.

"Busy tonight," he said to her.

The girl shrugged, glass of wine in hand. Her eyes were already a bit heavy. "It's like this all the time."

Nathan looked around. "Nice place."

"Haven't been here before?"

"I'm from out of town. Doing a corporate photography project nearby."

"Are you kidding me?"

Nathan was given his glass of wine and handed the bartender a twenty-dollar bill. "No. They're very particular. But it's interesting work."

"Wow. That's cool. So you're a professional photographer?"

The bartender handed Nathan his change and he dropped some coins on the bar for a tip. "Yeah, it's interesting work."

"I love photography. I so, so want to go to college and be a photographer."

Nathan sipped his drink and nodded. "Good for you. Look, I don't want to impose. I see you're waiting for someone."

The girl used her hand as if to swat a fly. "She's got some bullshit exam that she decided she needed to study for." She shrugged. "Latin. I mean, what the fuck?"

Nathan grinned.

"So she's a no-show."

"Too bad," he said.

The girl leaned closer, her boozy breath warm and sweet. A faint whiff of expensive citrusy perfume. "Her loss. She wants to be a photographer too. War photographer."

"Good for her."

"So you're doing corporate work in town?"

"Yeah, private client. Financial services."

"Don't you find that a bit limiting?"

"They pay well. And that's a great thing, trust me. Money's always a good thing."

"I guess."

"They need some pictures of their senior management but also images of their building. They want a certain look, which is fine. But I'm trying to get them to go with black and white. That's what I like."

The girl touched her chest. "Me too. My God, that's amazing! Don't you think that's an amazing coincidence?"

Nathan said nothing and smiled. He hadn't felt so crazy in ages. Externally, he showed a sense of calm attention to the young woman. But inside he was screaming that he wanted to get the job done and move on to the next phase of his plan.

She began to talk almost without pause about everything under the sun: abstract art, modernism, cubism, Picasso, Renoir, the Magnum photography agency, Marilyn Monroe, the Beatles pictures in black and white, the assassination of JFK, the Zapruder color footage of the assassination, intimate portraits of Joni Mitchell she'd seen in some magazine, the granular quality of black-and-white photos, and all manner of photographic horseshit.

Nathan had never heard such a torrent of artspeak in such a short time. He felt as if his head were going to explode. Waves of bullshit she'd picked up from friends, coffee-table books on modern art, and no doubt from the *New York Times*. She didn't realize how much verbiage she was spewing. She seemed to think he was under her spell. The fact of the matter was he was very tempted to burst out laughing in her face. But that wouldn't achieve anything. Instead he listened politely, nodding sagely as she held court with him, a smiling assassin. Her lack of self-awareness was staggering. It was almost touching.

"Are you OK?" she asked, snapping him back to reality.

Nathan gulped the rest of his wine and put the empty glass on the bar. "I'm fine, thanks," he said. "Just a bit distracted thinking about a call I have in an hour. I'm trying to set up a time to meet this guy later in the year."

"Is he in the industry?"

"Yeah, he is."

"Stop teasing. Sorry, I didn't catch your name."

"I'm John. John MacKay. He's an old friend of mine from when I lived in London."

She sipped the rest of her glass of wine and smiled. "How exciting. Is he well known?"

Nathan frowned as if he were thinking hard. "You could say that."

"What's his name?"

"David Bailey . . . That name mean anything to you?"

"Are you kidding me? You know David Bailey?"

"Sure. I occasionally stay at his place in London if I'm working in the UK. I used to drink with him, hang out. He's a friend."

"Are you fucking kidding me, John?"

Nathan grinned.

"Seriously?" she said.

"I need to talk to him about an assignment I have coming up in London. He's helping me find the right assistant. He's also great at coming up with ideas."

"Of course he is! He's David fucking Bailey!"

"He's a great guy." Nathan was elated at how well this was going.

The bartender poured the girl another glass of white wine, and Nathan asked for a bottle of Heineken.

"I can't believe you know one of my heroes!" she said. "That's crazy."

Nathan smiled.

"Have you seen his iconic photos of the Kray twins?"

Nathan nodded, thinking the name sounded like a 1980s pop-synth group.

"This must be fate."

"I guess so." Nathan took a gulp of his beer and turned to walk away.

"You're not leaving yet, are you?"

"Bathroom."

The girl smiled as Nathan headed through the bar to the bathroom. He checked to make sure the stalls were all empty. Then he called his handler.

Seventeen

"You cruel bastard. You're a fucking natural."

"Quick question," Nathan said.

"Sure," his handler said. "What do you need?"

"Where's Mark Mahoney right now?"

"What?"

"Where is he? Right now. At this moment."

A beat. "He's . . . hold on . . . he's at an Italian restaurant."

"For how long?"

"About fifteen minutes. Just sitting down to his entrée."

"Who's he with?"

"Journalist from the Toronto office."

"So his apartment's empty?"

"Mahoney's?"

Nathan sighed. "Yeah."

"It's empty. Hold on . . . I'm just gonna check the feed. Yeah, lamp on in the living room but all quiet. What do you have in mind, Stone?"

"I have an idea. A slight change of plan."

"You want to elaborate?"

"We kill two birds with one stone. If you pardon the pun. We show the girl compromised and out of it but put her in Mahoney's apartment.

I think that will give us leverage over not only her father but also over Mahoney."

"You want to take her there? You sick fuck," the handler said. "And because we have cameras operating, you thought . . ."

"Precisely. Get her there, pretend it's my place . . . and leave her there."

"Shit. Hold on, I need to OK this."

Nathan cleared his throat. "I need to go. Don't call my cell phone. Get back to me ASAP."

"Copy that."

Nathan washed his hands and walked back through the bar toward the pretty girl, who was now pouring herself a glass of wine from the bottle. Nathan picked up his beer and took a sip. He glanced at his watch. "Better watch my time."

"You're not leaving now, are you?"

Nathan gave her a pained look. "Got a few things to do before my call with David. Need to leave in a few minutes."

"Are you married?"

Nathan was surprised at the question. "No . . . I'm not married. Are you?"

The girl laughed hard. "Yeah, good one. Not something I'm aiming for. At least not now."

"So what's the plan for you? You gonna be a photographer?"

"I don't know. I hope so."

"Where do you want to study?"

The girl took out her cell phone and smiled at Nathan. "My dad wants me to go to law school. But I was hoping to get into the School of Visual Arts, in New York."

"Nice school."

"Where did you go?"

"Me? I didn't go to college."

Again the girl laughed hard. "Really?"

"Got a Leica as a present, and before you know it, I'm walking around the East Village taking pictures. Models. Actresses. Junkies. Homeless guys. Panhandler crazies. Hard-luck stories."

"That's amazing. Are you from New York?"

"Yeah, Lower East Side. It's all different now."

"Wow! I so want to go to New York."

"Great town. You'll like it."

The girl's glassy eyes stared at him as if she was lost in thought. "Sorry, I'm a bit fucked-up tonight, but you did say you're speaking to *the* David Bailey in an hour, right? I didn't know if I'd imagined that or not."

Nathan looked at his watch. "Actually, forty-five minutes to be precise."

His earpiece crackled into life. "Mahoney is out, we think for a couple of hours. He's meeting a colleague for a drink after dinner."

The girl smiled. "I'd love to hear more about you."

The voice in the earpiece. "His apartment is free. The four-digit code for his door is still 0911. Good luck."

The girl leaned in closer. "I said I'd love to get to know you better."

Her raised voice snapped Nathan out of his thoughts. "Sorry, I was miles away."

"I said I'd love to get to know you better."

Nathan checked his watch again. "I'm heading back to my apartment to edit a couple of pictures before I take the call. So I really need to think about heading back. It was really nice to meet you."

"John, I'm sure you're really busy, but is there any way I can see how you work? Maybe even . . . I don't know, say hi to David Bailey?"

Nathan put on a pained expression, as if it were a big ask. "I don't know . . . Don't get me wrong, I'm fine with it . . . It's just that . . ."

"You're married, aren't you?"

"No, I'm not married. But thanks for asking. Twice."

"Girlfriend? Boyfriend?"

"None of that, no."

"So you're unattached. How do you feel about me watching you doing some editing?"

Nathan smiled. "Sure. Why not? It's just a couple of minutes away."

The five-minute walk through downtown Toronto to Mahoney's luxury apartment felt strange.

"Is this it?" the girl said when she caught sight of the huge tower.

"Short-term rental."

Nathan punched 0911 into the security entrance pad and walked into the lobby with the girl. They rode the elevator to the top floor and walked down a corridor to the door of Mahoney's apartment. Nathan again entered the four-digit code and the door clicked open. He pushed it and they went inside. He made sure to lock it.

The girl walked into the huge open-plan living room. "This is like, wow!"

"Yeah, it's OK, I guess. Can I get you a drink? Coffee? Coke?"

"I'd love a beer."

"Beer. I'll see if I've got any left."

Nathan went to the kitchen, all granite surfaces and tiled floor. He opened the refrigerator. Inside were half-a-dozen bottles of Red Stripe. *Well done, Mahoney. Nice work.* He opened two of them.

"This is so fucking cool," she said.

"Yeah, it's pretty nice."

Nathan took out a packet of Rohypnol pills and crumbled three into her beer. They began to dissolve. Slowly. He stirred the sediment with a fork as it dissolved in the beer. Then he returned to the living room.

"So where's all your photographs and shit?"

Nathan handed her the beer. "Red Stripe OK?"

"Love it." She took a couple of large swigs from the bottle.

"I've got my stuff in a side room next door. But since I'm just here on a temporary assignment, most of my stuff is back in my main studio in the Village. In New York."

The girl took another swig of beer and closed her eyes for a second. She began to move her head from side to side, as if stoned. "I so want to be a photographer. I love photographs. It's such an amazing art form."

Nathan could see she was already falling under the spell of the roofies. The drug was working its terrible magic. It was odorless and tasteless. Ten times stronger than Valium. And fast acting.

He checked his watch. It had been three minutes since her first gulp. It usually took ten minutes to render someone completely unconscious.

"Take a seat on the sofa and I'll put some music on," Nathan said.

The girl's eyes opened for a few moments and began rolling around her head. She slumped down on the sofa. "I'm exhausted." She slugged the beer until it was finished and rested the empty bottle on her lap.

Nathan bent down, took the bottle, and put it on the table.

His earpiece crackled into life. "Heads-up, bro. Mahoney just got a call from his editor in New York. He finished his after-dinner drinks early, and he's headed back. The editor wants more information on the facility in Scotland."

Nathan looked down at the room-freshener plug, which contained one of the hidden cameras.

"We estimate four minutes, maybe less. Ideally, perfectly, we can get her and him in the picture. Two birds with one stone."

That had been Nathan's idea from the outset. But this was way too rushed and unexpected.

"Better get yourself out of there quick."

The girl moaned as she slipped into a drugged stupor.

Nathan waited a few moments until her eyes closed completely.

The voice in his earpiece: "This is taking too long, bro. You need to move fast!"

Nathan took some shots of her with his cell phone and sent them to the handler. Then he took a small bag of coke and sprinkled it on her T-shirt. He took some more pictures and sent them along.

Nathan got the beer bottle and put it on the sofa, as if it had dropped from her hand. He took some more photos and sent them to the handler. He got his bottle and placed it beside a cushion. She was totally out of it.

His earpiece hissed. "Shit! Mahoney is outside. He's paying the cab. Get the fuck out of there!"

Nathan's heart was beginning to race. He took one final look around and left the apartment, shutting the door behind him. He headed to the stairwell and walked slowly down the stairs.

"He's in the elevator! He's heading up!"

Nathan bounded down the stairs, reached the lobby, and headed out into the Toronto night as Mahoney exited the elevator upstairs.

Eighteen

A faint whiff of perfume and beer greeted Mark Mahoney as he opened the front door of his apartment. It usually smelled of beeswax. He flicked on the lights. The only person who had access was his cleaner, a woman who also cleaned the offices of the *New York Times*'s Toronto bureau.

He sensed something wasn't right as he hung up his coat.

The smell of booze only got stronger.

Lying sprawled and ashen faced on the sofa was a young woman, white powder on her T-shirt. Two bottles of his beer lying next to her.

Mahoney felt his legs nearly give way. "What the fuck is this? Hey! Hey!"

He stood over the girl, heart pounding, wondering what the hell was going on. Who was she? And why was she here? Was it some kind of joke? Was he getting punked?

"Hey, what the fuck is this? Get the hell out of here before I call the cops!"

The girl lay motionless. He stared down at the white powder.

"I said get the fuck up! Who the fuck are you?"

The girl moaned, completely out of it.

Mahoney raised his voice. "I'm going to call the cops if you don't get the hell out of here! What the hell are you doing here? Is this some sick fucking joke?"

The girl had slipped back into a deep sleep.

Mahoney began to pace the room, wondering if he was in the middle of a nightmare. He tried to make sense of it. How had she gotten in? Had he left his door unlocked? But no, he never did things like that. He was careful. Had his cleaner forgotten to lock up? She had been there in the late morning, and when he had returned, everything had been fine. So what had happened? Was this some druggie squatter?

Mahoney rubbed his face, trying to think. His cognitive abilities seemed to have deserted him. He wondered what exactly he should do. The most obvious choice was to call the cops. And say what? *There's a drunk girl covered in drugs lying in a stupor on my sofa, please arrest her. And by the way, I don't know who the fuck she is.* Who'd believe such a ridiculous story? Nobody, that's who.

His cell phone rang and he tensed. *Fuck.*

Mahoney picked up the phone and checked the caller ID. It was his executive editor at the *Times*, Mort Weiss. Shit. He pressed the green button. "Mort . . ."

"Hey, Mark, we OK to talk? Really interested to hear exactly where we are."

Mahoney looked down at the girl's unconscious body and closed his eyes. "Bit of a problem just now, Mort, sorry."

"Nothing serious I hope."

Mahoney racked his brains to come up with a plausible lie. "Got a . . . It's a bit of a nightmare. Got a . . . shit, a bad leak."

"That's not good."

"Water is pouring out of the bathroom. Don't know what happened. Just got back."

"No problem. You deal with that. We'll talk tomorrow, same time. How does that sound?"

"Thanks, Mort. Much appreciated."

Mahoney ended the call, his heart racing. It felt as if he was in the middle of a bad dream. Then it occurred to him: What if she'd slipped into a drug-induced coma?

"Shit, shit, shit!"

Mahoney kneeled beside the girl and tried to take her pulse. He pressed his finger against her skin. He started the stopwatch on his cell phone, but he couldn't detect anything. No pulse. "Oh shit, no!" he exclaimed. He kept his fingers on her wrist. Suddenly, he felt a beat. Very faint. And then another. She was alive. Thank fuck. He waited a full minute. He counted twenty-five beats. It was really weak. Shit.

He didn't have any choice. He had to call it in.

He called 911. He closed his eyes.

"Emergency, how can I help?"

"I think there might've been a drug overdose in my apartment, a young woman." Mahoney gave the address.

"Is this woman a friend of yours, sir?" the operator asked.

"No, she isn't. I came back to my apartment, she's lying there drunk, covered in fucking drugs. Can you please send the paramedics?"

"They're on their way, sir, as we speak."

"How long?"

"ETA two minutes."

"Please hurry!"

Mahoney ended the call and began to pace the apartment. He didn't know this girl. The poor kid was just there, lying on his goddamn sofa. Dear God, it looked shocking. Terrible. Oh Christ, he was going to take the rap for this. And what if she died?

The seconds dragged into minutes.

Eventually, he heard the sound of banging on his apartment door and opened up.

"Where is she?" the paramedic snapped.

"Living room. Please save her."

"What did she take?"

"I have no idea. There's a white powder on her. I just found her lying there."

The paramedics went to work on her. "Very weak pulse," said one.

Mahoney was pacing the room. "Please . . . you have to save her."

"What did she take?"

"I don't know. I just came home and there she was." His story sounded ridiculous, even to him.

"Sir, please, you need to help us!"

Mahoney threw his hands up. "I swear I don't know her. No idea."

"It looks like traces of cocaine on her body. Are you sure?"

"This has absolutely nothing to do with me."

The paramedic shook his head as if he didn't believe a word Mahoney was saying.

A few more paramedics arrived, strapped the girl onto a gurney, and wheeled her out into the elevator.

Mahoney watched in horror. He knew it wouldn't end there. And it didn't. A few minutes later, the cops turned up. His heart sank.

"You need to come with us, sir," one said.

They arrested him and took him in for questioning.

Mahoney felt like he'd entered a parallel universe as he was hustled to the cop car waiting outside.

"If she dies," one of the cops said, "you're in real trouble, my friend. You're a journalist, right?"

Mahoney could only nod. No words came out.

"I don't think your friends at the *New York Times* are gonna be able to help you, are they? They'll put as much distance between them and you as possible. But I guess you know that already."

Mahoney felt sick; he'd never felt so alone.

Nineteen

Nathan got back to his apartment, showered, and put on a fresh set of clothes. It was the dead of night and he couldn't sleep. He was so wired it was unreal. He picked up the remote and switched on the TV. He watched in real time as forensics officers photographed Mahoney's apartment. A couple of detectives were deep in conversation as they looked over the books on the shelves in the bedroom.

A short while later, his cell phone rang. "You watching your handiwork?"

"Yeah."

"How do you feel?"

"Just doing my job."

"To get her there, incriminating her and him, at his apartment—frankly, you're a dangerous genius, Stone."

Nathan stretched his arms. "We should be able to get the necessary leverage on the young lady's father. It's also a tidy backup plan to silence Mahoney."

"I guess my only concern might be if Mahoney decides to tough it out. What if he tells his wife what happened?"

Nathan sighed. "He's a smart guy. And I'm assuming he married a smart woman. And I don't know any woman that would believe that sort of story, that there was a drunk chick just lying there on his sofa, OD'd, covered in drugs, when he got home."

The handler laughed. "When you put it like that, maybe you're right."

"But if he doesn't back off, he's headed for a fall. A nasty fall."

"Is that what you have planned for Mahoney?"

"No. Still working on that."

"OK, first things first. The girl. Miss Blanc."

"What's the latest?"

"She's alive, throwing up all over the place, but she'll live. Currently in the hospital. Mom and Dad don't know yet."

"You want them to get a call?"

"Yeah, but only the father. We'll send some of the nice still photos of his daughter you took, without Mr. Mahoney in the picture."

"When?"

"When this call ends. We'll confirm when we've sent the photos, and then we'll give you his cell phone number."

"And I get to make the call?"

"You certainly do, bro."

"I'm assuming I can't be traced from my cell phone."

"Encrypted to make it untraceable. Stand by."

Nathan's handler was as good as his word. Ninety seconds later, a message pinged into his phone. It read, *Photos sent. Give this number a call.*

He walked over to the floor-to-ceiling windows overlooking downtown Toronto. The phone rang four times before it was picked up.

"Who's calling at this time of the night?"

"Mr. Blanc?"

"Who is this?"

"The guy who took the photographs."

A silence stretched between them.

"Are you still there, Mr. Blanc?"

"What do you want?"

"I want to talk."

"About what?"

"I think you know what. Do you mind if I call you Matthew?"

A pause. "Is this blackmail?"

Nathan smiled. "This is how it's going to work. We know who you are. We know all about you. And we respect that. We admire your work."

"I have no idea what you're talking about."

"Matthew . . . don't be like that. You know exactly what this is about. It's about the photos. Your daughter."

"Where is she?"

"She's in the hospital. But she's going to live."

"When I find out who you are, I will kill you. Do you understand?"

Nathan sighed. "Bravado. I respect that. I'd be the same way. Here's what's going to happen. You will visit your daughter. She will be mortified by this. And she will talk about having her drink spiked. That is all correct. So she's not to blame. I am."

"Who do you work for?"

Nathan sighed. "You're not making this easy on me, Matthew."

"Your accent isn't Canadian. You American?"

Nathan said nothing.

"What do you know about me?"

"I know you've been in contact with Mark Mahoney."

Blanc went quiet.

"Yeah, we know you met with him. And about the information you passed along. We just want you to know that it stops now. You will not be meeting up with Mahoney again or pass on any further information."

"I have no idea what you're talking about. You must have the wrong guy."

"Matthew, let's be very frank. We're playing nice. If we weren't playing nice, your daughter might be dead."

"You leave my fucking daughter alone."

"And we will, Matthew, I promise. Don't worry about that. She's a sweet kid. Big future."

Blanc said nothing.

"But that future might not be so bright or big. Can you imagine if pictures like that made their way to those fancy art colleges she wants to go to? You imagine how that would look. Not fucking good."

"So you're blackmailing me?"

Nathan sighed. "I'm being patient with you, Matthew. I'm being nice. I would hate these photos to be leaked to the press. *National Enquirer*. Shit, we could even upload the stills to YouTube. I believe there's video footage too. It would go viral. Imagine that!"

"Who do you work for?"

"I don't work for anyone. I'm just calling to advise you that you need to take on board what I'm saying, or these pictures will be everywhere. And you know how mean kids can be. There will be questions asked about you too. Has a Canadian intelligence operative been compromised? You know the kind of thing, Matthew. You've probably done it a hundred times before, exerting a little pressure."

Blanc sighed long and hard. "How do I know the photos won't be published?"

"You don't. That's the bottom line. But these photos will never be seen by anyone unless you break our agreement."

"There is no agreement."

"Of course there is, Matthew. You know as well as I do it's in your interests, and your daughter's, to keep this quiet."

"What about my country's interests?"

"Guess you'll have to make a choice. Choose well. Do we have a deal?"

"Yes, we do. You have my word. But these pictures must never be published in any form anyplace. Do you understand, you piece of shit?"

"I hear what you're saying, Matthew. I'm telling you loud and clear your daughter's secrets are safe with us."

Twenty

It was late the following morning when Nathan awoke. He showered, got dressed, and headed to a nearby diner. He knew he needed to focus on the job at hand. But he found he was thinking of what lay ahead. He was on his third coffee of the day when his cell phone rang. He recognized the number of his handler.

"Morning," the man said. "Very fine work."

"You think that will do it?"

"The guy knows it would be a nightmare for him at his job and for his daughter's career prospects. But especially with the drugs all over her. We hear he's already pulling strings with the police, and she'll be released with a slap on the wrist as long as Blanc vows she won't be going out on the town for the next six months."

Nathan smiled. "That works. And he won't be going near Mahoney?"

"I wouldn't think so."

"Where's Mahoney now?"

"Still being interviewed by the cops. Had a drug test, which came back negative. And an alcohol test, which also came back negative."

"OK, now that we've got Blanc out of the way, we need to focus on Mahoney," Nathan said. "We have incriminating photos as a useful backup. That should scare him off pursuing his investigation."

"Photos might come in handy if he gets spooked and heads back to New York. But we need to focus first and foremost on neutralizing this fucker."

"Do we have any indication when Mahoney will be back in his place?"

"In a few hours. In the meantime, I want you to take the SIM out of your phone and flush it down the toilet."

"Not a problem."

"Then go to the nearest shop selling iPhones and buy the latest model. We'll remotely access your phone and encrypt it, so you'll be good to go within ten minutes of buying it."

"What else?"

"Enjoy your breakfast. Rest up."

"Why?"

"You'll see."

Nathan did as he was told. He dismantled the cell phone he'd been given and flushed the SIM card down the toilet. Then he headed outside and dropped the iPhone into a trash can. He bought a new phone, then headed back to the apartment. He lay down on his bed and began to formulate a plan to finally neutralize Mark Mahoney.

Nathan reflected first on Mahoney's predicament. It was only common sense to realize that the discovery of the girl, covered in drugs, would rattle him. It would at a minimum, if the story got out, get him fired. Nathan had convinced his handler it was a useful fallback position. He had calculated that Mahoney could be manipulated during a face-to-face approach as part of his shadow plan. It was high stakes. And there was no going back now.

Nathan wondered if Mahoney would tell his executive editor. Would he tell his wife? Would the story be leaked by the police?

The more Nathan thought about it, the more he believed Blanc would stop contact with Mahoney. He knew people acted in their own interests when push came to shove. There was a possibility that Blanc might do the honorable thing and do what he thought was right for the country. But Nathan knew it was human nature to protect flesh and blood, just like he himself was doing with his sister. He was doing whatever it took to keep her alive. And he assumed Blanc would do the same.

Mahoney, on the other hand, was in a very bad situation. And he would know that. Being arrested for minor misdemeanors was one thing, but being arrested on drug charges, maybe even drugging a minor with Rohypnol? None of that looked good.

Nathan knew the girl wouldn't remember a thing. Perhaps only that she'd been drinking with a guy named John.

He felt himself drift off, thinking about how Mark Mahoney was going to react.

The sound of his cell phone ringing snapped Nathan awake. He took a few moments to get his bearings. He reached over to the bedside table and picked up his new phone. "Yeah?"

"Hey, Stone." The voice of his handler was cold and flinty.

Nathan rubbed his eyes. "What time is it?"

"Just after five. You doze off?"

"Yeah. So what's happening?"

"First, this new cell phone you're using has been updated with cutting-edge encryption. So you're good to go, bro."

"What else?"

"Mark Mahoney has been released by police. They're not convinced he's innocent. They say they're going to be carrying out further investigations."

"How's he taking that?"

"He's totally freaked out."

"What about the forensics team at his apartment?"

"They're finished. He only just got back in."

Nathan grinned. "What a mind fuck."

"Yeah, precisely. So, here's the thing. Our analysis shows that Matthew Blanc is cutting Mahoney out of his life. His daughter is now home. He picked her up from the hospital. And he's ensured the cops won't take this further. The chatter we're picking up is that the Fox has effectively pulled up the drawbridge. So we don't anticipate any more meetings between him and Mahoney."

"So what about our journalist friend?"

"I was just getting to that. We're watching him now. Sitting with his head in his hands on his living room floor."

Nathan went into the other room and turned on his TV to watch the feed of Mahoney. The plan was now under way. A plan that just might save him and his sister. But he also needed to convince his handler that he was finalizing plans for the endgame for the journalist. "I think we need to talk to Mark Mahoney. Exert some pressure close up."

The handler was quiet for a few moments, as if considering this move. "Talk to Mahoney?"

"I've got an idea. About the photos."

"You don't think a call would cut it? Remember, we've already exerted influence on Matthew Blanc. But we've still got to delete this fuck now. I don't see why we should complicate this. It's not like you to complicate things."

"Can I ask a question?" Nathan said.

"Sure."

"Mahoney's been investigating this facility in Scotland, and the death of Senator Crichton over there."

"Right. We believe he has serious amounts of data. We've tried to access it, but it's squirreled away in several military-level encrypted sites. We've intercepted one, but there are others. So, unfortunately we can't derail things that way."

"Mahoney, as far as I can tell from the file, is married, two kids, straight, family man, universally liked, all-around good guy."

"Right. So, next move, Nathan. What do you think?"

Nathan had been considering several options. He was still weighing up the best way to execute the shadow plan he was working on. "I think you should monitor him closely, see how he reacts. Who he contacts. If he talks to his wife and tells her the story, or his boss, we need to get in and neutralize very quickly."

"I can live with that."

"One final thing."

"What's that?"

"He was an embedded journalist with my unit during the Iraq War."

"Sure, we know that."

"And he knows what I looked like then."

"Right."

"But he won't know what I look like now, since the reconstructive surgery, will he?"

His handler was quiet for a few moments. "Where are you going with this, Stone?"

"He won't recognize me, right?"

"No, he won't, guarantee it."

Nathan smiled as his heart began to beat faster. He could see a way to make this work. It was opening up in front of him. "My original point about a face-to-face. That is something I'd like to move forward."

"You going to do him face-to-face, up close?"

"Maybe. I think I've got an idea."

Twenty-One

Wilson had been poring over the status reports of the operation in the small cottage where he was staying on a huge estate on a private island off the Gulf Coast of Florida. He'd heard from various sources in Canada, including Stone's handler and the psychologist. Had talked extensively to Fisk, the financial backer of the Commission, who was enthralled with the details and minutiae of Stone and his role in the operation. Now they were moving to a critical phase.

A knock sounded at the door. Wilson answered it to find three armed guards.

"Sir, I believe they're waiting for you," the most senior of the trio said.

He headed over toward the main building, flanked by the security detail, past more security, and down into the secure conference room in the subbasement.

The other members of the Commission nodded as he walked in, the door locking behind him.

Wilson sat down at the head of the table, as he always did. "OK, gentlemen, here's an update as promised. The operation to neutralize Mark Mahoney is well and truly under way. First, we have unmasked Mahoney's recent source in Toronto. Matthew Blanc, military attaché to the UN several years back. That name will no doubt ring a few bells around the table."

Everyone nodded.

"Very highly thought of, but in our business there's no room for sentimentality." He picked up a remote control and pressed a couple of buttons. Up on the big screen were pictures of Blanc's daughter, drugs sprinkled on her T-shirt. "These are stills taken by Stone within Mahoney's apartment. This not only incriminates the girl—and buys the silence of her mortified and, no doubt, alarmed father, who will see it for what it is, us exerting influence—but also provides us with a useful tool for blackmailing Mahoney as a backup." Wilson pressed another button, and a still image appeared of the distraught journalist kneeling beside the unconscious girl, holding her wrist. "We've put the screws on both Matthew Blanc, who is now backing out of any further involvement with Mahoney, and the *New York Times* journalist, who is our main target."

Richard Stanton pinched the bridge of his nose as he absorbed the information. "How do we know he's backed off? Do we have confirmation, or is this merely supposition?"

"Good point, Richard," Wilson said. "Back channels to Blanc have been established by two sources on the ground in Toronto. We've been told in no uncertain terms, and I quote, 'I'm out,' and 'Don't worry, I get the message. There will be no contact with Mahoney from now on. You have my word.' That's what Blanc said, since he doesn't want any incriminating pictures of his daughter getting leaked."

Stanton nodded. "So let's assume Blanc's out of the picture. This is interesting work by Stone."

"Stone constantly surprises us, as we know to our cost. We're just one step away, I think, from neutralizing Mahoney."

A few nods around the table. Stanton was the only one who didn't seem to agree.

"Richard," Wilson said, "do you have any thoughts on the operation so far? I know it's been a little more complicated than we'd imagined."

Stanton steepled his fingers for a few moments, as if gathering his thoughts. "I believe this is classic neutralizing. It's elegant in that we haven't had to leave a trail of bodies anywhere. Far better to dissuade and instill fear than to act recklessly. So all appears to be fine and dandy. But I am concerned that Mahoney still has to be dealt with more permanently. My other concern is that, since we kidnapped his sister, Stone will nurse a grievance with us."

Wilson sighed. "The psychologist's report didn't mention anything like that. Do you think that will manifest itself in unpredictability, or compromise our aims in some way?"

"I don't know. I think he's very smart. He's also very violent. But his love for his sister, the girl who killed their tormentor, is a love for someone who means everything to him. The psychologist mentioned in a paragraph of a report about Stone that there are depths to him that, and I'm quoting here, 'mystified and terrified in equal measure.' What I think he meant by that was that Stone, as we saw during the last operation, is always thinking ahead. But I will be happy when this operation is complete, since Stone not knowing if his sister is dead or alive every day could be doing untold damage to his head."

Wilson said, "You think there might be blowback for our actions? If so, how would that play out?"

Stanton looked around the room. No one else seemed concerned. "While I agree he's ideally suited for these operations, I think we haven't addressed this terrifying undercurrent in Stone. And I for one think we should consider releasing him from his obligation to us once this is complete. And we should respect that and adhere to it."

Wilson said, "I think the idea has some merit. But first things first. We shouldn't get ahead of ourselves. We don't know how exactly Stone will execute his task. He wants to get in close. He could just poison the fucker."

Stanton said, "It's not like Stone. And if that opportunity doesn't arise?"

"Stone is authorized to neutralize Mahoney in whatever manner he thinks is appropriate."

Stanton said, "The sooner this is done, the sooner we can get back to doing what we were designed to do."

Twenty-Two

Nathan was watching the feed of Mahoney as he moped around his apartment, the journalist unable to comprehend what had happened.

He watched as Mahoney poured himself a large Scotch and sat back on the sofa, classical music playing quietly in the background.

Nathan sensed the guy's anguish. It wasn't just the tight closing of his eyes or the occasional curse to himself. It was his general demeanor. The slightly hunched shoulders, as if bearing the weight of the world.

He wondered when Mahoney should be contacted.

The more he contemplated the situation, the more he tried to anticipate unforeseen events. What if Mahoney reacted by revealing everything to his wife? His editor? A friend?

Time dragged as Nathan watched Mahoney lying unmoving on the sofa. He wondered if the fucker was simply going to do nothing. That would make sense. Perhaps he was taking time to let what had happened sink in. Try and figure it all out. Maybe put it down to dumb luck. And then move on.

But he was a smart guy. He wasn't the type to assume this was coincidence.

The buzzer sounded in Mahoney's apartment. He seemed agitated. Stone watched as the journalist got up and checked the video intercom.

"Mark, guess who?" a woman's voice said.

"Honey, are you kidding me? Is that you?"

Suddenly, the voices of excited kids. "Daddy! Daddy! We're here in Canada to see you!"

Nathan watched in grim fascination, realizing he needed a new plan. "Fuck."

Mahoney pressed the buzzer to let them in. A few seconds later, his wife, carrying an overnight bag, and the excited kids appeared in the apartment as Mahoney wheeled in a large suitcase. The journalist shut the door behind him and hugged his wife and kids, who were jumping around like crazy.

"I missed you," his wife said. "Wow, nice place they put you in."

Nathan stared at the scene. He had never imagined this happening. This complicated things. He couldn't speak to Mahoney at the apartment. That was out of the question now.

His cell phone rang. "We got a problem, bro," his handler said.

"Yeah, no kidding."

"Quite a surprise."

"Did we anticipate her joining him?" Nathan asked. "Because I sure as hell didn't."

"He's been here for months and she's never even talked about visiting. We're scratching our heads like you. The question is, What do we do now?"

Nathan sighed. He took a few moments to let it all sink in. It wasn't good. They could be there for days, maybe weeks. Who knew?

His handler continued. "So we can't neutralize Mahoney at his place now."

Nathan nodded. "Out of the question."

There was a long pause before the handler spoke again. "We were hoping this might be finished in the next couple of days."

"It still might be."

"How?"

"There are ways. We need to get him out of the apartment."

"But to where?"

"I'll figure it out. That's what you guys pay me for, isn't it?"

"Get this done and you'll be one million dollars richer with your sister back, safe and sound, in her hospital room in Florida."

Nathan grew quiet as he contemplated his next move. "I might need to go dark to avoid being detected."

The handler groaned. "I don't know, bro. That's not how we usually do things."

"Trust me. I know how to pull this off."

"You wouldn't have any eyes or ears helping you."

"Just for a few hours. But I think it's important to not be linked back to you guys on this."

"So are you going to set something up? I need to know that."

"Let me handle this. It's complicated. But I got this."

"Make sure you do, Stone. For all our sakes."

Twenty-Three

Berenger had been reviewing the notes on how Nathan had entrapped the impressionable young woman with his tale of being a photographer. He was impressed with how Nathan's plan had evolved as the situation developed. It was brilliant. He began to look over the covert surveillance footage of Nathan. The easy way he engaged with the girl in Mahoney's apartment before he drugged her and then left her sprawled on the sofa, covered in drugs.

He watched the way Nathan had set it all up. The execution of the plan. Entrapment. But the way he managed to ensnare Mahoney in the actions as well was very gratifying to see.

His cell phone rang and he recognized the number. It was Nathan's handler. A man whose name he didn't even know, despite having worked with him in the past. He believed the man was from Texas, but that was all the information he had.

"Hey, Doc, you got a couple of minutes?"

Berenger stared at the image of the unconscious girl. "I was expecting you to call."

"What do you think?"

"You want me to try and establish the up-to-date assessment of where he's at?"

"Can he complete the operation? That's all I need to know."

"I have no doubt he can complete the operation. Absolutely no question about that."

"So we're good. On schedule."

"We're all these things. And more."

"What do you mean, *and more?*"

"I had previously formed the opinion that Nathan was dangerous."

"Well, he is, isn't he?" the handler said.

"Yes, I think his performance with that girl also shows stunning critical thinking. He engineered this himself. Quite brilliant. Which puts him on a whole new level."

"He's a cold-blooded killer, Doc."

"Yes, he is. But there's so much more. I feel like I'm only now starting to gauge the depths of his manipulative skills, how he deploys these skills, and how he can mask his emotions and his real intentions."

The handler went quiet.

"Nathan thinks long and hard when required to. He calculates. He plots. And he can switch off the physiological reaction that we all have to moments of fear. Have you ever watched any horror movies?"

"Not for a while. But sure, I've watched some."

"What's the scariest one you've seen?"

"Probably *The Shining*. Yeah, that scared the shit out of me."

"When you say it scared you, in what way?"

"I was so tense. My heart was beating hard. My palms were sweating. I was watching it with my girlfriend at the time, holding her hand in the movie theater."

"You old romantic."

The guy laughed. "And she commented on how sweaty my hands were."

"That's interesting."

"Why?"

"Someone like Nathan Stone would have a very different reaction."

"Shit."

Berenger leaned back in his seat. "Tell me, how has Nathan sounded to you?"

"Like he always does. Cogent. Strong. Assertive. Smart. But always thinking of angles."

"That's good, right?" Berenger asked.

"It's always a good thing in our business," the handler said. "Unfortunately, the last time, when Stone realized the operation was going south, in Scotland, and he was becoming the hunted, he turned the tables."

"He's got far more at stake in this operation, though, doesn't he?" Berenger said.

The handler sighed.

"I said, he's got even more at stake—"

"Yeah, I heard you. Doc, look, I'm not keen on getting psychoanalyzed. This is not what I do or care for. No offense."

"None taken. But you still haven't answered my question. Nathan has even more at stake now. His sister's life. His flesh and blood. The only thing that means anything to him, in whatever abstract sense anything matters to him at all."

"What are you looking to find out from me, Doc? I thought this was just a tool to know Stone's state of mind. And if he was ready to go."

"I'm trying to determine from those who know him—"

"No one really knows him. That's the thing. But you're right. Stone has even more at stake now."

Berenger sensed an apprehension in the handler, as if he was unwilling to open up and express his true feelings. "Listen, I want you to be up front with me. For me to understand the true position of Nathan Stone, I need you to be honest. Totally honest. And I can't have you withholding any concerns or aspects of this operation that we might be missing. What one person might view as insignificant, someone else might think is more important, do you understand?"

The man said nothing.

"I'm getting the feeling you're not telling me everything."

"Look, I get paid to run an operation. I know the kind of stuff we know. You have to have something a bit out of whack in your personality to consider doing what we do."

"Go on."

"I get paid incredibly well for the work I do. I'm sure you do too."

Berenger wondered what the man was getting at. "You're reluctant to jeopardize your large salary by criticizing any aspect of the operation, is that it?"

"Wouldn't you be?"

"What I know is it's my job to ensure the operation is completed by addressing the psychological needs, demands, and fears of the participants, and not just Nathan. He's only one piece of this jigsaw. So I want you to rest assured that whatever you say is confidential. But it's vital you speak your mind."

The handler was quiet for a few moments before he finally spoke. "His handler on the Scottish operation that went to shit, he was an old friend of mine from way back."

Berenger listened but said nothing. The handler needed space to speak.

"We worked out of a CIA satellite office not far from Langley. Special-operations type of gigs."

Berenger began to take notes.

"I knew him as well as anyone. He trained Nathan Stone. And he was killed by Nathan Stone. I still can't believe he's dead. He was my mentor. He taught me everything I know about this job. But more than anything, he talked about Stone. I was based at the facility in Scotland. And I was there that night Stone came back. It was like a blitzkrieg."

94

Berenger's mind flashed back to the incident. "I worked there until a couple of days before it all went south too. I'm well aware of what happened."

"I don't remember you."

"I was shut off from the rest of the team. Working exclusively with Nathan."

"So you know him pretty damn good already."

"As you say, as well as anyone can. But go on. You were talking about the death of the handler in Scotland."

"He told me he knew Stone had to be killed off right in the middle of the operation, and he called in a shadow team. This shadow team apparently found the senator's mistress, killed her, and buried her in the woods on an isolated peninsula in northwest Scotland. My friend said it was the saddest day of his life when he had to activate that team. A couple of guys who were tasked with killing Stone and the mistress so as not to compromise the mission."

Berenger thought of Nathan's cold, intense eyes.

"We all assumed Stone was critically injured, maybe fatally, since we couldn't contact him, but all the time, we now know, he was watching the shadow team. Dealt with them. And then returned to the facility to get his revenge."

"Are you saying you have concerns about Nathan on this mission?"

The handler remained silent.

"Can you answer that question?"

"I've had concerns from the get-go."

"Can you explain?"

"I told everyone we shouldn't use Stone."

Berenger was shocked at the revelation. "What was your rationale?"

"He's not only a killing machine but a killing machine that can turn into a wrecking ball. When he was threatened, he turned."

"You said you expressed those concerns?"

"I sent my concerns up the chain of command. But apparently they've been overlooked or ignored."

Berenger cleared his throat. He hadn't heard this story before. And it alarmed him. "You think because his sister is being held and being used against him, this might trigger him?"

There was a pause before the man spoke, his voice barely a whisper. "That's exactly what I'm saying, Doc."

Twenty-Four

Late the following afternoon, Nathan emerged from his apartment. He was still contemplating how to deal with Mahoney. He had left his cell phone behind, as he had told his handler he would. It was certainly problematic, the journalist's family turning up unannounced. But if there was one thing Nathan had learned over the years, it was that sometimes problems could also create opportunities.

A germ of an idea had begun to form, taken hold, and morphed into a plan. A plan that required a convergence of several factors.

He took a bus downtown.

Nathan bought a new iPhone at the Eaton Centre. He didn't want anyone to trace him. He headed to the *Times* bureau and called reception. "I need to speak to Mark Mahoney."

"I'll put you through."

A brief pause. "Mahoney speaking."

Nathan cleared his throat. "Mark, you don't know me, but I know you. I'd like to talk to you about something very important."

"I'm sorry . . . Who are you?"

"Let's focus on you for now."

"What are you talking about?"

"I'm talking about the girl covered in drugs. I'm talking about your investigation. I'd like to talk about that. You know what? I'd like to talk about a lot of things."

Mahoney didn't speak.

"Are you still there, Mark?"

"I think you must have the wrong number."

"I don't think so. So let's quit playing games. I want to talk to you face-to-face and explain what exactly happened."

"I really have no idea what you're talking about. This is very strange."

"It won't be half as strange if your wife finds out about it. Or sees the pictures. Very damaging pictures. Trust me. A lot of pictures. And they don't look good for you."

Mahoney sighed.

"Now, here's what's going to happen. I'm waiting outside."

"Excuse me . . . I have work to do. So if it's OK with you, I'd like to get back to it."

"Forget that. I'm by myself and I don't want to hurt you. I just want to talk to you. But do not under any circumstances bring any recording equipment, a cell phone, or electronic devices of any nature, am I clear?"

"I think I'm going to have to call the police."

"Go right ahead."

A deafening silence filled the air.

"You've already been interviewed by the police. I'm sure they'll be fascinated to know more about that evening. And so would your wife. She's in town, isn't she? Bit of a surprise for you, I assume."

"You leave my family out of this."

"I have no intention of bringing your family into anything. But that's why I want to speak to you. We'll just talk and walk, in full view. I'll be waiting outside. Wrap up warm, it's cold out here. And remember, no phones."

Nathan ended the call. He wondered if it would draw Mahoney out. He wouldn't recognize Nathan after his surgery. But maybe his voice would betray him. But he thought it was far hoarser than all those years ago, when he had been just a kid in Iraq and Mahoney the fresh-faced cub reporter.

A few minutes later, Mahoney emerged from the building across the street from where Nathan stood. He wore a burgundy scarf, a heavy coat, and a hat.

Nathan crossed the street and cocked his head. "Walk with me," he said.

Mahoney turned up his collar against the cold. "Who are you?"

"I'm assuming you have no cell phone or any devices on you."

"None at all."

"I'm going to trust you. And I hope you're going to trust me."

"Who the hell are you?"

"I'm the guy that was sent to kill you."

Mahoney glanced sideways at Nathan. "What the fuck is this? Are you shitting me?"

Nathan shook his head.

"Who wants to kill me and why?"

"It's complicated."

Mahoney strode on in silence for a few seconds. "You've been sent to kill me?"

"I'm an assassin. That's what I do. That's all I do."

"What the hell is this? We don't kill journalists in America."

"Not usually, no. But this isn't America, is it?"

Mahoney appeared to be in shock. His hands were shaking and his expression was pained, as if he were being eaten away at from inside.

Nathan spotted a bar up ahead. "You look like you could use a drink."

They crossed over and headed into the quiet little bar. Nathan got two beers and two Scotches. They sat down in a corner booth, away from the handful of people at the bar.

99

Mahoney picked up the glass of whiskey and knocked it back in one. He grimaced and took a couple of gulps of beer. "Christ Almighty."

Nathan sat down across from him. He knocked back the whiskey and also gulped some of the beer. He leaned in close. He could see the fear in Mahoney's eyes in fine detail. As if everything he had accomplished and achieved amounted to nothing. The family he loved, disintegrating. His reputation in ruins.

"So is . . . ? I don't know, this doesn't seem right."

"Relax. And listen to me. Now that we've established a few basics, I want to talk further about what the people that hired me want to happen to you."

Mahoney closed his eyes.

"The people who hired me want you dead. They will not be happy until you are dead. Now, the first part of the operation, that was my idea. And my bosses bought it."

"What are you talking about?"

"The plan went better than I had imagined. A girl was found unconscious on your sofa, a generous sprinkling of coke on her T-shirt if I remember."

"You did that?"

"Not important. What is important is that you're still alive, and you have a choice."

Mahoney knocked back the rest of the Heineken and shook his head, clearly struggling to take it all in. Possibly even in shock.

Nathan leaned in closer, his voice barely a whisper. "They want you to kill yourself. Failing that, I was tasked with assisting with your death. Do you understand what that means?"

Mahoney shook his head.

"They want you to have an accident, maybe a fall."

"Oh Christ."

"Keep it down. Like I said, that's what they want. And I've done this sort of thing many times. It's no big deal for me. I'm in town to make sure this happens. The first stage of the operation they believe was a backup. That's what I persuaded them it was. As I say, we have incriminating pictures. I'm assuming you haven't told your wife or employer."

"No, I haven't."

"I don't blame you. No wife would understand that. And no employer would either. Do you see how easy it was?"

Mahoney nodded.

Nathan ordered another two bottles of beer. "This isn't personal. It's just . . . well, your work is now coming into conflict with the interests of my client."

Mahoney stared.

"I think you know what I'm talking about."

"Crichton?"

Nathan nodded. "You're investigating the death of the senator . . . and I can assure you that no good will come of it. Now, as it stands you've had a little run-in with the police, and you've gotten off lightly. So far. But I have to warn you: that can change at a moment's notice." He pushed the second bottle of beer toward the journalist. "It's nice and cold. Take it."

Mahoney picked it up and gulped the contents of the bottle in one swig.

"Feeling better?"

Mahoney shook his head.

"I want to go through your current options. First, how would you feel if your wife saw the photos?"

"I would be devastated. So would she. And she'd take the kids back to New York, and I'd never see them again."

"That's the reality. OK, what do you think would happen if the *New York Times* board saw those pictures? How would they react?"

"They'd fire my ass."

"That's right. They would. And whatever lame excuses you would come up with would cut no ice with them. Can you imagine one of their

101

journalists, a senior award-winning journalist, still being employed after partying with a drunk girl, who's sixteen by the way, covered in cocaine? That might almost be OK in Europe. But in America? I mean . . . your career would be over. And that's best-case scenario. Professional ruin. Could you live with that?"

"No, I couldn't."

"So here's the thing . . . I'm going to ask you a question. And let's see where it gets us."

"Please don't play games with me."

"I understand completely. It's only natural to be nervous. Don't beat yourself up about it. OK, so if you had a choice, what would be your least worst option?"

"If my wife believed I'd wound up with a girl, drugs all over her, at my apartment, she'd leave and take the kids and I'd never see them again. That's the absolute worst option for me."

"So if the photos were leaked to your paper, how would you explain that?"

"I'd just resign before it got to that point. And end the investigation."

"So you're prepared to do that?"

Mahoney thought long and hard. "That would be the lesser of the two evils."

"I understand. That sounds reasonable. Except . . ."

"Except what?"

"Except the people that hired me don't just want for you to be shamed and lose your job. That's really easy stuff. What they want is you out of the game."

"Out of the game?"

"I don't mean out of journalism. I mean . . . Well, ultimately they want you dead so the investigation dies with you."

Mahoney closed his eyes.

"The photos were just a means of getting your attention. I've bought you some time. But the people that sent me need you to die."

"Oh Christ." Mahoney took a deep breath.

"Your wife would get a sizable payout from your life insurance if you had an accident. And you'd have a lovely obituary in the *New York Times*, penned by one of your pals, who would wax lyrical about how you were an old-school, hugely talented journalist, a man of principle and all that bullshit. That in itself is better than enduring a lifetime of shame surely."

Mahoney stared at him. "Why are you telling me this?"

"I'm getting to that."

"What a fucking mess."

"Yes, it is." There was an awkward pause, then Nathan continued. "Tell me, Mark, this investigation, it's dragged on for months, right?"

Mahoney nodded.

"What exactly do you know?"

"I know major parts of the story. I think I'm close to piecing together other aspects. There are still a few holes I need to fill in."

"Percentage terms, how much do you think you've got?"

"I think I've got seventy, maybe eighty percent of the story."

Nathan glanced around. The handful of other customers had now left the bar. Only a bartender cleaning glasses remained. "Look, I'm not going to make promises . . . but there might be a way for you to save yourself. I'm not guaranteeing anything—far from it—but it might just persuade them that you pose no threat to their operation."

"Please don't tease me . . . This is my life we're talking about."

"I get that. I'm not playing games, Mark. I'm trying to come up with a solution that might just save your bacon."

"What exactly would that be?"

"Tell me about your files. The notes. I'm assuming you have everything saved someplace safe."

Mahoney nodded.

"But being a smart guy, you don't just save it to the hard drive, do you?"

Mahoney said nothing.

"You need to help me, Mark, or the slender chance you've got will slip through your fingers. Understand?"

"Yes."

"So, you don't just save all your writing to the hard drive?"

"I back it up to the cloud."

"Smart guy. Military-level encryption?"

"Are you saying if you had all my notes, everything pertaining to the investigation, I might get to live?"

Nathan took a few moments before answering. "I can't give you my word. But I think your only hope of staying alive is to hand over, just to me, what you've got."

"And if I don't? What if I go on the run?"

"Then the photos will be unleashed on the world. You'll have crossed a line. And there's a pretty good chance you won't survive the fall."

Twenty-Five

Nathan let the words sink in as Mahoney mulled what he'd said.

"I have my own line," Mahoney said.

"What's that?"

"My family."

Nathan nodded.

"They don't know anything about this investigation."

"Tell me more about it."

"I love my work. This investigation is very important to me."

"As important as your family?"

"No. Never. But it means a lot to me."

"The people that sent me don't share your enthusiasm for this investigation."

"I'm sure they don't."

"Tell me, you say you've been piecing this together. What do you know?"

Mahoney sighed. "You're probably not the best person for me to share this information with."

Nathan smiled.

"What's so funny?"

"You. Trying to exert some leverage. I admire that."

"Bullshit."

Nathan shook his head. "You're probably looking at me thinking, *This is the last face I'm going to see*, right?"

"I don't want to think about it. Look, I get it. I'm fucked."

"You resigned to your fate?"

"I guess I could go to the police and tell them what happened."

"And the people who sent me will release the photos. Upload them to YouTube. You'd be arrested, charged, and your former life would be over."

"I'd be alive."

"Your threat would be neutralized. And besides, no one would believe the word of a disgraced journalist. Your credibility would be shot. And your family would leave you. Wasn't that your worst-case scenario?"

Mahoney closed his eyes as he got quiet again. "Why didn't you just neutralize me, as you put it?"

"I could have."

"So why haven't you? Is there some other reason you're not telling me?"

Nathan sighed as he looked around the still-empty bar. "You were sent an eight-page document by a man named Nathan Stone. It was an assassination list. And it had a list of twenty people these men planned to kill. Top of the list was Senator Crichton."

Mahoney said nothing.

Nathan stared at Mahoney. "And this was the basis for the start of your investigation. And like such things, it's grown wings. You're hearing about a second facility, right?"

"Maybe."

"But those eight pages, they also contained something else. The names on the circulation list. I believe the document was stolen by an NSA contractor, who had intercepted the information from supposedly deleted documents on an NSA server. Which was passed to a journalist . . . a libertarian blogger, I believe, in Washington, DC."

"How do you know all this?"

"I just do. I know more about this than most people. And I know a thing or two about how this whole thing started."

Mahoney stared at him. "I'm wondering, though, why you have access to all this information."

"I can't reveal that at this stage. Tell me, the names on the list. Retired generals, admirals, and Brigadier Jack Sands. What do you know about Sands?"

"How the hell do you know all this?"

"Just answer my question."

"Well . . . from the information I was given, I started inquiring about him. And he seemed to be the point man for this operation, on the ground in Scotland."

"Very good. He was. He's dead now, though."

Mahoney rubbed his face with his hands, as if this were all a bad dream.

"The others on the list. Five others. You have the names."

Mahoney looked at him for what seemed like an eternity. He leaned a bit closer, voice a whisper. "You know an awful lot for a guy that was sent to neutralize me."

Nathan said nothing.

Mahoney pointed at him. "Your voice . . . it's familiar."

Nathan shrugged.

"Yeah . . . I think I recognize it."

Nathan smiled. "I get that a lot."

"No, that voice is very familiar. I just can't place it."

Nathan looked around the bar as Mahoney tried to work it out.

"Fuck. It's *you*."

Nathan looked at his drink. "Took you long enough."

"You were the one. Your face . . . What happened to you? I remember Nathan Stone from an operating base outside Fallujah, but you don't look like the same man."

"I've changed."

"Oh Jesus Christ . . . So you were sent to kill me?"

Nathan sighed, crossing his arms as he leaned on the table. "I want to talk about the names on the list."

"You sent it to me?"

"Yes, I did."

"And you killed Crichton?"

Nathan nodded.

"I don't understand."

"What don't you understand?"

"Why would you turn up in person? Surely you knew I'd recognize you."

"Yeah . . . eventually."

Mahoney shook his head and finished his second beer. "And you put that girl in my apartment."

"Yeah."

"So you're interested in the names," Mahoney said, as if in a trance. "The names you sent me."

"What else do you know about them? What have you found out?"

"I know everything about them. Why are you so interested in them? Is that who sent you?"

Nathan sighed. "When you say 'everything about them' . . . do you know where they live, for example?"

Mahoney began to nod slowly.

"Their home addresses? These aren't the sort of people that will be in the phone book."

"Yeah, I know where they live." Mahoney showed his hands. "Hang on just a fucking minute . . . Why exactly do you want to know where they live?"

"I've got a proposition for you. Quid pro quo."

"What do you want me to do?" Mahoney asked.

"I want you to go back to your apartment. Take your wife and kids out for a pizza or something. Don't take your phone with you."

"Why not?"

"They'll be listening in."

"What else?"

Nathan leaned in closer. "Tell your family to go back to New York, something has just come up. Say you'll see them again very soon."

"Then what?"

"I'll be in touch."

"When?"

"Tell them to take the first flight out. Drive them to the airport. Go back to your apartment. Then we talk."

"About what?"

"About a plan I have that just might save your life."

Twenty-Six

Mahoney was in a daze when he left the bar alone. It wasn't just the booze. It was the shock. The terror that was rippling through his body. He walked the ten minutes back through downtown Toronto to his apartment after his terrifying encounter with Nathan Stone. He rode the elevator. His mind was racing. The same elevator Stone would've taken. And the same elevator that girl had taken, the one who had wound up on his sofa.

The more he thought about it all, the more he was starting to doubt his sanity. He felt as if he were losing his mind. His solid, respectable, middle-class life, the terrific salary, the accolades that came with the job, and all the trappings of being a successful American journalist.

Mahoney's mind went back to the targets on the kill list. He had checked and rechecked and found that all the remaining targets were still alive. He had reached out to the Feds to let them know but had never heard back. He was sorely tempted to contact the targets himself. But he was still unsure what to do, as he was still trying to authenticate the document Stone had sent to him.

Mahoney felt empty, his heart in his mouth, as he opened his apartment door. "Hey, I'm back," he said.

His wife hugged him tight. "You smell like a brewery."

"I'm sorry. Had to have a drink after work with a colleague."

"I've been trying to call you."

"You know what? I left my cell at work."

"Mark, how is that possible? You never go anywhere without it."

"I know . . . The thing's virtually attached to me. Just spaced out today, I guess. Crazy. So have you guys eaten?"

His wife shook her head. "We're starving."

"Good, so am I. Who wants pizza?"

The kids roared their approval and they headed out to one of Mahoney's favorite restaurants, Figo's, on Adelaide Street West. It wasn't long before they were chowing down on one of the most phenomenal pies. But his wife could tell he was distracted.

She touched the back of his hand. "You OK, Mark?" she asked.

"I'm fine. Why?"

"You just seem . . . not yourself. Did we come at a bad time?"

"It's never a bad time to see you guys. I love it. But I'm working on a deadline on a pretty important story. You know how it is. And to compound matters, the new executive editor has asked me to talk him through it."

"That's great."

Mahoney nodded. "It is. But I'm just . . . I don't know. It's good, but I feel like I'm drowning in this investigation. Really, really high-level stuff."

"Can you say what it's about?"

"I'm sorry, honey. I wish I could. It's a national security story, I can say that. But that's all."

His wife squeezed his hand. "We're getting in your way already. I can see that."

"I need space and time to focus on this story. It's a real quick turn-around. I feel like I'm juggling different things, meeting up with you guys, my beautiful family, deadlines, you know."

His wife smiled. "Honey, there's something wrong. I know it."

Mahoney ate a slice of pizza and dabbed his mouth with the napkin. "I wish you'd let me know, and I could've said maybe another week or two, and that would be perfect. It's my fault. I should've given you a heads-up."

"Honey, I love you, and if that's what you need, we'll head back to New York. It's only a short plane ride away. It's not a big deal."

"Can I make it up to you?"

His wife screwed up her eyes in mock indignation. "This better be good, Mark. And I mean you gotta hit this out of the ballpark."

"You always wanted to go to Europe, right?"

His wife turned and arched her eyebrows in surprise at the kids. "What does Dad have in mind, I wonder?"

"How about Italy? Lake Garda next summer for a full two weeks. Does that work?"

His wife bit into her pizza. "It works." She looked at her watch. "I think it's too late to get a flight home tonight, though."

"Stay tonight, grab a few hours' sleep, and then I can finish this goddamn project and get home to you in New York as soon as I can."

"You're incorrigible, Mark, do you know that?"

The following morning, bleary-eyed after a restless night, Mahoney sent off his wife and kids at the airport. There were tears, hugs, and no small amount of sadness. But he needed them out of the way. Things had gotten out of control. Dangerous.

His mind was processing so many thoughts as he struggled to comprehend how he was going to extricate himself from the mess he was in. Maybe he should just go to the cops. It would be the easiest way out. Perhaps the most logical.

But something within him begged him to think of his family. He was a naturally cautious person. If he was torn between choices, he usually did nothing.

He drove back to his apartment, showered, put on a fresh suit, brushed his teeth, flossed, and washed his mouth out with Listerine after the booze and pizza from the night before.

Mahoney headed into the office. Made some small talk at the water cooler. Then headed to his desk.

Waiting on his desk was a small unopened package marked *Private & Confidential, Mark Mahoney.* He waited until the other reporters were out of sight before opening it up. Inside was a brand-new iPhone with a note containing a number. Scrawled in ink were the words *Head to the bathroom, make sure no one else is there, and call this number.*

Mahoney's heart was beating fast. He tried to act natural as his fellow journalists dropped by his desk to chat about everything from the weather to the Blue Jays. Eventually, once he could see all the reporters were back at their desks, he headed to the bathroom with his new phone.

He made sure no one was in any of the stalls, went to the farthest one, put down the lid of the toilet, and locked the door. Once the cell phone was activated, he tried to dial the number. But his hand was shaking so badly he misdialed. He tried again, hand still shaking, and managed it on the second attempt.

Mahoney waited. It rang five times.

"I was wondering when you were going to call." It was the voice of Nathan Stone.

Mahoney felt ice in his veins. "So where do we go from here?"

"This is how it's going to work between me and you. First, if you don't do what I tell you, you will die. Either by my hands or someone else's. Second, your apartment is bugged from top to bottom. And the cell phone you usually use is being monitored."

Mahoney closed his eyes as a feeling of dread washed over him. He wondered if Stone was telling the truth. Was this just a trap to lure him to a location and then kill him?

"So the only safe way for us to communicate is via this phone. Am I clear?"

"You're going to kill me whatever I do, aren't you?"

"Not necessarily." Stone let the words linger in the air.

"Are you fucking with me again?"

"No. You're going to help me, and I'm going to help you."

Mahoney cleared his throat as he dropped his voice to a whisper. His mouth felt dry. "How am I going to help you?"

"You're going to give me the addresses of those people on the list like Clayton Wilson, the men who hired me to kill you."

"Why would that be of interest to you?"

"You've got to trust me. I want to help you. I have something you want. Namely, a chance to live. To get back to your wife and kids."

"So why do you need the addresses?"

"They have my sister."

"Your sister?" It sounded weird that a cold-blooded assassin even had a family. Much less one he cared about.

"My older sister."

"I don't believe you."

"Her name is Helen Stone. She was in a psychiatric hospital. But they took her. And they said I wouldn't see her again unless I neutralized you. That's what this comes down to."

Mahoney felt sick. It was then, in that moment as he was gripped by indecision and fear, he realized, as unlikely as it might have seemed, there was a connection between them. He wanted his family to be safe, while Stone wanted the same for his sister. They both needed the same things. He began to wonder if he shouldn't take a step back from the investigation. Was it really worth all this? His family meant everything to him. But it was clear that Stone felt the same for his own sister.

"This is all starting to sound a bit unbelievable," Mahoney said.

"It is what it is. I'm not lying to you."

"I don't know . . . This is a lot to take in. OK, here's a question. If you just neutralize me, as you called it, you'd get your sister back. Why not kill me and be done with it?"

"Because I don't believe their word means a damn thing, Mark."

Mahoney could see what Stone was thinking. And it terrified him almost as much as the idea of Stone killing him.

"They double-crossed me before. They called in a shadow team to take me out when the Crichton job went south."

"So what are you planning to do?"

"More like what are *we* planning to do."

"Nathan, what are you talking about?"

"You're going to accompany me for a few days while I take care of every one of them."

"'Take care of'? What does that mean?"

"You want me to spell it out? I'm going to kill each and every one of them."

"Kill who exactly?"

"The people who sent me. The Commission, as they call themselves."

"I'm a goddamn journalist . . . Are you insane? That's not what I do."

"Mark, listen to me. It's an easy choice. Your only chance of survival is to stick with me."

"And if I don't?"

A silence stretched between them. Eventually, Stone spoke. "Then I'll have to kill you myself."

Twenty-Seven

Nathan made the call to Mahoney from a diner. He suspected his apartment was bugged, perhaps even filled with cameras. He knew his own covert plan was at a critical phase. Mahoney could very well just go to the Feds or the police and get his family into witness protection. And that would leave Nathan and his sister at the mercy of the Commission. But there was another element to the plan he was about to embark on.

He returned to his apartment and saw he had three messages on his "official" phone. He listened to them. All from his handler.

Nathan switched on the TV showing Mahoney's empty apartment. Then he called his handler on the phone he'd been provided with.

"Stone, thought you'd turned tail."

"Yeah, good one. Not quite."

"Where you been, bro?"

"Just watching our guy. Checking what he was up to."

"The wife and kids turning up was not good. But they seem to have dropped off the radar. Said they were heading back on the first flight out. We checked, and they did. All very weird. And he seems to be going around without his cell phone."

Nathan cleared his throat. "It's OK. I was watching him the whole time, don't worry. The guy was at a pizza joint."

"With the family out of the way, I'm thinking you've got a clean shot at this. Time to take him down."

Nathan could tell his handler was getting antsy. The man wanted Mahoney neutralized sooner rather than later. It was a difficult balancing act for Nathan. His parallel operation needed more time and space. But he also needed to persuade his handler, through some misdirection, that the plan to kill Mahoney was imminent. "I've been giving this a lot of thought. I think it's vital that it looks like an accident."

"You want to elaborate?"

"I'd considered just saying that we wanted him to resign and not pursue the investigation. But that got more problematic and messy as I thought it through. I'm not convinced he would necessarily stick to that. I could see him agreeing to scrap the whole thing, resign from his job, but then privately take everything he knew to the FBI as collateral and protection for him and his family."

"I think the time for talking about blackmailing him has come and gone, and now it's all about deleting him."

"That's my gut feeling. I think it's best, now that his family is out of the way, to just get to it."

"OK, that works. Today?"

"I think so. After observing him and listening to him, I can see this is a smart guy who was rattled by this incident. But I think he'd be a thorn in our side if we didn't delete him completely. If we tried to silence him with the blackmail, we couldn't guarantee it would work. But with a fatal heart attack, he's out of the game."

"I'm with you on that."

"It could be the *Times* pursues the story with what they have. But I'll find out what he knows before I get rid of him."

"I think you're right, Stone. The fact this bastard managed to keep it together and not tell his wife and boss means he is going to tough it out. Or try and ignore it."

"I say I do him tonight. He either jumps or he's pushed. What're his plans today?"

"As far as I know from his calendar, he's in his office."

"I'm going to wait till later this afternoon, after his maid cleans up, then get in there and wait for him."

"Fantastic. Get some fresh air, bro. Relax. Then when you're ready, head on over. And let's get him done. Then we can finally get you back home—and your sister too."

Nathan had a shadow plan for the operation. A plan so out there it unnerved even him. He had crossed a line. And it felt good. He had resolved to save Mahoney. And in turn save himself and his sister. He couldn't see any other way out of it.

He showered, put on some clean clothes, headed out, and left the cell phone *they* had given him in his apartment. He pulled out his new cell phone and installed a little-known virtual private network for anonymity when surfing the net. Then he downloaded the Tor browser bundle. Within two minutes, he was up and running on the dark web.

He immediately downloaded a hacker app called locatethisprivate-number. Then he entered the cell phone number of his handler. A few moments later, it spit out the handler's GPS. It showed it was registered in the name, likely fake, of Clive F. Neilson Jr., of Remex Solutions, Toronto.

The shadow plan was under way.

Nathan saw from the GPS that the man was half a mile away. He bought a pair of shades and a Blue Jays hat from a street vendor and walked to the location, a glass high-rise office building.

He went into the huge lobby, where a young receptionist smiled his way. "Hello, sir, how can I help you today?"

"I'm here for an interview. Remex."

"That's on the fourteenth floor, sir. Do you want me to buzz ahead?"

"Thanks anyway, but they're expecting me."

The receptionist pointed to the elevator.

Nathan rode up to the thirteenth floor. He walked down a corridor and headed into a bathroom. He made sure it was empty. Then he pulled out all the paper towels and stuffed them in one of the trash cans. Then he took out a lighter and set it all ablaze. Before long, the fire began to take hold.

He placed the trash can underneath a smoke detector and headed out into the corridor. A few seconds later, a piercing fire alarm and flashing red lights wailed out across the building. Almost immediately the offices emptied as workers pushed past him.

"You need to get your ass out of here, man," a young guy said.

Nathan nodded. "Sure thing." He headed up a flight of stairs to the fourteenth floor and walked toward the door with the name Remex on it. He kept on walking past it.

He heard the sound of a door opening behind him. He turned and saw a man, tattoos covering his arms. Nathan recognized the guy immediately from his time in Scotland. He remembered those tattoos from his earliest days at the facility. The guy was always with Sands, his original handler, the one who had betrayed him. So he had to have been the deputy handler on the Scotland job. Nathan couldn't remember the guy's name. But that didn't matter. In an instant, his Glock was in his hand and his finger on the safety.

Nathan crept up on the guy as the door shut. He pressed the Glock to his head. "Not a fucking move!"

The guy froze.

"You got a security swipe card?"

The guy nodded.

"Nice and cool, swipe it and go back in."

The guy complied, swiped the card past a scanner. The door clicked open and Nathan pushed him inside.

"On your fucking knees!"

The guy nodded and did as he was told.

Nathan frisked the guy's jacket pocket. He pulled out a gun and a cell phone, which he put in his own jacket pocket.

"Stone? What's going on?"

Nathan kept the gun trained on him.

"You need to realize this wasn't me. I had nothing to do with taking your sister. I'm just a working guy like you. Trying to earn a living."

Nathan pressed the gun tight to the man's forehead. "OK, this is how it's going to work. I want the names and numbers of the men who are behind this."

"I don't know that."

"So here's the thing. I can make it painless. Or I can make the last moments of your life wretched."

The guy scrunched up his face. "I'm just following orders. We're just supposed to take down Mahoney."

"What else?"

"Swear to God . . . we gotta have him neutralized and out of here in seventy-two hours. Those are my orders."

Nathan pulled out the man's phone and pressed the home button. "What's your pass code?"

"Stone, please, this is—"

Nathan pressed the gun even tighter into the man's scalp. "I'm going to count to three. And then you die."

"022101."

Nathan tapped in the numbers and the menu appeared. He recognized 22101 as the zip code of the CIA at Langley. He pulled up the contacts and saw there were only six, including the psychologist, Berenger. "Does this have the contacts of those involved?"

The guy nodded.

"Are these specially allocated cell phones?"

"Yeah, everyone that works for us has a specially encrypted phone."

"You need to update your security, my friend."

The man was breathing hard, red in the face. "What do you want, Stone?"

"I got a question for you. One question. If you can answer it, you live."

"And if not?"

"Then you die."

The fire alarm seemed to be getting louder. "What do you want to know?"

"Where's my sister?"

The guy kept his head bowed and began to moan. "Richard Stanton knows about that I think."

"Where's she being kept?"

"I don't know."

"Do you have a code name for me for this operation?"

The handler groaned but said nothing.

Nathan pressed the gun tighter to his head. "Tell me."

"Plastic Man."

"How very original. After the work I had done on my face."

The handler nodded, head bowed.

"Neat."

"Nathan, believe me, I had nothing to do with what happened to your sister."

Nathan looked around the open-plan room with big screens on the walls, blinds pulled down. "So this is your nerve center. Is this where you see what Mahoney is getting up to?"

"Yeah."

"And me?"

"No."

Nathan didn't believe him. "Where are they?"

"The Commission? They were down in Florida . . . but they meet all over the country. New York too."

Nathan scrolled through the messages. "Tell me about Clayton Wilson. What's his code name?"

"Patriot One."

Nathan could see the members of the Commission had been given a unique name with a number from one to five. "How do you usually communicate with him?"

"Always encrypted message."

"Always?"

"I swear."

Nathan scrolled through the text messages. "Clayton likes updates, I see."

"Likes to be kept abreast of what we're doing. Sure. Progress. Short and sweet."

"Tell me about the second facility in Canada."

The guy sighed. "It's impregnable. You'll never get near the place."

"I never asked you that. Did I ask you that?"

The handler closed his eyes tight, as if fearing a bullet at any second.

"I just asked you about it. Describe it. What goes on there?"

"Look, it's secure. They've upgraded everything to biometrics and retina scans, etc., etc. Trust me, it's a fortress."

"They said the same about the facility in the Outer Hebrides. You remember what happened there?"

The guy said nothing.

"What's the purpose of this facility?"

"Just like Scotland, this is a black site. Owned by a private corporation."

"Plausible deniability."

"Pretty much."

"What else do you know about the place?"

The guy got quiet again.

"Cat got your tongue?"

"I heard there's a big operation planned. That's all I know, bro."

"An operation planned within the facility?"

"I don't know. That's just what I heard."

"So you've been there?"

"No. A guy who works there said they were on lockdown for the next week. That was a day or so ago."

"So for the next six days they're on lockdown. Why?"

"You know how it works, Stone. I don't know. He doesn't know. He just knows something's going to go down."

"And it's not connected to Mahoney?" Nathan said, putting the guy's cell phone in his back pocket.

The guy shook his head.

"What's the rationale for getting him out of the way?"

"He knows too much."

"So do you. So do I."

"Nathan, gimme a break."

"Where is this place?"

"It's a huge private island in the middle of a lake in Northern Ontario. Got a landing strip. The works." Nathan figured this was the place he had been taken to blindfolded.

"Hands on your head and get to your feet. And nothing stupid."

The guy complied.

"I'm going to give you one choice."

"Don't kill me, bro. I've got a kid, just a girl. She needs me."

"Here's the deal: you walk out of here right now and you disappear. If you do that, you can live."

The guy nodded. "I can disappear. I can do that."

"That's good. You and your daughter move away, someplace far. Get a new ID. Shouldn't be too difficult. What do you say?"

The guy nodded.

"But you need to leave right now."

The guy stared at him. "You want me out now?"

"Right now, no turning back." Nathan cocked his head to the door. "And don't try and alert them. First thing they'll do if you turn up at the facility unannounced is kill you."

"Understood."

"Go!"

The guy brushed past Nathan and was out the door in a second. Nathan's plan was under way.

Twenty-Eight

Nathan made his way out of the office building, mingling with scores of other workers as the fire alarms continued to ring out. They were evacuated down a stairwell and escorted to the rear parking lot. Dozens of office workers were hanging around as fire trucks pulled up.

Nathan ignored it all and made his way by a circuitous route back to his apartment. He gathered his things—9mm Glock, ammo, cell phones—and put them in the false bottom of his backpack. He got outside before he used the new iPhone to communicate with Mahoney.

"How are you?" Nathan asked.

Mahoney sighed. "I can't do this."

"Then you leave me no choice."

"I think I'd rather take my chances with the cops."

"Good luck with that."

Mahoney groaned. "Listen, I'm serious. I think the cops are my best bet."

"Then what's stopping you?"

A long silence. "Nathan, you scare me. I'm losing my mind. Please . . . I'm begging you."

"Mark, do you think the people that sent me won't be able to get to you? Trust me, they can get to everyone. And I mean *everyone*. Anyone can be neutralized."

Mahoney was quiet.

"I could make one call," Nathan continued, "and those photos would be released to your wife, Twitter, Instagram, the Associated Press, *National Enquirer*—you name it, they'd get it. And of course your bosses at the *New York Times*."

"This is fucking outrageous."

"Of course it is. That's why it works."

Mahoney said nothing.

"I need to find my sister. I don't believe they'll return her."

"So why did you agree to this operation?"

"I had no choice in the matter. I had to agree to it or they would've killed her, then me, when the time came, and they would have gotten someone else to kill you. *Capito?*"

"I'm fucked whatever I do."

Nathan sighed. "Same as me." He realized he had crossed a line. It had been a hasty decision. He knew it would be only a matter of time before news of the handler's absence was uncovered. But he knew how it worked. He couldn't just sit and wait and rely on them to make good on their promises.

The more he thought about it, the more he realized the facility could be sending someone to downtown Toronto to find and kill him at that very moment. Maybe a team.

He knew it must be a similar facility to the one he'd been kept in in Scotland. A black site to hide those about to embark on covert operations. Operations that weren't authorized by anyone. At least officially. It was *the deep state*.

Nathan had been hearing that phrase more and more lately. Some thought the very notion of the deep state was just a conspiracy theorist's projection of what, in their eyes, the shadow government was capable of. Pulling the strings, manipulating policy and policy makers: a covert alliance between the military-industrial complex, the Pentagon, and Wall Street. He was but a very small cog in the machine. They used phrases like *special operations*. But he could see how people thought the deep state was penetrating and influencing their country through corrupt politicians, an all-powerful collection of intelligence agencies who worked in secrecy with, by and large, a malleable media, and organizations like the NSA, able to extend their tentacles to all corners of the web, monitoring and manipulating the virtual as well as the real world.

Mahoney spoke, disturbing Nathan's train of thought. "Why do you need me?"

"I want to keep an eye on you."

"So you can kill me when this is over?"

"You know more about what happened than just about anyone alive. The information you have could help me. And maybe . . . maybe even save my sister."

"You're throwing that guilt trip on me?"

"It is what it is, man."

"If I go to the cops and let them know what I know, I'll be fine."

"You're not thinking this through, Mark. I thought you were a smart guy. Listen to me. You might be fine in police custody, maybe even an FBI safe house, but they'll sure as hell get to your family."

"What if they're taken to a safe house too?"

"Do you know how long it takes to organize that stuff? A long time. Weeks if you're lucky."

"I'm fucking scared. This is not the world I live in."

"It is now. So you need to make a decision."

"And if I don't?"

"You're publicly destroyed by these photos, your family life blown to hell, and your career ruined. There will also be charges. Drug dealing to minors, anyone? You'd never work again. And I'm talking instant—it would take seconds. Bang! You're dead, metaphorically speaking."

"I could write a book."

"Good luck finding a publisher if you're drugging children."

Mahoney was quiet for a few moments, as if reflecting on his predicament.

"Are you really going to walk away from this story? There's a Pulitzer in it, no question."

"My family comes first. My career a distant second."

Nathan was doubtful. He'd known only one journalist. Her name was Deborah Jones, an investigative journalist with the *Miami Herald*. She'd uncovered the missing twenty-eight pages of the 9/11 report that a computer hacker had tried to leak to her. But as Nathan kidnapped her, planning to kill her, she had driven her car straight into the Florida Everglades, fighting Nathan until he passed out. He was dragged unconscious from the water. But she had battled to the bitter end, not only for her right to live but for the story she'd fought so hard for.

He sensed Mahoney was the same: an obsessive journalist who wouldn't give up on the story. But Nathan had no way of knowing for sure.

"This is seriously crazy, you know that, right?" Mahoney said.

Nathan thought the journalist's tone had softened. "Maybe."

"So why do you need me?"

"You're good cover. If I get stopped with a *New York Times* journalist beside me, I'm less likely to be detained by cops."

"I wouldn't guarantee that. Cops hate journalists."

"How much cash have you got?"

"What, right now?"

"At your apartment here in Toronto. That you could access immediately."

Mahoney sighed. "Why do you want to know that?"

"You ask a lot of questions."

"I'm a journalist. It's what we do."

"We'll need to rent cars, take buses, trains, planes, whatever, to get where we need to go."

"Shit, you're serious."

"Mark, I'm running out of patience. Trust me, if I have to get the photos released, so be it. So stop fucking around. I'm asking you a question. How much money can you get your hands on?"

"We have a checking account."

"How much is in it?"

"About sixty thousand dollars I think."

"Would you be able to withdraw ten thousand dollars?"

"What? My wife would know immediately."

"Make up some story. That's what you do, right, stories? So make up a goddamn story."

"So you want me to come with you. And you're going to kill people."

"Honestly? I don't know yet."

"So I'd be an accomplice."

"Don't be so dramatic, Mark. Besides, you could write a book about it. Blackmailed, threatened at gunpoint, blah, blah, blah."

"Now you *are* fucking with me."

"OK, time's up. I need an answer. Either you come with me—and no, you don't have to kill anyone, but you do have to do this—or your life won't be worth shit."

"What if I said I'll do it? What guarantee have I got?"

"I don't do guarantees."

"I need to make sure my family is safe. Maybe I should warn them."

"The best way to protect them is to listen to me. Do as I say. Get some sleep tonight. And tomorrow we go with the flow."

Twenty-Nine

Just after eight the following morning, Nathan arrived at Toronto's Union Station. He was dressed to impress. He wore a navy blazer, black polo shirt, nice jeans, and brown leather brogues. A short while later, he saw Mahoney.

"I must've lost my fucking mind," the journalist said.

"Get over it."

They boarded the Amtrak Maple Leaf train bound for New York Penn Station.

Nathan picked a table with no one near them ahead of the twelve-hour journey.

As the train pulled away, Nathan looked across at the journalist, who was scanning his iPad. He was checking his emails and reading articles from the *Times*.

Nathan sent a message from the handler's phone to Wilson with a false update saying the neutralization was "imminent." He wondered how it would all end. He had put in progress a series of events, and he didn't know how they would unfold. He wondered if maybe he should have just continued with the mission. That thought was eating away at him from the inside.

Would he be signing his sister's death warrant? Would he be signing his own?

The more he thought about it, off and on, as the hours passed, the more Nathan began to realize he might be in the final hours of his life. The decision to allow the handler to escape was high risk. It was just a matter of time before they realized the handler had gone, if they hadn't already.

Then again, maybe his luck would hold. Nathan didn't think the handler's office would be cleaned. It would be accessible only to him and him alone. Secure.

Police stopped the train at the border and all the passengers' passports and IDs, including Nathan's fake one, were checked with their tickets.

Eventually, nearly an hour later, the train continued its journey to New York.

Mahoney looked up from his iPad. "This is never-ending. Ten hours to go. There's got to be a better way of traveling."

"There is. But the beauty of this, and bus and car, is that it's a lot less intrusive than air travel. Fewer cameras. Less focus on bags. Stuff like that."

Mahoney closed his eyes for a moment before he looked out of the window.

"Relax. You worry too much."

"I have a family."

"So do I. And she's mentally ill, a sister who needs around-the-clock care in a specialist hospital."

Mahoney nodded. "I'm sorry . . . I didn't mean to suggest otherwise."

"Don't sweat it. Tell me, the Commission members in New York. What are their exact locations? I know New York better than anyone."

"Trust me, I know New York too."

Mahoney stared at him. "Where are you from?"

"The Bowery. Lower East Side."

"It's changed. And I mean *changed*."

"I know."

"Still has its moments. But now it's all ethnic restaurants, college bars, that kind of thing."

Nathan was quiet as his mind flashed back to his days in his shithole of a room with his sister. His memories of New York were always dominated by the pervasive smell of piss, mostly his own, wetting the bed as a boy, afraid of his father. But also the stinking garbage on the streets, the smell wafting through the vents in the wall and cracks in the windows.

The crazy wild-eyed heroin addicts roaming the streets. Looking to score. Some carried knives for protection. Some carried knives to get money. Mostly they just lay around, out of their fucking minds, as the city carried on around them. Walking over them. Walking around them. Trying not to make eye contact.

Nathan pushed those thoughts and memories to one side. "OK, let's focus on the names on your list."

Mahoney was ghostly white.

"I said let's focus on the names on your list."

"I heard."

"So we have five current members of this Commission. The man that chairs it is . . ."

"Clayton Wilson, ex-director of the CIA."

Nathan made a mental note. "And he lives where?"

"He lives in McLean, Virginia."

"Handy for Langley."

Mahoney didn't smile.

"Who else?"

"Richard Stanton. He's also CIA. Retired general Adam C. Johnson, retired admiral Charles Coleridge, and another former director of the CIA, Crawford McGovern."

Mahoney nodded.

"And they get paid for this, or do they just volunteer their services for the good of the country?"

"Clayton Wilson is mentioned in the Panama Papers."

"What's that?"

"It was a massive leak that showed thousands of names of wealthy individuals, like Clayton Wilson, using shell companies for tax evasion."

"And the rest of the Commission?"

"Cayman Islands companies. Shell companies. Set up for zero tax."

"Nice. Interesting that these superpatriots make sure Uncle Sam doesn't get their money, huh?" Nathan checked the special GPS tracking app he had installed on the handler's cell phone. It showed them each at different locations at that moment, all on the East Coast.

Mahoney shook his head, holding it in his hands. "This is insane."

"It could be worse."

"How on God's earth could it be worse?"

"Just shut up and stop bitching."

"Yes."

Nathan contemplated the scenario he was mulling in his brain. He checked the cell phone identity for Clayton Wilson and it showed his location in McLean. "What do you know about Wilson?"

Mahoney closed his eyes and shook his head. "You're taking the fight to them. This is insanity."

"I used to be in the army. And you learn to fight. And scrap. Do whatever you have to do to survive. Your deepest, darkest instincts kick in when you're in the middle of hell."

Mahoney said nothing.

"One of the first things I learned was not only how to kill but how to get your retaliation in first. Don't wait for people to come to you. Go after them. Make them scared. Make them less powerful."

"So what are you planning to do?"

"You don't need to worry about that. Is Clayton Wilson married?"

Mahoney sighed and nodded. "Yes."

"Family."

"He's got a son."

"Just one?"

"Why are you asking about his family?"

"Just curious. Tell me, you're the journalist. How do you go about finding out who has family and who doesn't? How do you do that?"

Mahoney cleared his throat. "I usually draw on different source material. It could be an official CIA press release from years ago, giving some details about the person. Also newspaper articles about him. And then pull together any number of magazine articles. If they're a director of a company or an adviser, which they all are, that company might release details. Nonexecutive director, that kind of thing."

Nathan contemplated this information for a few moments.

"What are you thinking?" Mahoney asked.

Nathan pulled out his cell phone and searched for "Clayton Wilson." It showed hundreds of articles, including the transcript of a speech Wilson had given at the Global Security Forum, held at the Center for Strategic and International Studies a few years back. Wilson mentioned how his work had affected his family over the years. Namely, his wife and his son. Nathan then looked up Clayton Wilson on Wikipedia. He scrolled through the page, reading about Wilson's elite background, his fast-track progress through the CIA, postings in shithole bureaus around the world, etc., etc. It said his son, Marshall Wilson, was president of Wilson Equity, a bespoke equity derivatives company with handpicked, high-net-worth private clients looking for spectacular returns. The company's main office was located in Midtown Manhattan, close to Columbus Circle.

He reflected on this as the train cut through the lush countryside.

The journey dragged as passengers got on, lugging huge suitcases, backpacks, bags, and God knew what else.

Nathan liked to carry the absolute minimum with him. A backpack had to have everything in it.

His mind was racing as he thought ahead. He was already figuring it out. He began to imagine a scenario. A playbook. He knew it was nuts. He knew these were powerful people. And he knew their tentacles would extend beyond the Commission.

He began to think of their privileged lives. They had directorships. They were individually wealthy. Advising hedge funds and banks on geopolitical strategies. He'd read all about how generals hooked up with Wall Street. Everyone was in it. Lining their pockets. No questions asked.

The corporations were grateful for the most senior people within the military-industrial complex, whose departments were in charge of multibillion-dollar contracts. But they also knew their way around Capitol Hill. They had political links. They knew people. They knew the judges. The powerbrokers in New York. DC.

The more he thought about it all, the more depressing Nathan found it.

He bought Mahoney and himself some sandwiches, snacks, bottles of water, and coffee.

"Tell me about your sister," Mahoney said.

Nathan cleared his throat, never comfortable opening up. "She's my big sister. I love her. She's got no one apart from me. And I do everything in my power to make sure she has what she needs."

"You said she was in a hospital. Do you mind me asking more about that?"

Nathan did mind. He was quiet as he wondered whether to talk to Mahoney. But he figured he needed to keep the reporter on his side for as long as he could. "My father was not a good man."

Mahoney listened. "In what way?"

"How do you mean?"

"I mean in what way was he not a good man?"

Nathan shrugged. "You know how it is."

"No, I don't."

135

"My father was a violent alcoholic."

"I'm sorry . . . Shit."

"You wanna know about my life? He beat me. He beat my sister. We were tiny. Scrawny little things. Malnourished. He spent whatever cash we had on liquor. And women. We scavenged. Like feral dogs."

Mahoney closed his eyes.

"She protected me by killing him. So they put her away."

"What about you?"

"What about me?"

"How did you get involved in . . . um . . . your line of work?"

Nathan stared out at the rolling hills and tiny hamlets of upstate New York passing by. "My line of work . . . Nicely put."

"So how did you get into whatever it is you do?"

"I was first and foremost a good fit from the outset, I think."

"How?"

"I had the right psychological profile. Ruthless, cold-blooded, a certain moral ambiguity."

Mahoney stared at him. "I'm sorry."

"What about you? Your life?"

"What do you want to know?"

"How did you get into journalism?"

"My father was a journalist. I followed in his footsteps after Yale."

"Yale? Wow. Smart boy."

"Not really. Went to a good prep school, and from there Ivy League was the next step. Great teachers."

Nathan nodded. He felt envious of such a privileged childhood. His own brutalized upbringing had prepared him to fight, if nothing else. He remembered street fights with toughs from Alphabet City. Nasty little Puerto Ricans who were quick with knives. He had gotten cut too many times to count. He'd been beaten up. Slashed. On his back. Arms. Hands. Neck. It was bad shit. He'd been kicked unconscious. A skinny little white kid fighting for his life in an urban jungle. But fought he did. And he survived. And learned. Slowly, he learned.

He learned how to fight back. He learned not to show fear. The fear might have been gnawing away at him when he confronted some street thugs. But his face didn't betray his emotions. Poker-faced as he approached them. Sometimes he smiled. That always unnerved them. And he had stood his ground to protect himself and his friends. Eventually, they stayed the fuck away from him.

Nathan's mind flashed to his youth. The stinking streets and alleys he knew around his neighborhood. The smells of burgers and puke and hot dogs and booze and smoke. He saw things. Things that were ingrained on his soul. His mind. He saw terrible things. Sometimes he dreamed of those days.

The rats emerged from storm drains and ate the remnants of sodden, moldy old pizza slices cast aside the previous night by drunken stragglers. Nathan saw it all. The dark side of the city. Living in the shadows, his sister gone.

They didn't tell him where she was. Not then. Not ever. He'd had to find her.

He retreated into himself, day by day consumed by rage and a black anger that was eating him alive.

Nathan was tested in the military. Then he was retested by the CIA. They seemed pleased with his profile.

Within months, Nathan was in Iraq. He realized he could handle the mayhem. The undiluted horror. A lot of the other tough kids in his unit were scared shitless. He never was. To him it was an adrenaline rush. It was out of control. There were no rules. No right and no wrong.

The war never ended for Nathan. It lived on in him. Each and every day.

Thirty

Berenger was sitting behind his desk, waiting for Stone's handler to call. He'd been told to expect a call an hour earlier. But still nothing.

He got up from his seat and stared out at the ashen skies over Toronto, the skyscrapers in the distance, wondering if the handler had other issues he was dealing with. He knew the handler would be overseeing Stone's actions and couldn't be disturbed for any reason. It was possible the man had other, more pressing matters to attend to.

Berenger reflected on his role in such shadowy operations. The confidant of the assassin. The man who analyzed Stone to see that he was psychologically prepared. Attuned. Ready. Nathan was his patient.

He thought back to the Scottish facility, where Stone had been taken after his reconstructive facial surgery. Stone looked different, but he was still wired the same. The same raw power and visceral anger boiling over. Strangling a perfect stranger on request. That had shocked even Berenger. He'd thought that since Stone had been away from killing and maiming and assassination for years between his near drowning in the Everglades and getting to Scotland, he would have turned away from his former life. Sickened by it perhaps. But nothing was further from the truth. If anything, Stone had returned more focused, and utterly terrifying.

Berenger was lucky not to have been at the Scottish facility after Stone's assassination of Senator Crichton. But the blowback had been unbelievable. His response cold, calculating, and beyond anyone's powers of understanding.

Stone had brought the facility to its knees, burned it to the ground, and made it out unscathed. No one had foreseen that, least of all him.

Berenger reflected on what the handler had previously said. Stone shouldn't have been chosen after that incident. He had been surprised by the handler's candor. The more he thought about the man's opinions of Stone, the more he wondered if the Commission had gotten it wrong. Horribly wrong. But he also knew there were two parts to the operation. First, Stone deleting Mahoney. That was the minor part. Then the main act. Once Stone was back in Florida, or wherever he wanted to go, the second stage would commence. A second stage that Stone didn't know anything about. Classic compartmentalization.

Berenger's thoughts again turned to the professional killer. Stone was not only dangerous. He was brilliant. Lethal. And almost certainly the perfect assassin. But his response during the operation in Scotland, coupled with his sister's kidnapping to exert leverage on him as payback, did give Berenger pause for thought.

Interestingly, his own views on the matter hadn't been sought.

Berenger wondered why that was. He was already consulting within the secret facility, no more than ten miles away. And he understood protocol was essential to curtail any leakage.

He knew more about the psychological makeup of Nathan Stone than anyone. But occasionally, very rarely, he detected signs of humanity in his brown eyes.

Usually it was when they talked about his sister. That was it. His love for his sister. His eyes softened, or at least they appeared to.

What was so interesting about him were his mood changes. He might appear to be in a docile mood one minute, answering questions pleasantly and occasionally with humor. But unpredictably, a switch seemed to flick in his mind. Sometimes the wrong word, phrase, or tone, and Stone's icy gaze would be on him. Like he had been triggered.

He knew Stone could kill him with his bare hands. He sensed it. He saw the way his eyes stared longer than was comfortable, lingering just enough to instill fear and uneasiness.

Truth be told, Berenger was fascinated by Stone. Other psychologists and psychiatrists dreamed of having such a complex, fascinating, multifaceted character with unimaginable layers to analyze and interact with.

Berenger closed his eyes. His mind drifted back to the secret room in his Toronto apartment. The door he always kept locked. Three walls plastered with pictures of Nathan Stone and newspaper clippings. *New York Post* reports the day after Stone's father was murdered by his sister. Forensic photos from inside the bloody crime scene in the one-room apartment on the Bowery. Photos of detectives scouring the scene. Photos of Helen Stone, the sister, wild-eyed, in a police mug shot. But mostly photos of Nathan. As a child. As a boy. As a teenage delinquent. As a young man. As a soldier. As a CIA operative. And now.

He would often touch the photos and imagine the horrors Nathan had seen. The nightmares he had endured. What was inside his head? *Really* inside his head? He sometimes dreamed of Nathan. He had imagined Nathan's silhouetted figure at his bedroom door, standing, watching him. In the dream, he was lying alone, frozen in terror, not daring to breathe. The dream had become recurring. And it always ended the same way. Nathan would walk toward him. Step-by-step. Closer and closer to him. He felt he was being suffocated by his spectral presence. Invariably, he would wake in a cold sweat, gasping for air, shaking like a leaf.

His secret room was his sacred space. The place where Berenger went to think about Nathan. To wallow in his world. To get closer to him. He had begun to fantasize more and more about Nathan. About his actions. About his needs and desires. No one knew. No one could ever know. It was his secret.

The more he thought about Nathan, the happier he got. He realized only too well that he had slipped under Stone's spell. Had become fixated on him. Fascinated by him. He felt a frisson of excitement in his presence. Knowing Nathan would soon be killing another human being.

Berenger had begun to visit New York. He wanted to see where Nathan had grown up. He wanted to see the tenement where he was born. He wondered about Nathan as a child. He visited his old school. He took photographs. He hadn't uploaded them to his laptop. But he would. They would add to his collection. Even his wife didn't know about his fixation. He sometimes snapped in a blind fury if she asked why she couldn't clean his study at home. No one entered that space. They hadn't for years. It was his area. The same as the room in Toronto. A shrine to Nathan Stone.

He often wondered why Nathan taunted him. Mocked him. Berenger felt angry with himself that Nathan could see the fear in his eyes. It often felt to Berenger as if Nathan was turning the tables on him. But it also felt as if Nathan was controlling him.

Berenger's thoughts turned to the operation as he wondered if Nathan would soon be closing in on his prey.

Thirty-One

The train had just left Poughkeepsie, about eighty miles north of New York City, and took on new passengers as they headed south to Manhattan. Nathan figured they were about ninety minutes away.

He stared out at the bleak surroundings, then fixed his gaze on Mahoney. "I've been thinking," he said.

"About what?"

"About you."

"What about me?"

"Where do you live?"

"That is not going to happen . . . So forget that."

"What did you think I was going to say?"

"That you wanted to stay with me. Well, no."

Nathan shrugged. "It was just an idea."

"'Just an idea'? My family are lovely, innocent, beautiful people. You're . . . Well, you know, you're a bit different."

"I think that's an accurate description. Aren't you curious? Don't you want to get to know me better?"

"I'm curious about a lot of things. I'm curious about how the world operates. Geopolitical currents and undercurrents. The state of our country. Public schools. The environment. The lack of investment in people. Gimme a break. You're killing me."

Nathan grinned. "You're making light of your situation."

Mahoney seemed to find the funny side of things for the first time in twenty-four hours. "I agree with what you said. I am, my own fears and neuroses aside, rather curious about you."

"That's good. We're making progress."

Mahoney glanced at his watch. "I haven't been home for months. I can't remember the last time."

"This is good then, isn't it?"

Mahoney looked away.

"What do you do for fun, Mark?"

"Why do you want to know?"

"I'm curious. I thought all journalists had to be curious."

"You're not a journalist. And I don't believe you're asking because you're interested."

"So why am I asking, Mark?"

Mahoney shrugged. "I don't know. It gives you a thrill knowing you can scare me. Then you can worm your way into my world."

"I've already done that, Mark."

Mahoney sighed. "I like football. Happy?"

"Giants?"

"Yeah, who else?"

"Love the Giants."

Mahoney closed his eyes. "This is weird. You do know that, right?"

"I'm aware this is slightly unusual. But hey, it's life, right? We take the rough with the smooth, the ups with the downs."

The train was powering through the rural surroundings of upstate New York. Fields. Rivers. Space to breathe.

"I like it here," Nathan said. "Nice and quiet. I like quiet."

Mahoney forced a smile.

"New York City is constant noise, isn't it?"

"I guess," Mahoney said.

"I used to like that. But as you get older, it's awful. You wonder, *What the fuck am I doing here?* At least, that's what I thought before I joined the army."

"So you volunteered for Iraq?"

"Out of the frying pan and into the fire."

Mahoney got quiet for a few moments. "I don't want to go with you once we get to New York. I don't want to know what you're going to do. I don't want to be an accomplice."

"Don't worry, I've got it under control."

Mahoney bit his lower lip, as if thinking hard. "You're going to ask them where your sister is."

"You ever heard of an asymmetric response?"

"Yes, I have."

"That's basically what I'll be doing."

"This is a surreal conversation."

Nathan leaned closer. "I know. Crazy, right?"

"You're going to kill these men?"

"I don't know. It depends."

"On what?"

"I have to roll with whatever scenario I'm faced with. I might not be able to get close to them. They might be surrounded by people. So I'll have to improvise."

"Is that a metaphor?"

"I like to call it *neutralize*, Mark. Far more antiseptic and pleasant to the ear."

Mahoney cleared his throat. "I don't want to be around you . . . when you do whatever it is you're thinking of doing."

"Where do you live, Mark?"

"Please . . . I can't tell you."

"Mark, here's how it's going to work. I hold the aces, and you have to take it on the chin. So, I'm going to ask again: Where do you live?"

"Chelsea."

"I already know that. And your address?"

"Shit."

"Chelsea's nice these days, I've heard." Nathan sighed. "So what's going to happen is, I'm going to let you return to your family, while I attend to a couple of bits of business."

"Then what?"

"Then I'll spend the night at your place."

"Never in a million years."

"Mark, I will not harm you or your family. I'm figuring out a way to save them."

Mahoney leaned in close, finger pointed. "Don't even think about it."

"Mark, be quiet and listen. Once I sort out my business, I will head over to your place, and you will say, 'Here's a friend of mine from Canada. He's originally from New York, and he's going to be visiting his sister, but she's out of town until tomorrow.' What do you say?"

"Just for one night?"

"I don't know. We'll see what transpires."

Mahoney just stared at him, color draining from his face.

Thirty-Two

Clayton Wilson was shown to a discreet table at Cafe Milano, in Georgetown. The rheumy-eyed man he'd met at the Army and Navy Club, wearing an expensive gray suit, white shirt, and tightly knotted black tie, was waiting. The man nodded and sipped from a glass of white wine as Wilson sat down.

The waiter smiled. "Something to drink, sir?"

"Talisker. Neat. And a great bottle of French red for the table, two glasses."

The waiter gave a deep bow. "Very good, sir."

The man opposite him was smiling. "I like a man that drinks, don't you?"

"Indeed."

"Good to see you again, Clayton."

Wilson smiled. "And you." He looked around the restaurant. "Nice place."

"Haven't been here in years."

Wilson smiled. He'd known the man for decades, since Wilson had joined the CIA. John Fisk Jr. was a reclusive financier. A billionaire many times over. And he had been one of the first to approach Wilson about his plans for the Commission.

The waiter returned with the glass of single malt and a bottle of red. He poured out two large glasses of the wine, took their dinner order, then left them to it.

The man's eyes bored into Wilson's, as if he was trying to determine what kind of man he really was. Was he a steady man? A man to be trusted? "So gimme where we're at. I believe we're still not over the line."

Wilson nodded.

The man's facial expression changed. "Should I be concerned?"

"About?"

"Well, first, the gentleman you've chosen to represent our interests. Mr. Stone."

"He's interesting, I'll give you that."

"He's also pretty wild, I'm led to believe. What happened in that place . . . ?"

"It was messy. You're right. But we came to the conclusion that it was far better to compartmentalize, thus keeping leaks to a minimum. Also there's a strong incentive for him to complete this task. So we can move on to the main event at the end of the week."

The man smiled.

Wilson said, "I appreciate we invested a significant sum of money into him and the facility in Scotland."

"I know. I picked up the tab."

Wilson nodded. "We lost some good people. Lessons were learned."

The man lowered his voice to a whisper. "He did manage to complete the core task we set him."

"He most certainly did. And this will be a way for him to repay the costs we incurred because of his . . . misguided approach."

"You're squeezing him where it hurts."

"That's one way of looking at it."

The man leaned closer. "He owes us. So it's only right that there's payback."

"Did you get the secure message I sent with regards to future financing?"

The man nodded. "Yes, I did."

"What are your thoughts?"

"I believe you need fifty million to guarantee a five-year timescale of future events."

"That's correct." Wilson picked up his malt whiskey, smelled the peaty aroma, and took a small gulp. He felt it warming his insides.

"That feel good?"

"Indeed."

The waiter returned with plates. For the rest of the three-course meal, they engaged in small talk. The weather. Real estate prices in DC. Afterward, after finishing the wine, the man patted Wilson on the back of his hand.

"The money's already been transferred into the Caymans account. Fifty million. So you can continue the work for another few years."

Wilson felt a great sense of relief. He had hoped and prayed that the fuck-up in Scotland wouldn't derail the man's financial support. "You're a true patriot."

"Let's clean up the loose ends before the big show."

Wilson knew he was alluding to neutralizing Mahoney ahead of their big objective. "It's all under control."

The man got up from the table and shook Wilson's hand. "Make sure it is." Then he ambled out of the restaurant to the street, where a limousine would take him back to his six-bedroom, ten-thousand-square-foot Georgian estate.

Wilson finished the rest of his whiskey and allowed himself a small smile.

Thirty-Three

The train pulled into Penn Station later that evening.

Mahoney, a migraine coming on, looked at Stone. "What's the plan?"

Stone stared at him with cold eyes. It was as if he was determining whether Mahoney was in any way a risk to him. But then again, maybe he was just trying to figure out when he should kill him. "I'll call you first."

"You can't stay at my house."

"I'll decide that."

"No, that's where you're wrong."

"I know where you live."

Mahoney felt sick as his stomach and throat tightened. "My family has nothing to do with this."

"They do now. So here's what's going to happen. I'm going to head off into the city and see what's going on. And you . . ."

Mahoney sat rooted to his seat as terror washed over him.

"You will return to your family, enjoy your time together, and we will meet up again sometime in the next day or so."

"I don't want you coming to the house."

"Like I said, I know where you live. But your family is not at risk. I give you my word."

"Your word? The word of an . . ."

"I said, I give you my word."

Mahoney nodded. "I guess that'll have to be good enough."

"If you go to the cops, all bets are off. Do you understand?"

Mahoney sat silently in shock.

Stone got up from his seat. "You worry too much."

Mahoney was in a daze as he watched Stone disappear in the midst of a throng of people at Penn Station. It was a fifteen-minute walk to his apartment in Chelsea. Thoughts were swimming around his head the entire time, almost threatening to overwhelm him.

He took the elevator to the eighth floor and opened his apartment door.

His wife looked astonished as he walked in, his two daughters throwing themselves at him.

"Mark," she said. "Oh my God, I can't believe you're here!"

Mahoney hugged her tight and pulled his kids close. He felt pent-up emotion and fear building up inside him and broke down, sobbing hard. "I missed you."

His wife extricated herself from his grasp and held his face in her hands. "Honey, what's wrong? This is so unlike you. First you tell us you have work to do, and now you're back in New York. What's going on?"

"I don't know." Mahoney began to conjure up a white lie. "My doctor says I'm working too hard. And he thinks seeing my family would be good for me. I felt really bad saying you had to get back home. It was really inconsiderate of me."

"Don't worry about that, honey. That happens. You look terrible."

Mahoney felt tears on his cheeks.

"Honey, this is so unlike you."

Mahoney could only nod.

"Where're your bags?"

He dabbed his eyes. "I don't have any. I left all my stuff in Toronto."

"Mark . . . are you kidding me?"

Mahoney shook his head as she wiped the tears from his eyes.

"You're gonna be fine. I'm glad you're home. And I agree with your doctor. You work too hard. You're going to give yourself a nervous breakdown. Didn't I say that last fall?"

Mahoney smiled. His wife had an uncanny knack of always making him feel good, even when he felt like shit. "Yes, you did."

After a few minutes of his wife and kids coming to terms with his sudden arrival, Mahoney showered and was glad to get into fresh clothes. His wife fixed him a pastrami sandwich, which he wolfed down.

He lay back on the sofa as he felt himself drifting off. His wife was stroking his hair. She put on some Bach. The music washed over him. Relaxing him, knots of tension in his neck and back melting away.

He needed time and space to think. He let his mind drift. To wander. He thought of sun-kissed picnics in the Hamptons the previous summer. It was an idyllic August week. The kids paddling knee-deep in the ocean. The breakers crashing onto the golden sand.

His mind switched back to the present. He needed to reconsider his options. He could go to the police. But Stone had said *they* could get him here. Anywhere. He could confide in his wife. But that would just terrify her and the kids. The whole thing could spiral out of control, ending with Stone turning up and killing them all.

Then he began to think maybe he should take his wife and kids and go on the run. Or maybe into FBI protective custody.

Mahoney's thoughts were racing away with him. His deepest fears were beginning to seep out of the darkest recesses of his mind. *Help me. Help me. Think!*

The baroque music was wafting over him, working its magic for a few moments, allowing him to dream of possibilities.

Then in his mind's eye he saw Stone, unsmiling. Had he been sent to kill him? The same guy who had sent him the documents. It had all begun with Stone. Emailing the intercepted message that should have been deleted from an NSA server. The list of five men—the Commission—who drew up an assassination list of men and women they wanted to kill. And the reason? Because these people, including the late Senator Brad Crichton, wanted to move away from the postwar world of US global domination, regime change, and all the rest. The endless wars. On and on. Millions of dead. Weapons to suppress, maim, kill, and buy. Uncle Sam had the best weapons, after all.

Now he was on the list. *Fuck.*

The more he thought about it, the more he wanted to run. Run far away. Run now. That made the most sense. At least at that moment. Then again, What if? What if Stone found them? What if *they* found him? He thought of the power they possessed. The contacts. The intelligence networks. They'd be found. And someone else would kill them. Of that he had no doubt.

Mahoney's stomach knotted as he began to realize the uncertainty of going into hiding. Drop off the grid? Get rid of all cell phones and electronic devices? But since 9/11, surveillance cameras were everywhere in New York. Even in the outer boroughs. Train hubs. Airports. Bus terminals.

Then again, maybe he should risk it?

Doubts were going off in his head like firecrackers.

"Honey?" The soft voice of his wife recalled him to the present.

Mahoney opened his eyes.

"Are you OK?"

"I'm just worn-out. A lot of things on my mind."

His wife kissed him on the forehead. "You worry too much. You always did."

Mahoney smiled as he closed his eyes. He felt a blanket being wrapped around him as his children were stroking his hair.

"Daddy, we love you," his younger daughter said.

Mahoney felt tears on his cheeks.

"Daddy, what's wrong? You don't seem very happy."

Mahoney opened his eyes. His younger daughter's beautiful blue eyes were staring back at him. He pulled her close. "Daddy is just very tired because I've been working really hard for several months, seven days a week."

His daughter said, "That's every day, Daddy."

"I know, honey."

"Mommy was sad when you sent us home."

"I'm sorry, honey. I really am. I'm behind on my work and I'm under a lot of pressure."

"Well, I'm glad you're home, Daddy."

Mahoney hugged her tightly, never wanting to let her go. "I'm glad to be home too, honey."

Thirty-Four

The following morning, Nathan left the budget hotel room near Penn Station where he'd spent the night. He stopped off for a cup of coffee. Then he took a ten-minute subway ride to Columbus Circle. His head was swimming with ideas, permutations, and possible scenarios as he walked a couple hundred yards to a tower three blocks from Central Park. He walked up the steps and through some glass doors, cameras watching his every move, before he strode through the marble lobby to the huge black-granite reception desk.

"Good morning," Nathan said. "I'm here to see Marshall Wilson."

The young woman smiled. "Certainly, sir. Can I have your name please?"

"Name's Stanton, Richard Stanton, friend of Marshall's father." It was a lie. A big lie. But Nathan knew brazenness was underrated.

"What's the nature of your business, sir?"

"I've been asked to convey an urgent message to Marshall in person by his father."

A grave look crossed the receptionist's face. "Very good, sir," she said. The young woman pressed a couple of buttons on a phone beside her. "Janet, I have a Mr. Richard Stanton, friend of Mr. Wilson's father, here to convey an urgent message. Can I send him up?" She nodded. "Thanks, Janet." The young woman turned and smiled at Nathan.

"Eighty-third floor. Out of the elevator, turn right, and Janet will show you in."

Nathan nodded. "Appreciate that, thank you."

Nathan walked across to the elevator and rode it to the eighty-third floor. The doors opened, cameras watching his every move. He headed to the outer office. A middle-aged woman with blond hair was smiling behind a desk. "Mr. Stanton?"

Nathan nodded. "This is an urgent family matter. I've been sent by Marshall's father. Do you mind holding all calls for the next fifteen minutes so we're not disturbed?"

A look of concern overtook the woman's face. "Of course."

The woman ushered Nathan down a carpeted corridor to a corner office. She knocked and showed him in. Marshall Wilson was on the phone and motioned for Nathan to take a seat. Then he motioned for the woman to leave the room, which she did.

Wilson was wearing black slacks, a pale-blue Oxford button-down shirt, striped maroon tie, and expensive black shoes. He winced as he continued a conversation. "Tell them we either go in at 2045 or we let them stew. That's where I am, Frankie. That's it." He ended the call and shrugged, looking over at Nathan. "I'm sorry, you're a friend of my father? I don't think we've met."

Nathan got up from his seat and walked up to the handsome financier. "Name's Stanton. Richard Stanton."

"What's this about? And . . . have you got any ID?"

"Of course." Nathan reached into an inside pocket and pulled out the Glock. He strode up to Wilson Jr. and pressed the cold metal tight to his forehead. "So this is what's going to happen. I'm going to ask questions and you're going to comply."

Color drained from the young man's face. "Who the hell are you?"

"A guy your father knows."

"Do you want money?"

Nathan smirked. "Money . . . Do I look like I want money?"

"I don't know."

"Hands on your head."

Marshall Wilson complied.

"Where's your cell phone?"

The guy pointed at his jacket hanging over his chair.

Nathan rifled in the inside pocket with his free hand. He retrieved the phone and put it on the desk.

"Please . . . what's this all about?"

Nathan took a couple steps back. "Empty your pockets. Wallet, keys, etc. on the desk."

Wilson complied. "What do you want? I can get you anything you want. Do you need money for drugs? Or just drugs? I can get those too."

Nathan stepped forward and pressed the gun tightly to Wilson's mouth. "You're starting to piss me off now."

Wilson blinked away tears.

Nathan picked up the cell phone. "Stop crying, son. I'm not going to hurt you. As long as you do what you're told."

Wilson nodded, and a wan smile crossed his face.

"So, what's on your calendar today?"

Wilson shrugged. "I've got a lunch this afternoon."

"With who?"

"My father."

"Clayton Wilson?"

The kid nodded. "Please don't hurt me. I have no idea who you are or what you're here for."

"Where's the lunch?"

"Vaucluse. It's a French brasserie."

Nathan grinned. "Sounds like my kind of place."

"I don't understand what you want."

"You got a bathroom?"

The kid nodded. "Over there. Please don't hurt me."

Nathan cocked his head and followed the guy into the spacious en suite with an adjacent shower. He shut the door behind him.

Wilson began to cry, and a wet stain appeared on his crotch.

Nathan said, "Turn around. Face the shower."

The kid complied.

Nathan pressed the gun to the back of his head. "I want you to count backward from fifty, and then I'll be gone."

Wilson nodded. "Please don't hurt me."

"I'm not going to hurt you. So count backward."

"Fifty, forty-nine, forty-eight, forty-seven, forty-six, forty-five . . ."

Nathan said, "Keep going."

"Forty-four, forty-three, forty-two, forty-one . . ."

Nathan took out the fentanyl nasal spray from his blazer pocket. He stepped forward and sprayed it twice into Marshall's nostrils. The trader gave a garbled moan and collapsed in a heap on the floor tiles. He was incapacitated in seconds and would be out of it for hours.

Stone stared down at the young man sprawled on the floor. It looked like he'd passed out. Shallow breathing. He locked the en suite door from the outside before he took the elevator to the lobby and headed out onto the streets of New York.

Thirty-Five

Clayton Wilson was nursing a Scotch at his favorite cigar bar ahead of another hearty lunch. He enjoyed the small talk with the bartenders as he savored a robusto-sized Ramón Allones cigar. But he was distracted, his thoughts turning to matters closer to his heart.

He couldn't understand why Stone's handler hadn't given him an update from the situation room in Toronto. He wondered why that was.

The operation was set up deliberately in a cell-like structure, so Stone's handler was unaware of what and who were involved at the secret facility that they'd developed. His job was simply to be the eyes and ears on Stone, working essentially remotely.

Wilson didn't and couldn't interfere in the day-to-day functions of this framework. The systems had been set up by Richard Stanton to ensure secrecy. But also so those involved in the component parts at the lower levels would be unaware of the big picture. It was deemed that Wilson had to be insulated from any aspect of the operation. So calling the handler directly was strictly not allowed, as it would compromise the Commission. However, for updates and in emergency situations, the handler could contact Wilson on his military-grade-encrypted cell phone.

His cell phone vibrated in his pocket, and he wondered if this was the call he was waiting for. News that Mahoney had been neutralized was all he wanted to hear. The code words *He no longer lives at that address.*

Wilson reached into his pocket and took out his cell phone. It was a text from his son, Marshall.

Running a little late. Will join you as soon as I can. M.

Wilson's thoughts turned to his son. He'd scrimped and saved as a young man to help the boy attend an elite prep school, Phillips Academy, at Andover, in Massachusetts. Hundreds of thousands plowed into school fees and then college tuition. But his son had blossomed. He'd learned the ropes at hedge fund managers in Connecticut and then formed his own business there in New York City. The contacts he'd nurtured over many years were willing clients, keen on serious investment returns.

His son worked sixteen-hour days seven days a week, providing everything his wife and kids could wish for.

Wilson loved the way his son hugged and cuddled his children, unlike how he himself had treated Marshall, with a disciplined and more old-fashioned style of parenting.

His cell phone vibrated again. He checked the caller ID and saw it was Richard Stanton.

"Richard, it'll have to be brief," Wilson said. "I'm meeting my son for lunch."

"I'd been hoping to hear that we had concluded matters."

Wilson turned away from the bartender, lowering his voice. "You're not the only one. I expected word last night. The last time I spoke to him, it was imminent. Those were his words."

Stanton went quiet for a few moments. "Do you think everything is OK?"

"I suspect there's been some change of plan, probably fine-tuning preparations to get it done."

Stanton said nothing.

"You're not convinced?"

"I know the handler, our point man. He's the best there is." A ringing sounded in the background. "That's a call I need to take. We'll speak later tonight."

Wilson finished his drink and left a twenty-dollar tip for the bartender.

"Enjoy your day, sir," the man said as Wilson left.

Wilson left the premises and walked to the French brasserie. He was shown to his usual table, tucked away in a discreet corner far from prying eyes. His seat was facing the wall, the way he liked it. He ordered a bottle of still mineral water and a glass of Sancerre.

The waiter returned with the glass of wine and he took a large gulp.

"Very good," he said.

The waiter smiled, gave a respectful bow, and left Wilson alone with his thoughts.

Over the years, as he had watched Marshall become a father, the more he had begun to realize what he'd missed all those decades earlier. But it was a different time then. A different way for men to behave.

His job, he'd been told by his authoritarian father, was to provide and protect. And he had done this. But the natural way his son had bonded with his own children was something to behold. Wilson felt oddly envious.

He sipped some more of the Sancerre, savoring the subtle flavors.

There was a tap on his shoulder and he turned around.

Staring down at him was Nathan Stone, grinning like a madman.

Thirty-Six

Nathan sat down and ordered a glass of "whatever he's having twice, please" and smiled across the table at the corpulent figure of Wilson. "I love this place, Clayton. I can see why you like it."

Wilson looked at Nathan as if he'd seen a ghost, his face turning a sickly shade of gray.

"The thing is, being away from New York for so long, it's great to see a nice part of the city. They say downtown's where it's at these days. But I don't know. This is pretty good, right?"

Wilson leaned in close. "What the fuck is this?"

Nathan grinned. "Always liked the feel of the old-money side of town. Great access to Central Park, right?"

"I asked you a question."

"Clayton," Nathan said, his voice now a whisper, "here's how it's going to work. I'm going to talk and you're going to listen."

"I have no idea what this is all about, but you need to get out of here before I call the cops."

"Really? And say what exactly, Clayton? 'Yeah, there's this guy, we hire him to kill people for us, and he seems like he's ready to go fucking rogue again. Can you help me?'"

Wilson stared at him.

"So are we good?"

"What do you want?"

Nathan felt seriously crazy. "Why does everyone think I want something? I don't understand."

The waiter arrived at the table with two glasses. "Are we expecting your son for lunch, Mr. Wilson?"

Wilson looked up with hooded eyes. "He's running late."

The waiter gave a polite nod and left them alone.

Nathan put the glass of Sancerre to his lips and breathed in the fragrant bouquet. "Fine wines at lunch, Clayton, huh? What a great way to live. Bet they didn't serve that at the Langley cafeteria. It's a bitch trying to get executive chefs with top-level security clearance. But hey, someone's got to do it, right?" He took a small gulp and savored the cool wine as it slid down his throat.

Wilson's face flushed with anger. "What do you want? Do you want to get the conversation started?"

Nathan grinned and shook his head. "Do *I* want to get the conversation started? Is that the bullshit terminology that's in vogue just now? I mean, Clayton, really, language like that!"

Wilson began to grind his teeth.

"Have we become, as a species," Nathan continued, "so afraid to call a spade a spade that our language is now too warm, fuzzy, non-threatening? Politically correct speech as opposed to free speech. You know what I'm talking about?"

"Sounds like you've been reading up on cultural Marxism."

"Indeed I have. What a revelation that the Frankfurt School had such an impact on America via our once-great colleges and universities. Gender. Race. Ethnicity. Sexuality. We're supposed to care about shit like that. Changing our actions and thoughts to make us afraid. Afraid to say what we think. What we want."

Clayton sneered. "I want you to tell *me* what the fuck *you* want."

"That's better. That's a whole lot better, Clayton. I like that." Nathan knocked back the rest of the white wine and sighed. "What do I want? I want my sister back."

Wilson just sat and stared, his gray-blue eyes unblinking.

"Do you want to know why?"

Wilson said nothing, like he was still in shock.

"She's family. The only family I've got. And you had no right encroaching on her life."

"How did you find me?"

Nathan just smiled.

"You've crossed the line."

"I've crossed the line? Are you kidding me?"

Wilson took a sip of his wine and flashed a fake smile at the waiter. Then he leaned in close to Nathan. "You better not be here when my son arrives."

"Why not?"

"He's a friend of the mayor. The cops love my son. He invests their hard-earned money in emerging markets and tech firms for them. One call and they'll blow you to pieces. And I mean they shoot first, then ask questions."

"You really don't get it. It's like you and your kind are impervious to what's going on in the real world. Content to play little games. Is that what this is about? Playing geopolitical games. I wonder what the cops will think when I tell them you and your gang—because that's what you are—got Senator Brad Crichton deleted."

Wilson looked long and hard at Nathan, as if studying him. "I don't think this is the right place or time to discuss such matters, do you?"

"Quite the contrary. This is the perfect place."

"Do you think this is going to end well?"

"Depends who we're talking about, Clayton. Where I'm sitting, I'm not worried, let me tell you that. How about you?"

"Do you think this will end well for your sister, Nathan?"

"I guess we'll find out soon enough. What about you?"

"What about me?"

"How do you think things will end up for you?"

Wilson edged a couple inches closer. His breath smelled of cigars and booze. "Don't fuck with me."

"But I am fucking with you. Question is, How are you going to respond?"

Wilson was breathing hard. "You were supposed to carry out a job for us."

"You haven't answered my question. How are you going to respond?"

"You need to keep your side of the deal."

"Thing is, Clayton, there was no deal. A deal requires mutual agreement. This is a one-way street, isn't it?"

"You need to finish the job. And then we'll talk."

"You don't seem to have figured out that your position is weaker than you think."

"Anything happens to me, your sister . . ." His words trailed off as he finished his glass of Sancerre. The waiter approached and refilled his glass and Nathan's before leaving them in peace again.

"You're going to kill her anyway, aren't you?"

Wilson's cheeks flushed.

"I've already factored that into my calculations. So you see, Clayton, I have absolutely nothing to lose."

"She's still alive. And she'll stay that way."

Nathan smiled. "As long as I proceed with the request?"

"Yes, the request needs to be fulfilled, and then, and only then, will you two be reunited."

"Where is she? And no bullshit."

"She's safe."

"Where exactly?"

"And why would I tell you that?"

Nathan smiled, enjoying the verbal joust. He looked over at the other diners in the brasserie. "Nice crowd." He faced Wilson. "Just to be clear, are you refusing to tell me where my sister is being kept?"

Wilson said nothing, sipping his second glass of wine. "You need to choose, Nathan. Do you want this charade to continue, or do you want to move on with your life? I'm giving you the opportunity to move on. Your actions in Scotland were . . . somewhat erratic, shall we say. And they cost people I know, good people, an awful lot of money. It was extremely troubling. I thought you'd see the opportunity to redeem yourself as the act of kindness it was intended to be."

Nathan mimicked Wilson's mannerisms and voice. "I never had you figured as a humanitarian, Clayton."

"You know nothing about me, son."

"I knew you were going to be here for lunch, didn't I? How would I know that?"

The waiter approached slowly, and a silence hung over the table. The man cleared his throat. "Apologies for interrupting, gentlemen, but are we still waiting for the younger Mr. Wilson?"

Wilson said, "I can't wait any longer. I'll have my usual. Veal with caramelized onions. And a bottle of Sancerre and two fresh glasses for the table."

The waiter nodded. "Very good, sir." He turned to Nathan. "And you, sir?"

"The same as my gracious host, thank you so much."

The waiter smiled. "Very good choice, sir."

He took the menus off the table. A few moments later, he returned with the bottle of wine and refilled their glasses.

Wilson toyed with his glass of wine before taking a large sip. "Very nice."

Nathan's gaze wandered around the room. "So this is what it's all about, right? The freedom to choose. The freedom to sit in restaurants.

The opportunity to live as free men and women. You gotta love this country."

"I do. From the very depths of my soul. And that's why we do so much to protect it, don't we?"

The minutes dragged until the food arrived. Nathan was devising a plan in his head as he ate the delicious food.

"This is great, Clayton. Knockout."

Wilson was chewing hard on the succulent veal. He leaned in close. "I know what you're going to do."

"And what's that?"

Wilson pointed the fork at him. "You're going to threaten me. Maybe harm me. As leverage."

"I love your imagination, Clayton. Really refreshing."

"Listen here, son, I've been all over. You don't fucking scare me. Nothing scares me."

"Is that your final word?"

"What the fuck do you want? Be reasonable!"

"My sister returned unharmed to me."

"That could happen. But we need business to be taken care of. That's not up for negotiation."

Nathan sensed that Wilson might be slightly more amenable after the drinks. "You need to do me a favor."

"What?"

"I need to know where she is."

"Why do you need to know that?"

"Put yourself in my position. Wouldn't you want to know?"

Wilson paused from eating and was quiet for a couple of minutes. "I was wondering why I hadn't heard from the handler."

"So was I. I thought the whole thing had gone south."

"And you decided to try and find me."

"I haven't heard from him in thirty-six hours."

Wilson turned and looked around as the restaurant door opened. "My son is running late." He turned to face Nathan. "Listen, I don't want you meeting him."

"Why not?"

Wilson shook his head. "I just don't."

"Well, you need to call them. Right now. And say you want her moved."

"It's more complicated than that."

"No call, no deal. I'll just hang around until your son turns up."

Wilson pulled out his cell phone and dialed a number.

"Tell them it's only a text message from you that can change this decision."

"Trent? Yes, I'd like the patient moved to the original residence." He frowned and nodded. "With immediate effect. The decision is final, unless I contact you by text." He sighed. "Got it?"

"I want to speak to her," Nathan said.

"Get the girl on the line."

Wilson handed him the phone, and he pressed it tight to his ear.

"Hello?" The shaking voice of his sister.

"Hey, sis, guess who?"

"Nathan, they say we might be going somewhere."

"Ask them where." His sister repeated his request. A man's voice said, "Back to your room at the hospital."

Nathan said, "See, I told you it was going to be fine. Just do as the men say and you'll be fine. I love you." He ended the call and knocked the cell phone against a glass, seeming to drop the device under the table. "Damn." He reached under, pulled the syringe that contained the depolarizing agent from his pocket. Then he gently jabbed it into Wilson's right knee. There was a sound of moaning. He took the syringe out of Wilson's leg and placed it carefully back in his inside pocket.

Nathan sat back in his seat, Wilson's cell phone in his pocket, and saw Wilson—his back to the rest of the diners—drooling, face dark red, clutching his chest, eyes wide open.

He took a few moments to savor the horror in the man's eyes.

Nathan slowly got up from the table and calmly walked out of the restaurant, past the other diners. The drug, sux, which he had decided not to use on Mahoney, had paralyzed Wilson, inducing a massive heart attack.

Nathan headed down the East Side street and dropped the syringe into a storm drain, knowing that in less than ninety seconds Wilson would be dead. He hailed a cab.

"Where to, pal?" the driver asked.

"Chelsea. West Twenty-Fourth Street."

The driver pulled away.

Nathan was on the move again. He looked back and saw the waiter standing outside looking around, as if they'd suddenly discovered Wilson gasping for breath. Nathan took out Wilson's cell phone and scrolled through the emails. He saw invites to a "members only" meeting at an island in Florida. He scrolled further back, ten months earlier, and saw an invite from Wilson to the rest of the Commission to another "emergency members only" meeting in New York. It listed an address. The code for the entrance to the townhouse in the Upper East Side used exclusively for "our business meetings."

He copied and pasted the exact wording of the email, changing the date to the following evening at nine. Then he wrote a one-sentence addition:

A situation has arisen and we need to meet to discuss our options in NY, usual address.

Then he sent it to the other four men.

Thirty-Seven

Mark Mahoney was forcing himself to put on a brave face in the kitchen of his Chelsea loft apartment on West Twenty-Fourth Street as his wife made him coffee. The kids were playing games noisily on the PS4 in the next room.

Mahoney looked out the window, the world going on around him as usual.

"Honey," his wife said, handing him a cup of coffee, "I'm worried about you."

Mahoney snapped back to reality. "No, I'm fine. Like I said, just been at it too long."

"I'm wondering if this assignment, and being away for so long, is hurting our relationship."

Mahoney nodded and gulped some of the fresh coffee. "I don't know. My mind's racing a bit. My heart's pounding."

"I think we should get you checked out. Dr. Merton will see you whenever it's convenient, you know that. Remember when you had that spell about a year ago?"

"That was just low blood sugar. I'm fine."

"Did you eat the banana I gave you?"

Mahoney rolled his eyes. "Yes, I ate my banana."

His wife looked hurt at his snappish response.

"Sorry, I didn't mean to bite your head off."

"I know." She sighed. "How long do you think you'll be back for?"

"Not sure. I thought I was locked on to this story, but now I'm not so sure."

"What's changed?"

"*I've* changed."

His wife nodded empathetically.

"It doesn't seem so important. I want to be with you and the kids. All the time. Every day. I want to work from home. How does that sound?"

"My God, Mark, that's great. Unexpected but great. Are you sure? What about money?"

"I've just got to clear my head."

His wife sipped some of her coffee, cradling the mug in her hands. "Do you need some time to think?"

"I've got so much to think about."

"Go outside and get some fresh air. Go for a walk. You're back in New York. Go enjoy it."

Mahoney gulped down the rest of his coffee. "I just wanted you to know I love you. I hope you know that."

"I want you to be happy, Mark. If work isn't making you happy for whatever reason, leave."

"We've got commitments, though. Private school fees aren't cheap. And that's before we talk about the rent for this apartment."

"Hey, if necessary, we take the kids out of school, put them in public school, or I'll teach them here."

"You'd do that?"

"I'll do whatever it takes to keep us together and happy. And as it stands, my husband isn't too happy. I get that. So let's think about how we can deal with it."

Mahoney put down his empty coffee mug and embraced his wife. "You're too good for me."

"Enough. Get some fresh air. And get yourself moving. I'm convinced that's part of your problem. You don't exercise enough."

Mahoney knew she was right. He was wrapped up in his own little world, oblivious to what was going on around him. "Maybe you're right." He pecked her on the cheek. "I'll be back in an hour or so."

"Be good. And relax. You're home."

"I know."

It felt good to get out of the apartment, but his head was still swimming with thoughts and fears. He felt trapped. Claustrophobic. He headed down the street and up to the High Line, built thirty feet above street level on an old rail line. People lounged on wooden benches, some staring down onto the streets below. He could see New Jersey across the Hudson. He walked and walked along the green corridor, an oasis in what was a grimy part of town just a couple of decades earlier. Now it had been reborn.

He felt the cold November air rouse him from the virtual stupor he'd been in over the last twenty-four hours. He wondered what he should do. Should he believe what Stone had said about not telling a soul? Should he trust Stone at all? The whole idea was so ridiculous it was laughable. Why the hell would he trust an assassin? A man who'd been hired to kill him.

The more he thought about it, the more he began to feel the doubts and fears creeping back into his thoughts. His mind flashed to images of Stone staring back at him in the bar in Toronto. The fear that had begun to eat away at him then still hadn't subsided. Stone wasn't there, but yet he was. He'd burrowed his way into Mahoney's head. He felt as if the fear was clouding his judgment. Maybe it was.

He walked the length of the one-and-a-half-mile route. It felt good.

Mahoney didn't want to go back home yet. He needed to be by himself, let his thoughts clear. He got off the High Line and walked a few blocks to Billymark's. It was a classic rough-around-the-edges dive bar not far from Penn Station. It was filled with postal workers, a few construction workers, and Chelsea locals as usual. A couple of young women were playing pool.

He ordered a Miller High Life and sat on a stool.

The bartender was wiping the surfaces. "Haven't seen you around for a little while, Mark."

"Been out of town."

"Working on a story?"

Mahoney took a gulp of his beer. "This and that, yeah."

The bartender's name was Benny, and he was a good guy. Mahoney was usually more than happy to engage in conversation. As a journalist, that was what he did. He talked to people. Found out what was going on. But that afternoon, his thoughts were elsewhere.

Benny seemed to sense that. "Let me know if you need anything."

"Will do."

Mahoney often disappeared to Billymark's for an hour or two when he was in town, usually on the weekend. He hadn't been in for almost a year. But the familiarity of the old place, the pictures of the Beatles above the bar, the griminess, it felt strangely reassuring. The guys at the *Times* nowadays didn't frequent bars the way they used to. As a young reporter, he'd enjoyed drinking with Jimmy Breslin. He was a tough, brilliant reporter and not afraid to drink hard.

Mark had lost count of the number of times he'd listened as Breslin had talked about riots, about growing up in Queens, about all the underappreciated people in the city, the men and women who did the dirty jobs. The people like Benny who didn't want to achieve or even strive to achieve. Even if they did, he was interested in those on the periphery of the city. Those not striving to be something or someone. They just worked to survive. To live. To keep their head above the water.

Drinking in Billymark's reminded him of his old life, before he headed up to Canada. He began to think how he'd scribbled notes sitting on the same barstool when he had first started out on the investigation. It was a phenomenal story. And he was finally close to understanding the machinations of those who'd ordered the killing of Senator Brad Crichton. He'd started writing his story for the *Times* a few months earlier. But now the story was growing arms and legs. And every day, every word he wrote, it became stranger and more frightening. Now the story was seeping into his family life. He was becoming the story, or at least part of the story. He wasn't immersed in it anymore. He was being engulfed by it.

That wasn't a good thing.

Mahoney nursed the cold bottle between his hands as he turned and watched the girls playing pool for a few moments. They were laughing and joking, knocking back shots. Maybe they were from a local college, maybe just passing through, it didn't matter. In bars like the one he was sitting in, everyone had a story. About their life. And their loves. And their hopes and dreams and fears for the future.

Mahoney drank his beer, thinking of heading home. He felt slightly detached. As if his life had come apart at the seams. He was used to structure. But now, in the last twenty-four hours, his ordered world had been shattered.

A second chilled bottle of beer was placed in front of Mahoney.

"What's this?" he asked Benny.

Benny pointed to some construction workers at the end of the bar. "They thought you looked a little down, thought you needed cheering up."

Mahoney forced a smile and lifted the bottle, toasting them. "Thank you."

The biggest of the construction guys picked up his beer and walked over to Mahoney. "You OK?"

"Not having a good day. Lot of stuff going on."

"You wanna join us for a drink?"

"Thanks, but I'm just going to enjoy this drink and get back to my wife."

The construction guy grinned. "Story of my life. Enjoy your beer, my friend." He patted Mahoney on the back. "Don't worry, man.

Tomorrow, whole new day." He went back to his buddies, leaving Mahoney alone with the beer. He nursed it for a few minutes, before downing the rest quickly. He felt a rush to his head, a strangely numbing effect.

Mahoney handed Benny a fifty-dollar bill. "Get the guys and yourself a beer."

Benny shook his head. "Are you sure?"

"Get them all a beer. I'll see you around."

Mahoney walked out of the bar into the chilly late-afternoon air. He'd been gone for a couple hours. But he felt slightly better than when he left.

He took the long walk back to his apartment. The familiar smells, vendor stalls . . . He walked some more of the High Line and then headed home.

Mahoney opened his front door and saw his wife was smiling.

"Have you been drinking?" she said.

"Stopped off for a couple beers."

"Guess who's here?" she said.

Mahoney's heart nearly stopped. He shrugged.

"A friend of yours from Toronto was visiting a friend nearby and decided to drop by. Isn't that nice?"

Mahoney's stomach tightened and he felt sick. A feeling of dread washed over him. "That's great." He followed her into the living room.

Sitting on *his* sofa, drinking a cup of coffee, watching Fox News, was Nathan Stone. "Mark, I hope this is OK. I thought I'd drop by when I finished my assignment."

Mahoney felt as if he were losing his mind. His sanctuary from the bustling streets of Manhattan. And now a trained assassin was sitting in his living room, as if he were an old friend. "Hi . . . This is a surprise."

"I'm not intruding, am I?" Stone said. He was a brilliant actor. Terrifying. His eyes were sparkling. "You said to drop by when I finished my work."

Mahoney nodded. "That's right." He turned to his wife. "This is great. Can I have a couple of minutes alone with my friend?"

"Sure, honey. Can I get you a cup of coffee?"

"I'm good."

"Can I get you or your friend a sandwich?"

"We're good, thanks," Mahoney said.

His wife smiled and shook her head. "How about Chinese tonight?"

"Sounds good."

She looked at Stone. "Would you like some too?"

"Sure, count me in."

Thirty-Eight

Nathan followed Mahoney into his study and closed the door behind them. He sat down on the sofa and looked around. "What's on your mind, Mark?"

Mahoney pulled up his seat beside Nathan. He leaned close and whispered, "What the fuck are you doing? Are you planning to kill us here? Is that it?"

"Don't be so dramatic, Mark. You need to lighten up."

Mahoney pushed his face up close to Nathan's. "You leave my family alone."

"Your family isn't in danger from me, I can assure you."

"Do not dare fuck with them."

"I have no intention of doing so."

"Those are the rules. Kill me. Discredit me. Do what you want with me. But do not lay one finger on my family."

"You have my word."

"Your word? Are you kidding me?"

"I've given you my word. And I am a man of my word. Trust me."

"Except I don't trust you, do I?"

"Trust me, and you'll live. But if you don't trust me and start overthinking this, you'll be dead meat."

"I want you out of here. Now."

"I'll be on my way. But first, I need to eat. I'm starving."

They ate their Chinese food at the huge table in their dining room, much to Mahoney's discomfort. His wife and the kids seemed impervious. Nathan loved the noodles, crab Rangoon, fried beef, and fried rice, gorgeous food he hadn't eaten in he couldn't remember how long.

Nathan forked the beef and rice and shook his head. "This is wonderful." He turned to face the kids, who were smiling. "When I was your age, trust me, I didn't get food like this."

"Are you from Toronto, Mr. Stone?" Mrs. Mahoney asked.

Nathan smiled and looked around the table. The children, who were both eating Cantonese seafood soup, and Mahoney's wife, were smiling. By sharp contrast, the face of the *New York Times* journalist Nathan had been assigned to kill was waxy, his eyes hooded. "Where do you think I'm from?"

One of the kids said, "Boston!"

Nathan shook his head. "A bit closer than that."

Mahoney's wife shrugged. "I can't quite place your accent. There's a slight twang to it. You know, like a Southern drawl."

"I get that a lot. I've lived down in Florida for a while, but no, I'm from New York City. You believe that?"

The kids both shouted, "Yeah!"

Mahoney's wife said, "Were you brought up here, Mr. Stone?"

"Call me Nathan. Born and bred. Lower East Side, Bowery. A different place than it is today."

"What exactly do you do, Nathan? I don't think I remember Mark mentioning you."

Nathan looked across at Mahoney, who shifted in his seat. "Mark, do you want to explain, or shall I?"

Mahoney cleared his throat. "Nathan does research and things like that for us."

"And you're back in New York to visit family?" his wife asked.

"Yeah, family, old friends, and I remembered that Mark gave me his address if I was ever in New York, so it was very fortunate that you all were home."

Mahoney stabbed some noodles. "Nathan, what are your plans while you're in town?"

"I don't know. I'm hoping to see a show, maybe meet up with some old friends later. You want to join us?"

Mahoney was chewing his food and turned to his wife. "Honey, you mind if I spend a couple of hours with Nathan?"

His wife rolled her eyes and smiled. "You just got home, and I feel like I've barely seen you."

"I'll make it up to you. I just feel like hanging out for a little while."

"You guys," his wife said. "It's almost like you never grew up."

Mahoney looked at Nathan. "Is it OK if I tag along?"

"The more the merrier," Nathan said.

After their takeout and some small talk, Mahoney got his jacket, pecked his wife and kids on the cheek, and headed out with Nathan. They didn't speak until they got to the Westside Tavern.

Mahoney ordered two large beers and they sat down in the back corner.

"What the fuck was that all about?" Mahoney asked.

Nathan took a large gulp of the beer, which tasted good. He leaned in close, voice a whisper. "Listen, you fuck, I could've wiped you out twenty-four hours ago. And you're still whining."

"Are you kidding me? I'm supposed to be grateful for you turning up at my home? Where my family lives?"

"I'm trying to save you."

"What do you mean?"

"You're only alive because of me. Without me you'd be dead."

178

Mahoney drank some beer, his eyes downcast.

"So get down from your high horse."

Mahoney's forehead was beading with sweat. "Do not visit my home or be in touch with my family again. Am I clear?"

"Fine. Whatever. I have to say you've got a really nice family. Very sweet."

"Shut the fuck up about my family."

"Do you know how lucky you are?"

"Yes, I do."

Nathan drank some more beer. "Do you know where I've been?"

"I don't want to know."

"You're a journalist and you're not interested in what I did? Even when it concerns the Commission?"

Mahoney's gaze wandered around the bar for a few moments before he made eye contact with Nathan.

"I want you to know that my action in not killing you has almost certainly signed my death warrant. Today I took out Clayton Wilson."

Mahoney rubbed his hands over his face. "Stop, I don't want to hear that."

"I want you to know these things."

"So I'm now an accessory after the fact, as well as probably about to be assassinated? Well, that's just great. Thanks for that. And who's going to kill me now? You still penciled in for that?"

"That's enough. I've signed my own death warrant. I get that. And I'll deal with that. You? The people who asked me to kill you were Clayton Wilson and his gang. That's one down. Four to go."

"Oh, Jesus H. Christ, you have gotta be kidding me."

"Do I look like the sort of fuck who jokes? I want you to know that your only chance of making it through this is to hope and pray I can kill the rest of them before they kill us."

Mahoney's hand was shaking as he lifted his beer. His gaze was darting around the room as if he was struggling to take it all in.

179

"Take your time. Remember to breathe."

"Is this your idea of a joke?"

Nathan grinned.

"Well, you know what? It isn't funny."

Nathan watched a couple guys enter the bar, sizing them up. Young, white, unshaven, slightly scruffy. Maybe college kids from NYU.

"I can't live like this. I just can't. I feel like I'm having a breakdown."

"Do you want some advice?"

"Advice? From an assassin? Gee, I'm not sure."

"Sarcasm doesn't suit you, Mark."

Mahoney closed his eyes for a moment. "Advice. Yeah, sure. What?"

"Listen very closely. I'm going to disappear for a day or two."

"Disappear? Disappear to where?"

"I'm going to take care of business."

Mahoney turned away. "I don't want to know."

"You need to know. Look, if you haven't already figured it out, I'm not going to kill you. I'm trying to help you."

Mahoney just stared at him. "Why?"

"I don't think you deserve to die. Besides, my sister is safe now."

"How?"

"Clayton Wilson made it happen before I killed him."

Mahoney shook his head. "Shit."

"You need to move out of your apartment for a while."

"While you take care of business?"

Nathan nodded. "I'd like you to take your family and go somewhere. A quiet place. A place where people don't know you. A place not owned by you or in your name."

"My in-laws have a place."

"Where?"

"An old colonial in the Hamptons near the beach."

"The Hamptons is good. Go there. Tell your wife and kids you need a break by the ocean."

"For how long?"

"Take a week. Maybe two. I'll let you know when it's safe to come back."

"What exactly are you going to do? I mean . . . what the hell is going on?"

"Like I said, I'm taking care of business."

"Why?"

"Because if I don't kill the rest of the Commission, they'll have you neutralized sooner rather than later. Me too." Nathan pulled out Wilson's cell phone from his jacket. "This belonged to the chair of the Commission."

"Oh my God."

"I checked, and it's got all the numbers of the other four. But I think there will be a lot of information on this phone. Perhaps incriminating evidence. Evidence you might be able to use if you play your cards right."

Mahoney stared at it as if transfixed at the prospect of what it contained.

"Do not go to the cops, the Feds, or tell a soul about what happened. If you do, then all bets will be off and I will come back for you, and this time I won't be trying to help. I never picked you as my target. They did. But if you cross me, be under no illusion, I will fucking delete you from the earth, so help me God."

Thirty-Nine

It was dark and Berenger was sitting alone in his Toronto apartment, watching TV, when his cell phone rang. "Yeah?"

"You don't know me but I know all about you."

"Who's this?"

"I'm a friend of Clayton Wilson. My name is Richard Stanton."

Berenger picked up the remote control and switched off the TV. His senses were switched on. "You must have the wrong number."

"I've been informed by our facility—you know the one I'm talking about—that the Plastic Man has dropped off our radar."

"What?"

"I just contacted the facility fifteen minutes ago, and they said there was chatter on their Toronto police radio scanner about some fire at a business in downtown yesterday. It was evacuated apparently."

"So what connection is that to our operation?"

"The address corresponded to the office suite an acquaintance had been renting. The man who was handling the Plastic Man."

Berenger wondered what was going on. "That is strange."

"Damn right it is. Haven't heard from the handler. It's like he's dropped off the grid."

Berenger said, "And no one's made contact with the Plastic Man?"

"Not a word. I've sent people from the facility over to his apartment, but he's not there. It's under surveillance, but so far nothing."

Berenger began to pace the apartment. "The handler called me."

"What?"

"The man who oversees the Plastic Man."

"When?"

"Thirty-six hours ago, maybe more."

"About what?"

"He was trying to determine if the Plastic Man was ready for the operation after I'd carried out the preassessment."

"Is it usual for him to contact you about such matters?"

"Not really. In fact I can't remember the last time he called me looking for clarification or verification."

"You think there was something bugging him?"

Berenger nodded. "Yes, there was."

"What exactly?"

"He had doubts about the Plastic Man."

"What sort of doubts?"

"He was against the Plastic Man carrying out the operation as planned."

"What? Are you serious?"

"He had grave concerns about his suitability for the job, especially in light of what happened in Scotland. He said he had voiced these concerns to Mr. Wilson."

There was a pause as Stanton digested this information. "I wasn't informed of any concerns. At all. At any time."

"I can't comment on that, sir."

"I've been trying to contact Clayton, but I haven't been able to get through. Not to voice mail or anything. It's just ringing and ringing. But we did all get a message from him with an update."

"I can't imagine that's typical of Clayton."

"Quite the opposite. He was always available on the phone. Night and day. No matter what."

"The handler called it. He said he didn't like the Plastic Man working on this assignment."

"If we'd heard any dissenting voices like that of the handler, we would have gotten someone else."

"So why do you think Clayton was so adamant about using Nathan?"

"He figured the Plastic Man owed us, and this was us making him pay. Turning the screw."

"And how's that working out?"

"What a mess. What a fucking mess. And it might not end like this."

"What do you mean?"

"I mean, I think this could get worse. We thought we were playing it cute with the Plastic Man. But he's like a wrecking ball. There'll be nothing left at this rate. But the fallout and blowback could be even worse. And that's before we can even contemplate the main event in a few days' time. This might even put that in jeopardy."

Berenger's mind flashed back to sitting face-to-face with Nathan, his facial features expertly crafted and sculpted to show a different man from before. Cutting-edge technology and the best surgeons money could buy had created a monster. He remembered the coldness in the eyes. But also the way Nathan had commanded the room. Not overtly, but sometimes with a cutting remark, a comment that illuminated some of the rage within him, or perhaps it was the way Nathan had stared so long and hard at him, as if trying to determine if he should also be killed. It unnerved him, despite his being a highly experienced psychologist who was an expert in Special Forces psychology.

He had half expected Nathan to strangle him for any imagined slights or for an offhand comment.

"Are you still there, Doc?"

"Yes, I am. Sorry, I was just thinking about my last meeting with him."

"That's history. We need to think about the here and now."

"I agree."

"What are your thoughts on what I've told you?" the man asked.

Berenger sighed. "I think when you finally speak with Clayton—"

"I'm meeting with him tomorrow night."

"Good. So you need to all speak openly and get everyone's views. What you've told me indicates there's some dysfunction in the decision-making."

"What else do I need to know about the Plastic Man? What advice would you give?"

"He's the most dangerous man I've worked with. You probably know this already, but if I were in your shoes, I'd make sure the Plastic Man was neutralized first and foremost."

"Then what?"

"Then, and only then, should you get a replacement to complete the job once and for all."

Forty

It was nearly night and Nathan was sitting in a dark, shitty room in a hostel in Chinatown in the Bowery, just a few blocks from the one-room hovel he had grown up in. The memories flooded back. The terrifying face of his father staring down at him. Beatings. Unimaginable cruelty.

Nathan had considered getting a room in a hotel uptown. But he knew it was far easier to escape detection and blend in among the working-class people who still inhabited this relatively sketchy part of downtown Manhattan. No one asked questions. You just paid in cash and you got a hotel room. Uptown? More questions, raised eyebrows. It would have been easier for him psychologically. But his main focus was staying out of sight for as long as possible.

He looked out through a tear in the nicotine-stained lace curtains at the still-bustling street. Bangladeshis, Chinese, African Americans, crowds of white kids, every facet of New York, all contained in one of the city's oldest and grittiest neighborhoods. But the gentrification signs were there. Swanky new hotels opening up farther down the block where there had once been abandoned lots. Crumbling tenements being turned into offices or new apartment blocks. It was just a matter of time before the rents and prices headed skyward. And what of the working class then? They would inevitably have to move out. Brooklyn. That was gone. Prices skyrocketing. If you were lucky, you could get a shithole apartment in Crown Heights. What a mess.

Nathan had grown up in a nonworking-poor household. His father was a bum. He didn't know if he'd ever worked. Maybe the odd shift at the Hudson River docks. He couldn't ever remember his father getting up at the crack of dawn for work. That was when he usually stumbled in, if he came home at all.

He looked around the sparse, cramped, six-by-four room. It stank of piss, maybe from the mattress. Who knew? He remembered his father saying—in one of his rare sober moments—that he'd stayed in the same hostel for a few nights. It was called something else then, the Lodging House or something like that.

He wondered if his father had stayed in this same shitty room, maybe with a prostitute.

The more he thought about it, the more he felt the anger start to well up inside him. The crazy, leering eyes, the filthy hands raining punches down, the smell of sour rotgut whiskey on his breath, the screaming in his face as he cowered. At times it felt as if it would never end. And it never would have if his sister hadn't put an end to it all. She hadn't told Nathan what she was going to do. She just lay on the dirty mattress, similar to the one he was lying on now, with scissors sharpened—she would tell him later—on the stone stoop outside the apartment.

A flash of metal as she stabbed the blade straight into his heart. Down and down, the blood spurting out of their father's shirt, incredulity on his face as he fell to the floor. Then she stabbed him maniacally in the head and neck and back and neck and head, again and again and again until he no longer moved.

Nathan remembered trying to scream but being too afraid. His sister was drenched in their father's blood, and so was he. He tasted it on his tongue and began to wet himself. Then he cried and cried before the screams eventually came from deep within him, deep down in his guts.

Little had his father known, as he spent what would be his last drunken hours carousing or sleeping or fighting in a flophouse like this one, that his daughter was waiting for him, feigning sleep.

They knew he was going to come home that night. His money would have run out. And he would take shelter in his shitty one-room apartment on the Bowery, no more than half-a-dozen blocks away from where Nathan now sat.

Nathan and his sister had cowered in fear for so long, been absent from school for so long, that everyone had forgotten about them. They had only each other. Not a soul came to their rescue. Existing like feral cats amid the filth, the cold, the suffocating heat in summer, going out of their minds, retreating into the comfort of insanity as they lost their will to live.

But something within his sister had fought back. Thank God. She had to do it. If not for her, they would both be dead.

She had refused to lie down and die. From that moment on, Nathan learned to fight back. Not be afraid of anyone. Take the beatings. The hate on the street. And turn that rage into fuel for his resentment. He became tougher. Harder. More resilient.

He lay down on the bed and stared at the shadows on the ceiling. He listened to the honking cars outside, the shouts and screams from the same streets he'd once run around in, barking dogs. He had been part of a pack. And now here he was, all these years later, alone in the same lousy streets his father had called home, the same streets that made him.

There was the sound of raised voices and a commotion outside.

Nathan got up from the bed and peered through the tear in the curtains. He saw a man with four fierce-looking dogs on a leash. The guy's face was bathed in a ghostly glow from a streetlight. Nathan stared at the guy's face. He looked familiar. And then he remembered. Jesus Christ, he knew the guy. Zico, a neighborhood kid. A violent fuck. Out of control. Nathan used to run around with him way back in the day. And here he was, still hanging around.

He wondered if he should talk to him. But as he was working, that was a no-no.

That said, the guy was always respectful when talking about his sister. Wasn't pure mean like the other fuckers. He was mean in a good way. Taking the fight to people who wanted to fight. But shit, here he was, still doing what he was doing all these years later.

Nathan headed outside and walked up to the man. "Hey."

Zico just stared at him.

"Nice dogs, man."

Zico stared at him long and hard, the dogs straining at the thick leather leash. "Easy, guys." He stared at Nathan for what seemed an eternity. "Who the hell are you?"

"I'd hug you, man, but not with those fucking dogs." Nathan shrugged. "It's Nathan. Nathan Stone."

Zico grinned. "What the hell? You look completely different."

"Accident. Plastic surgery."

"Fuck. I haven't seen you in a long time. A lifetime, I think. Way back when."

Nathan nodded. "Yeah, way, way back when. Long time."

"Are you kidding me? What's going on?"

"With me? Just doing a little work in town. Thought I'd spend a few hours in the old neighborhood, you know, before I have to leave again."

"So where the fuck you been? The last I heard, you joined the army."

"Yeah, for a while. Moved on since then."

"Man, you look real weird. Yeah, you look different. Your face, I mean. Are you OK?"

"I'm good."

Nathan said, "Look I'd love to have a drink, but I have to head off real quick. You got a number I can reach you at if I get back into town?"

Zico handed him a business card. "Twenty-four hours a day. Whatever you need, Zico can get. And by the way, if anybody's fucking with you or wanting to fuck with you, you let me know." He cocked his head in the direction of the dogs. "You should see them in action."

"What do you mean, action? You mean against other dogs?"

"No, man, better than that. Sometimes I have to set them on the opposition."

"What kind of opposition?"

"Drug dealers I don't like. Gangs. Kids these days. They're fucking crazy. I'm not affiliated anymore. So I have to look out for my interests. And these bad boys will deal with any threat I face."

Nathan looked at the card, which listed a cell phone number. "You gotta gun?"

"Have I got a gun? Course I've got a fucking gun. But I've been training these crazy fucking dogs for years. Meanest, baddest fucks around. And you know what else? One time, about a year ago in Queens, deal went sour and I had to set my dogs on the guy. Filmed the whole thing."

Nathan tried hard not to wince.

"Man, you need to get with the program. Pinhole camera on each of the collars. HD-quality film. Then uploaded it to YouTube. Made a fortune. Released a fucking DVD as well. I'm thinking about live streaming too."

Nathan looked at the dogs warily. He wasn't a fan of dogs. He wasn't a fan of cats either. Actually, he didn't really like pets at all. "Look, I've got to get some shut-eye."

Zico tugged at his dogs. "You need any help in town, you just let me know, man, and I won't let you down."

Nathan grinned as his crazy old friend headed down the street and the dogs snarled and scratched each other. He headed back inside the hostel and back into his room, locking his door.

He lay down on the bed, his mind flashing back to his days on the streets. Foster homes he'd been thrown out of. And he was feral. The same as the rest of the guys who hung around with Zico, including a whole bunch of sociopathic lowlifes.

Over the next hour or so, his thoughts began to come together. Thinking of the old days. But he couldn't escape the encounter with Zico.

Eventually, Nathan closed his eyes and felt himself drifting off to sleep, thinking only of the following evening and the remaining members of the Commission.

Forty-One

Nathan awoke in a cold sweat from a nightmare in the squalid hostel. He'd dreamed he was being chased through woods by headless figures. His heart was beating hard. Outside on the street, there was the sound of beeping from a garbage truck reversing and the clatter of trash cans being emptied.

He got up and pulled back the curtains. Down on the street, a couple of Latino guys were squaring up to the black driver of the garbage truck, who was telling them to fuck off.

Nathan walked across the room and splashed some lukewarm water on his face from the cracked ceramic sink. He put on his clothes, picked up his backpack, and headed out to a diner on East Houston Street. He loaded up on caffeine and pancakes. He popped a couple of strong steroid pills laced with amphetamines, washed them down with black coffee. He looked around at the faces and realized he was from another time. The people in the diner seemed relaxed. He guessed they were educated, some students. But certainly a different crowd than the one that used to hang around back in the day. Then it was crazies, homeless druggies shooting up in the street, cyclists being thrown off their bikes, their bikes being sold six blocks away to other lowlifes, people walking imaginary dogs, and the downright dangerous muggers, thugs, and all manner of street freaks.

He got his coffee refill and stared out at the street. He was a fucking relic, like Zico, from a forgotten past. A ghost who'd returned to the same streets he knew so well.

He looked across at a streetlight and remembered it was the very same one where he'd gotten his head smashed in by a gang from Alphabet City before they'd stomped him unconscious.

It had taken him months to recover. But recover he did.

He got stronger. And smarter.

Until one day Nathan's path inadvertently crossed with the leader of the gang's, a sixteen-year-old who was already pimping. And the guy was infamous for cutting his "girls" if they ever looked at him the wrong way.

Nathan's mind flashed back to the early hours of a freezing January night. The guy had emerged from the shadows farther down the street, grinning like a jackal, holding a knife.

He taunted Nathan. The kid was laughing as a few of his friends watched from the sidelines. It was then, in that moment, alone, staring into oblivion, Nathan decided he'd had enough. He crossed the street, picked up a scaffolding pole, ran up, and smashed it down hard. The guy went down, blood spilling out the back of his skull.

Nathan had shown no mercy. He smashed the metal pipe down onto the fucker's skull and face until the guy was battered unconscious.

The attack was over before it began.

Nathan had stared down at the pool of blood congealing around his cheap sneakers.

It was at that moment he realized he'd crossed a line. No one ever fucked with Nathan after that. Word got around. *Avoid that crazy white kid from the Bowery.*

A good-natured waitress clearing her throat beside him snapped him out of his reverie.

"Would you like anything else, hon?" she asked.

"No, I'm good, thanks." Nathan put down a fifty-dollar bill. "Keep the change."

The waitress looked at him as if he'd lost his mind. "Are you kidding me?"

"Take care."

The hours dragged as Nathan considered the best way to deal with the remaining members of the Commission. They'd each responded to the message from, they believed, Clayton Wilson, confirming they'd be at the meeting place at 9:00 p.m. sharp.

He considered various options. Should he get a gun? A knife? Something else?

He really needed to see inside the townhouse to know what he was working with. He might be walking into a trap. He wondered if he should kill them outside the townhouse when they pulled up in their cars or cabs. But that solution had its own issues.

What if they had bodyguards? Guys like that, he imagined, would have personal protection.

The more he thought about it, the more he believed they'd be protected. Even if he got past their security detail, they might also be armed themselves.

He thought of taking them out sniper-style.

That in itself could be problematic. He'd get one. Maybe two if he was lucky. But three would be a stretch, let alone four. And there would be no guarantees. What if they were wearing bulletproof vests?

Nathan pushed those thoughts aside and left the diner. He caught a bus uptown and made his way toward the address. Down Fifth Avenue and then East Sixty-Eighth Street until he caught sight of the stunning five-story limestone townhouse. Black front door, original stoop, brass knocker. He walked down the street, his senses switched on.

He headed back onto Lexington and bought himself a pair of expensive shades. Then he headed farther down and into Barneys, on Madison Avenue, where he bought a navy jacket, pale-blue Oxford shirt, new Versace jeans, and tan wing tips. He put them on in the changing room, asked the assistant to cut off the price tags, and paid in cash, much to the assistant's bemusement.

"Man, you going to a party?"

Nathan smiled. "Yeah, something like that."

He handed the kid a twenty-dollar bill as a thank-you and made his way back to the townhouse, shades on, the new clothes having changed his appearance even more. He climbed the stoop and keyed in the access code, and the door clicked open.

He headed inside. A towering atrium stretched before him, black-and-white-tiled floors polished to a shine.

He took out his Glock and pulled back the slide.

He headed down a corridor, down a winding staircase to the basement, which led him out into a small back garden. He looked around the rest of the basement. Gas boiler. He flicked it open and turned it off.

Then Nathan headed back up onto the ground floor. It was quite possible he was being watched on surveillance. But he figured there would be no need for evidence of any meetings or appearances. Higher and higher he climbed through the townhouse. Five bedrooms, six other rooms, including a library. Adjacent to the library on the fifth floor was a room, oil paintings on the wall, oval table with a dozen large bottles of water and glasses too. The blinds were drawn. It was situated at the rear of the building.

On one wall, a gold-leaf mirror hung above a fireplace. Nathan kneeled down and examined the fire. It was a gas fire, a modern one, although it blended in very well with the old room.

He wondered if this was the room they used for their meetings. It looked like it was set up for one.

Nathan opened his backpack and rummaged inside for a screwdriver. He loosened the fake coal display and saw the pipe that led to the gas element. He loosened some wooden molding on the floor, where the valve was housed. Then he removed the valve and carefully replaced the molding, gluing it back in place. Then he put the fake coal display back on top of the gas element.

Nathan headed back down to the basement and spotted the gas line regulator hidden in a tiny cupboard in the basement. He removed the valve there as well.

He went up to the ground floor, where the kitchen was. It was all granite surfaces, expensive ceramic floors, with a faint smell of pine as if it had been cleaned that morning.

Sitting on top of the worktop was a microwave. He raked through some drawers and found a metal container, which he placed in the microwave, carefully shutting the door. He checked the time on his cell phone. Then he set the microwave's delayed-start function to begin at 9:19 p.m. that evening.

Nathan headed down to the basement one more time and switched the gas on. Then he headed back up the stairs, out through the tiled lobby, and through the heavy front door, automatically locking it behind him. Inside he heard the alarm resetting.

He disappeared down the street and melted into the crowds.

Forty-Two

Mahoney was wrapped up against the deep chill, walking along a deserted beach near East Hampton with his wife and kids. The sky seemed like it went on forever.

"You look happier out here, Mark," she said, linking arms with him.

"Maybe we need to consider moving out of the city."

"What about the kids' school?"

Mahoney's kids attended a prestigious private day school in Manhattan. "I'm sure there are good schools out here."

"There are."

"So why not move out here? We can get a little cottage, maybe rent your parents' place for a year or so if they'd allow us."

"They're members of the Maidstone Club. I'm not sure they'd want to go without golf in the summer."

"Jesus Christ."

"Oh, honey, they like their hobbies. Is that so bad?"

"No, it isn't so bad. It's just that I'm starting to feel better already. It's so much quieter here."

The sun was sinking lower in the sky, a pale-crimson glow washing over the beach as the waves crashed onto the cold sand.

"Sure, now it is. But you know what this place is like in the summer."

Mahoney nodded, remembering from past visits how insane the crowds were from May till September.

"Jam friggin' packed."

"But the rest of the time it's like this," he said.

"True."

"I could get used to this."

"What about your job?"

"I've been thinking about that."

"What have you been thinking about? How stressed you are?"

Mahoney felt the cold wind on his face, smelled the salt in the air, and sighed. "I don't want to work in journalism anymore."

His wife took a few moments to answer. "What?"

"I know, it's out of the blue. I'm just . . . I don't know, I feel like I need a change."

"What kind of change?"

"The sort of change where I can see you and the kids every day. Where I can maybe write a book."

"A book? About what?"

"Maybe about what I've been working on."

"Will the *Times* allow you to do that?"

"My contract just mentions not working for competitors—you know, like the *Post*."

"I don't know, honey . . . This is all so out of character."

"I feel like I need a change. A major change. A change of pace. A change of scenery."

"Shouldn't we talk it over?"

Mahoney shrugged. "Isn't that what we're doing?"

"Well, no, honey. You're basically just throwing this curveball at me. First you asked us to leave Toronto because you were stressed and on a deadline. Then you turn up back in New York without any notice.

Now you're talking about leaving your job. And writing a book? It's like you're having a breakdown."

Mahoney had never been good with confrontation. He wasn't one of those journalists who could walk up to a door, knock on it, and ask for a quote. He found it uncomfortable. He would much rather have the time and space to research and write stories, investigate events, unearth news, write features. But even that, since Nathan had turned up in Toronto, had lost its shine. The whole journalism thing, which he was immersed in to the exclusion of his family life, had left his world hanging by a thread. He didn't know what to do. He felt sufficiently cowed by Nathan to just do as he said. It wasn't the tough thing to do. It wasn't the brave thing to do. And it probably wasn't the smart thing to do. But it was his call, as he was unable to burden his family with such news.

He closed his eyes as they walked on the beach, the kids running along the waterline farther down the sand. He felt scared. Racked by uncertainty. And guilt. His family was at risk, and he hadn't told them.

"Darling, what's wrong?" his wife asked. "I know you, Mark. I can tell there's something terribly wrong. Oh God, what is it, Mark? Is it a girl? Have you met someone?"

Mahoney shook his head.

"Please, Mark, you're scaring me now."

Mahoney wondered what to do. He'd wrestled with what to do. He couldn't find a solution. He couldn't bear to tell her. He was scared of the ramifications. But could he really, in all conscience, just leave her to wonder why he was acting so strangely?

"Is it a midlife-crisis sort of thing? Talk to me, Mark."

"I feel sick," Mahoney said.

"You feel sick? Something you ate? What?"

"I feel sick that I haven't . . ."

"Haven't what?"

Mahoney pulled her close. He looked around at the perfect scene. The sound of the ocean crashing onto the shore was a balm to his soul. "I haven't been totally honest with you."

His wife just looked at him.

"I feel ill about what I've got to tell you."

"My God, Mark, please, you're killing me. What is it?"

Mahoney felt a pain in his chest. He took a large intake of breath. He wondered if he was going to have a panic attack. The scale of what was happening was almost too much to bear. "I'm going to share this with you and you alone. I couldn't share it a few days ago."

"Please don't say you've met someone. Please don't say that. I couldn't bear that."

"You can't share what I'm about to tell you. With anyone."

"OK."

"Promise?"

"Yeah, I promise."

"What I'm about to tell you concerns a major secret investigation I'm working on. Two people at the *New York Times* know about this. And me. That's why I've been in Toronto."

"Please, Mark, what is it?"

"I'm investigating the murder of the late senator Brad Crichton, in Scotland."

"Didn't he fall to his death climbing or something?"

Mahoney shook his head. "He was killed by an assassin."

His wife didn't speak, as if she was taking it all in.

"The assassin's name is Nathan Stone."

"The guy who had dinner with us the other night?"

Mahoney nodded. "Nathan killed the senator, but his girlfriend managed to escape for a while. Until a second crew of assassins killed her. And they were subsequently killed by Nathan."

His wife put her fingers to her temples.

"Nathan Stone was subsequently assigned to kill me."

"Oh my God!"

"In Toronto."

"The guy at our apartment?"

"That was him."

"You told him where we lived?"

"He already knew. He knows everything about me."

"This is our family we're talking about, Mark. Our family. Our children. Me."

"Listen to me, the people who assigned Stone to kill me kidnapped his sister to ensure he would carry out their plan. But he's flipped or gone rogue or something, and he's vowed to kill the people who ordered his sister's kidnapping and the hit on me."

"This is like a nightmare. A living nightmare. We've got to get out of here."

"Nathan Stone . . . I sat down with him."

"The man in our apartment?"

"Yes! The man in our apartment. Nathan told me to leave the apartment in Chelsea."

"This is nuts. Mark, we've got to go to the cops. The FBI. Anyone."

"No. We can't."

"What do you mean we can't?"

"Nathan said not to go to the cops."

His wife turned away and ran her hands through her hair. "Mark . . . he's going to kill us. He's going to kill us out here."

"I don't think he will."

His wife turned to face him. "What? Are you serious? How do you know he won't kill us? He was hired to kill you, didn't you say that?"

Mahoney nodded.

"This is a nightmare. I'm going to wake up." She looked farther down the beach as their daughters walked along the shoreline. "Come back, kids!" she shouted.

The children waved at her.

201

"I said come back here! Right now, do you hear?"

The children reluctantly started walking toward them.

"If what you're saying is true, Mark, the right thing to do, and the smart thing to do, is contact the cops. The FBI."

"Stone said not to do that. He said these people would get to me or to you wherever they put us."

"And you believed him?"

Mahoney looked out at the ocean tossing and turning, waves crashing onto the shore. "So help me God I did."

Forty-Three

Nathan watched from farther down the street as a couple limousines pulled up outside the Upper East Side townhouse. He was standing nearly two blocks away eating some tacos beside a food truck with a perfect line of sight. He had dumped the clothes from earlier and bought a pair of Levi's, a black T-shirt, and a jacket, along with some black Nikes.

Nathan finished the food, wiped his mouth and hands, and dropped the wrapper in a bin. He reached into his jacket pocket and pulled out the new compact binoculars he'd bought. He saw three men, in their seventies, being led inside by a team of bodyguards. It was a classic formation, shielding front, rear, and side.

A huge bodyguard entered the code into the keypad—the same one he'd used earlier—and pushed the door open. He held it ajar as the men stepped inside, security teams following. Two stayed outside guarding the entrance, one speaking into a cell phone.

Nathan wondered where the final member of the Commission was. He watched and waited. He checked his watch. It was now 9:01 p.m. He scanned the windows of the various floors. Faint light glowed from behind the drapes in the library on the fifth floor. He believed the men would be meeting in the adjacent room, to the rear of the building.

A tap on his shoulder and Nathan turned around. Two cops were staring at him.

"What are you looking at, sir?" the burlier of the two asked.

Nathan's senses were all switched on. He smiled. "Just testing them out in low light, Officer." He handed them to the cop. "See, try for yourself."

The cop looked over the binoculars for a few moments. "We were observing you. Looked like you were spying on the building farther down the street."

Nathan grinned. "Not exactly, Officer. I'm a birder, just so you know."

"A what?" the cop said.

"Bird-watcher. Just spotted some finches in the trees down the road. Really beautiful birds."

"Can I see some ID, sir?"

Nathan pulled out his wallet and showed him the fake ID.

"You're a long way from home, sir."

"I love New York in the fall. Heading down to Central Park tomorrow to do some real bird-watching."

The cop handed back the ID and the binoculars. "You enjoy your stay in New York. Take care."

Nathan smiled. "Thank you, Officer. Stay safe."

He waited until they'd disappeared out of sight before he put the binoculars back in his pocket. Checked his watch. It read 9:11. His cell phone showed it was 9:13.

A message flashed on the phone he'd taken from Clayton Wilson. It was from Richard Stanton. It read:

Apologies, flight delay and I'm running late. Just landed at JFK and huge lines. Will be at least an hour before I'm there. Regards, R.

Nathan took one last look down the street. Everyone was inside apart from the two guys still by the door.

It would soon be time.

He turned and headed away from the townhouse, back toward Fifth Avenue.

A few minutes later, the sound of a huge explosion shook the ground and split the chill in the New York night.

Forty-Four

A couple of hours later, Nathan got a message from Richard Stanton on Clayton Wilson's cell phone. It read:

What the fuck is going on, C? You OK? Did you hear what happened? I just arrived. The place has been taken out. Please advise.

Nathan took a few minutes to consider his next move. He wondered if he should arrange to meet up with Stanton and delete him. But he thought his luck might just be about to run out.

He'd taken care of his handler, Clayton Wilson, and three members of the Commission. But Richard Stanton still eluded him.

He began to run through some options as he tried to concoct an assassination strategy. He wondered if he could take him out from afar. Darkness would make that difficult. Besides, it was always best to hunker down for a few days before attempting a sniper attack.

Slowly, his thoughts began to clear. He needed, in military terms, what was called an asymmetric response. Nathan assumed Stanton might bring a bodyguard to any suggested meeting. Then again, he might not if he was asked to come alone. But he needed a method that would not only attract Stanton but also wouldn't leave any trace of Nathan.

It was then that an idea began to form. Very slowly at first. His mind flashed back to the meeting with Zico. A crazy, irrational, money-driven psychopath.

Nathan took out the business card, printed on cheap paper, and dialed the number.

"Yo, who the fuck is this?"

"Zico, it's Nathan."

"Hey, man, what's up?"

"You said if I needed help you'd be there."

"Fucking right."

"I need your help. And I need it now. And I'm willing to pay."

"Pay for what?"

"I want a custom service, Zico."

"Yeah, I'm your guy."

"But you need to be discreet. Can I count on that?"

"Nathan, discretion is my middle name."

"Then this is what I want you to do."

Nathan caught a cab to the West Village and sent a text message to Richard Stanton from Clayton Wilson's cell phone. It read:

Family emergency, sincere apologies. What a mess. We've been compromised. And I believe I know who it is. Meet face-to-face to discuss. Security is doing a sweep of the location as we speak. Ground floor, the site of the old Keller Hotel, currently empty, Barrow Street entrance, just off the West Side Highway. 0100 hrs.

Almost immediately he got a reply.

Will do. R.

Nathan asked the cab to drop him off a block away, outside the Rockbar. It was a gay bar on Christopher Street. He walked around the corner and along West Street. Saw the dilapidated hotel sign and turned down Barrow. He used a knife to pry open the padlocked door and headed inside. The smell of dust, damp, and decay rushed at him.

Light was coming in from the street through cracks in the boarded-up windows. He headed up some rickety stairs to the next floor. A lot more light was coming in through the upper windows.

Nathan was satisfied there was enough light to see, but not too much.

He headed higher in the building to the top floor and located a set of stairs that led out onto the roof.

Nathan pushed open the sealed roof hatch, pulled himself up and onto the gravel roof, shutting the hatch tight. He crawled over to the edge and surveyed the scenery of the West Village. He turned around and saw the car headlights on the West Side Highway.

He pulled out his cell phone and lay still. He watched and waited. Sirens sounded in the distance as a cop car, red and blue lights flashing, screamed down the West Side Highway.

It was 0029 hours when Nathan saw a small white truck pull up farther down Barrow Street. Out jumped Zico with his four dogs. He watched as his psychotic old friend walked his dogs up to the front door of the abandoned hotel and took off their leashes. Then he opened the door Nathan had unlocked and pushed them inside. Zico slipped in behind them, carefully shutting the door after him.

Forty-Five

Nathan checked his watch. It was 0050 hours. He pulled out his cell phone and sent another text message to Richard Stanton. It said:

I'm here. Security is in place inside. Are you on your way?

A couple of minutes later, Nathan received a reply.

Cab heading down Bleecker Street. ETA 5 mins.

It wasn't long before a cab came down Barrow Street. Nathan watched as it pulled up next to the hotel. He saw Richard Stanton, a silver-haired man wearing a navy suit, no tie, with a cell phone pressed to his ear, emerge from the cab.

Stanton ended the call, put his phone in his jacket pocket, and headed inside the abandoned hotel.

The door slammed shut.

Nathan crawled over the roof space and pressed his ear to the wooden hatch. Then an ear-splitting scream emanated from deep within the bowels of the run-down, derelict hotel.

A ping to his cell phone. A link.

Nathan clicked it and saw a live feed of the dogs growling over a prostrate Stanton, whose eyes were filled with fear.

Nathan sent Zico a message. *Get the dogs out of there now.*

Zico did as he was told.

Nathan opened the hatch and headed down into the hotel. He pulled back the slide of the Glock and moved stealthily down the creaking stairs to the former lobby of the old hotel, cloaked in near darkness.

A silhouetted figure lay in the far corner, breathing hard.

Forty-Six

Nathan felt wired. He could make out the shape of the man illuminated by a single shaft of light coming in through the boarded-up windows. He stared down at the man as his sight adjusted to the near-pitch-black darkness.

Nathan pointed his gun down at the figure. "On your knees, hands on your head."

The man complied.

Nathan reached into the man's jacket pocket and pulled out a cell phone.

"What's your name?"

The man let out a long sigh. "Nathan?"

Nathan scrolled down a list on the phone. "Are you Richard Stanton?"

The man gave a small groan. "Where are the dogs?"

"Stanton?"

"Where's Clayton?"

"It's over."

Stanton began to laugh. "Good one."

Nathan pulled back the slide. "You think this is funny?"

"You have no idea. No fucking idea what's going to happen to you. You're out of your mind, son."

"Stanton, you lost."

"That's where you're wrong. You lose."

"What do you mean? I killed the other fuckers."

"It's not over, Stone."

"What do you mean?"

"I mean . . . Mahoney. We'll get him. No matter what. Not me. But someone."

"What are you talking about?"

A deathly smile. "I knew what you did. I have the authority. I couldn't contact Clayton. So I took precautions before I came here. Mahoney dies."

Nathan said nothing as he contemplated what Stanton was saying. He scrolled through the messages on the cell phone. A text message had been sent from a cell phone to Stanton's number just over an hour ago. *"En route to EH,"* Nathan said. "Who or what is this?"

"A man from the Canadian facility is en route to kill him. Probably arrived by now. We know more than you do. A lot more. So . . . you see, our work will continue. After we're gone."

"Why are you telling me this?"

"So you know that you failed. How does that feel?"

In the distance came the sound of police sirens. They sounded like they were getting closer.

"What's the name of the guy you sent?"

"Go to hell!"

"EH. Is that a place?"

Stanton began to laugh. "You're so fucked!"

"EH . . . East Hampton . . . You sent someone to East Hampton?"

Stanton was laughing uncontrollably, as if taunting him. "Just fucking kill me, tough guy!"

Nathan pressed the gun into Stanton's mouth, turned away, and pulled the trigger.

Forty-Seven

It was the dead of night.

Mahoney was sitting with his wife in the living room of the East Hampton cottage, watching Fox News with the volume off. The kids were sleeping upstairs as they continued to argue over the chain of events unfolding around them.

"Mark," his wife said, "I feel like I'm going in circles. I still don't get it."

"What don't you get?"

"You're not a stupid person. In fact you're really smart. But I can't fathom why you can't see what I see. We need to go to the Feds, if nothing else to protect our kids."

Mahoney felt as if his world was coming apart at the seams. "This is difficult to explain. But as I've said over and over and over again, if he wanted me dead, he could've killed me."

"Yeah, but as I've said over and over again, what about the people that sent him?"

"I didn't think you'd understand my thought process on this."

"Oh really? Why's that, Mark? Is it because it relies on us agreeing to the whims of a psychotic assassin?"

"Nathan Stone is a psychotic assassin, I know that. But I believe somewhere deep within him he's a person of his word. I don't know why that is."

"I'm sorry, Mark, but I think you've lost your fucking mind, excuse my French."

"What other choice did I have? Go to the Toronto cops while Nathan Stone heads down to New York to kill my family?"

"He's playing you, don't you get it?"

"I get it alright. Don't worry, I get that I'm being played. But sometimes you just have to take life as it comes. I didn't wish any of this on us. It was these people, the Commission, that wanted me dead, not Nathan."

"Sounds like you've got a bad case of Stockholm syndrome."

"Maybe I do. Maybe it's a survivalist trait, praying that I and my family don't get killed. I didn't know any other fucking way, do you understand?"

"You made the wrong call. And here we are, arguing about it in the middle of nowhere."

"I don't think a cottage in East Hampton is technically the middle of nowhere."

"We're a mile from the town of East Hampton, alone on the beach. No one will hear us scream."

"Oh stop it! Enough!"

"Mark, I will not stop it! This is our family. And you decided not to tell us our lives were in danger."

"They were trying to blackmail me too!" The words were out before Mahoney realized it.

"What do you mean?"

"They . . . Nathan brought a girl back to the apartment, my apartment, drugged her. They bugged my apartment, set up cameras."

Mahoney's wife looked aghast. "Are you fucking kidding me? This is getting worse. A girl? Tell me about the girl."

"I didn't know her."

"What?"

"He met her in the bar and wanted to blackmail me by taking a picture of her drunk, covered in drugs."

"OK, I think I've heard enough. I'm going back to New York with the kids."

"You need to listen to what I have to say."

"I've heard enough! Drunk girls! Drugs! Have you lost your fucking mind?"

"Actually, yes, I think I might have. But you have to believe me. Their backup plan was that I would abandon my investigation, or the pictures would be uploaded to the internet, sent to you, the *New York Times*, uploaded to YouTube, every-fucking-where, do you understand?"

"Mark, I'm having trouble understanding all this. Tell me about this girl. I want to know about the girl."

"She was the daughter of a Canadian intelligence officer. Two birds with one stone, forgive the pun."

His wife was silent for moment. "Intelligence officer's daughter . . ."

"Nathan wanted to silence him. And me at the same time. He knew his daughter's life would be fucked if there were incriminating photos of her with drugs. But it worked on another level by putting her in my apartment. Making me look complicit."

"And you've never met her before?"

"As God is my witness, absolutely not."

"And this was part of a backup plan by Nathan Stone to get you off this investigation. And silence the Canadian?"

"Got it."

His wife got up and started pacing the room, agitated, eyes bloodshot from lack of sleep. "I'm scared."

"Nathan has become entwined in my life."

His wife was pacing back and forth, shaking her head. "I can't believe he was in our house. And you knew about him."

"I had no fucking choice."

"Would you sacrifice us to stay alive? Is that it?"

"No. That's not it. That's not it at all. Never. I don't believe he's going to harm me or you, and I felt like I had to go along with what he said. I was desperate, going out of my mind." Mahoney rubbed his hands across his face, feeling trapped, scared, and unable to figure out his next move. "I'm not good at this sort of thing. My world is about words. Establishing facts. Narratives. Investigations. Building up relationships. This world . . . I don't know anything about it."

"I still don't understand why he didn't just kill you."

"He said he wanted the details I had on the Commission. They took his sister so he would take this job. And he just went rogue, I guess."

"He can't be trusted."

"I know, but—"

"But that's just the thing. You *do* trust him."

Mahoney sat with his head in his hands. "He said we'd be safe here. Why would he say that?"

"Mark . . . look at me. I have no idea why he said that. Is it because he wants us out of the way so he can kill us at his convenience, away from the city?"

"He could've killed me anytime. He could've, God forbid, killed any of us if he wanted to. But he didn't."

"OK, that's it. You've lost it. I'm taking the kids back to the city. You can wait here for your new crazy friend to turn up. And who knows? He might just show up with another drunk girl!"

She stormed out of the room.

"Where are you going?"

"I'm packing a bag, and I'm going to drive the kids back to the city."

Mahoney got up and walked to the bottom of the stairs. He heard his wife opening and slamming closet doors.

"OK, kids!" his wife shouted, switching the lights on upstairs. "Sorry but we have to go."

The oldest groaned, "Mom, it's the middle of the night. What's going on?"

"We need to go!"

"Go where?"

"Back to the city."

"Why?"

"I can't say. I just want to go."

Mahoney's cell phone began to ring. "Shit."

"Don't answer it!" his wife shouted down.

Mahoney went to the living room.

"Do not answer it!" his wife shouted from upstairs. "Do you hear me?"

Mahoney reached for his cell phone and answered. "Who's this?"

All he heard was the sound of fast-moving traffic, as if the person was traveling at high speed.

"Who's this?"

Eventually, a voice crackled to life. "Mark?"

"Yeah, who's this?"

"It's Nathan! Listen to me, you're in immediate danger. They sent another operative. They're going to kill you. I tracked his phone. Three minutes ago, he was at East Hampton Airport."

Mahoney felt himself go into shock. "What?"

Nathan shouted, "Someone's going to kill you!"

"Jesus Christ! Where are you?"

"I stole a bike . . ." The line began to crackle. ". . . Hampton."

"Sorry, I'm losing you. What?"

"I'm passing Southampton. He's going to get there first."

Mahoney felt panic begin to set in. "What do I do? Tell me what I do."

"Hide!"

Suddenly, the line went dead as they were plunged into darkness.

Forty-Eight

Nathan was speeding along Montauk Highway doing ninety, pushing a hundred, careening around winding corners as he sped into the night, hunched low on the bike. Towns whizzed by. The occasional light. Oncoming trucks passed, and their headlights flashed as he accelerated to one hundred ten, the powerful BMW bike nearly too much for the speed and the conditions.

His helmet was voice activated.

"Call the previous number!" he shouted behind his visor, gripping on for dear life.

The call rang and rang, but no one was answering.

"Call the previous number!"

It rang. And rang.

Nathan was focused on the road and realized the attack was probably going down at that moment. He sensed the assassin sent by Stanton to kill Mahoney might already be there. So why the hell was he getting involved? This wasn't his fight. He was only concerned about his sister.

But was that really the case? Did he feel obligated in some way to Mahoney? The problem was he hadn't felt obligated to anyone in his whole life, apart from his sister.

The trees blurred as he sped by. The headlights of the motorcycle showed the asphalt ahead. Had he lost his mind? Then again, maybe he was thinking clearer than he ever had.

"Call the previous number again!"

It rang. And rang. Then a voice answered, "Who's this?" It was Mahoney. He sounded frightened.

"Mark, get yourself out of sight!"

"Nathan, my wife thinks you're coming to kill us. She's scared."

"Tell her she's wrong. The guy who's coming to kill you is almost certainly outside your house right now."

"I don't know if I believe you."

"Believe me!"

"Why? How do you know that?"

"Richard Stanton told me right before I killed him."

"Jesus Christ. The lights went out a few minutes back. We're in total darkness."

"He cut the power. You have to get out of sight. Can you do that?"

"My wife is going out of her mind!"

"Hang in there. I'm heading toward East Hampton."

"What for?"

"I'm going to try and help you."

"You're going to kill me, aren't you?"

A rabbit ran out onto the asphalt and Nathan had to swerve to avoid it. "Negative. But someone else is. Someone from the Canadian facility's been dispatched."

"Hang on . . ."

Nathan wondered if the signal was fading as he went flat out on the bike.

"Nathan!"

"What is it?"

"My wife said there's a guy."

"Where?"

"Outside. I think he's broken into our car."

"He's disabling it so you can't escape. He's already cut the power. Call 911!"

"I did, but it just rang."

"Fuck. Have you got a gun?"

"No."

"Then get a knife. Get everyone in the house a knife. Take your cell phones and your family."

"Where?"

"Is there a basement?"

"Hold on . . . My wife says there's a basement under the kitchen. It's a storage space."

"Get down there!"

The line was breaking up.

"Where is he?" Nathan shouted.

Nathan heard Mahoney ask his wife.

"We can't see him."

"Mark, how far are you to the nearest house?"

"A couple hundred yards. Maybe a bit more."

"Fuck. I've got a fix on your location from this call," Nathan said. "I'll find you. But you need to—" The line cut out. "Are you still there?"

Mahoney was breathing hard down the line. "He seems to be going around the side of the house."

"Fuck. Get to the basement. Now!"

"What if we can't get there in time?" Mahoney asked.

Nathan was accelerating to 120 miles an hour, tearing hard toward the lights of East Hampton a few miles ahead in the distance. "Get down there now! If not, he'll kill you. All of you."

Forty-Nine

Mahoney ran up the stairs to the kids and his wife, who were crouching in an upstairs bedroom. "Everyone! Downstairs to the basement!"

His wife said, "Mark, I'm scared. Why isn't 911 working? I've tried texting my friends too, asking for help. But nothing."

Mahoney had read about signal jamming. He wondered if that was what this guy was doing while he was disabling the power. But he didn't want to freak out his wife further. "It's probably a computer glitch or something. Listen, we need to get downstairs. As a precaution."

His wife nodded and gathered the kids.

Mahoney led them downstairs in the dark. He picked up a couple knives, some barbecue skewers, and a flashlight from the kitchen drawer. Then his wife showed him the stone cover on the kitchen floor that led to the basement. He pulled it open.

"We used to hide down here as kids. It was like a play area," she said.

Mahoney shone the flashlight down so his family could see where they were going. Boxes, old chairs, and a chest of drawers lay scattered among the dust. His wife went down first as Mahoney handed her the kids. "Get in there and hide."

He turned. Outside he spotted the silhouette of a moving man.

Mahoney was gripped by a terrible fear as he descended the stairs and got out of sight. He switched on the flashlight and it picked out his wife and kids huddled in the corner. He pulled back the four-inch-thick stone cover and turned it clockwise, locking it from the inside.

He handed his wife a knife and armed himself with a barbecue skewer.

The kids were crying as his wife held them tight.

"Are we going to be OK?" his eldest daughter said. "Is the bad man coming to hurt us?"

Mahoney hugged them all tight. "Daddy's here. And I'm going to look after us all."

"Promise?" the youngest one said.

"I promise."

"Swear and hope to die," his eldest daughter said.

"I swear I'll look after you all. Let's be brave. And let's pray that someone is watching over us tonight."

"What if no one's watching over us tonight?" his youngest daughter said.

Mahoney hugged her tight. "I'll be watching over you. I promise. And I want you to know that the Mahoneys don't roll over and die. For anyone. We can fight too."

His wife blinked away the tears. "I'm scared."

The sound of a window smashing in the kitchen echoed above their heads.

Fifty

Nathan voice activated the overview map on his visor as he gave the details. Within seconds, the GPS voice in his ear was guiding him. "How long until destination?"

"We estimate you will be at your destination in two and a half minutes."

Nathan cranked up the speed some more as he got closer to East Hampton. He felt his blood pressure skyrocketing as he gunned the bike to the max toward its destination, praying he wouldn't be too late.

He sped around more corners and tore down Main Street, hoping there were no cops hanging around.

Closer. Closer.

The bike was roaring and vibrating as he squeezed every bit of juice out of the engine, closing in on God only knew what.

Fifty-One

Mahoney pressed his ear against the wall. He detected the faintest vibration, as if someone was walking about above their heads in rubber-soled sneakers or shoes. He switched off the flashlight, plunging them into darkness.

"Daddy, put the light on."

"Darling," he whispered, "we can't make any noise. No noise. And there can't be any light."

The girls and his wife sobbed as they huddled tight.

The sound of creaking timbers and joists continued as he heard footsteps above them on the kitchen floor. His kids were whimpering. He whispered, "Be very still and good."

His youngest was now shaking.

The footsteps headed through the kitchen. It sounded like the guy was upstairs. Going from room to room. The fear was palpable in the cold, dusty basement.

Mahoney held his trembling daughter tight.

The heavy footsteps returned above them. The sound of pots and pans crashing, as if the man had walked into the overhead utensils gantry. The sound of a chair being dragged along the floor.

Mahoney wondered if the man was using the chair to check for hiding places above the refrigerator and freezer. He wondered if he would notice the stone cover with a ceramic tile surface.

Every second seemed like minutes. A chasm of despair was opening up as they huddled in the pitch-black basement. The pitiful moans of his youngest daughter echoed in his ears.

Mahoney stroked her hair, praying she could contain her childlike fear of the dark, as the assassin was bearing down on them.

Suddenly, the sound of tapping on the stone cover.

Fuck.

Soft moaning from his daughter.

Mahoney held his breath as they huddled together.

The sound of more tapping.

Mahoney wondered if he was checking whether it was solid underneath. He knew at that moment the man would try to get in. He felt the terror seep into his very soul. He gripped his daughters tightly with one arm.

Suddenly, gunshots were fired rapidly onto the stone cover above. Then more.

His youngest daughter screamed. "Daddy!"

Mahoney held her and switched on the flashlight. He looked at his wife, who was hugging their eldest daughter. He whispered, "We can survive this. Let's be brave. And let's have faith."

His wife's eyes were closed, tears streaming down her face.

Rapid handgun fire sounded from above. Everyone tensed up, his youngest daughter covering her ears. "Make it stop, Daddy!" she said.

The gunfire made a hairline crack in the stone cover.

Faint light from the moon outside spilled in from the kitchen.

More gunfire hit the hairline crack in the cover, which was splintering.

Mahoney switched off the flashlight again and they were in near-total darkness. A sliver of light came through the ragged crack in the stone. Then a rifle barrel appeared and a hail of bullets tore into the stone basement, ricocheting off the walls.

A piercing scream from his wife. "My leg. I'm hit, Mark!"

Mahoney felt a surge of anger rise to the surface. He scrambled to her side. He ripped off his shirt and tore it into two strips. He felt her warm blood on his fingers as he wrapped the material tight around the gunshot wound.

"Fuck!" she snarled.

Mahoney gripped the skewer tighter. He leaned in close and whispered, "We can do this. I'll kill this fucker if I have to."

The bullets were being fired into an area two or three yards from them. The man couldn't aim the rifle at their exact location.

His wife was screaming in pain. "Mark!"

Mahoney tightened the ripped shirt around her thigh. "I'm sorry, honey," he said. "We need to slow the blood."

The gunfire abated as Mahoney's family sobbed and moaned, interspersed with his wife's screams of agony.

The heavy footsteps moved away. A few seconds later, they returned. The man shouted, "Not long now, folks!"

The kids began to scream and his wife was whimpering.

"Don't be afraid." The guy was toying with them.

Mahoney gripped the skewer hard. He anticipated what he would do when the man finally broke through. He would have to rush him. Adrenaline was coursing through his body. But with no outlet.

His eyes were becoming slowly accustomed to the near-zero light. At the far end of the basement were old packing crates, perhaps left by his in-laws when they had moved in. He wondered how he could use them.

Then came the sound of a power drill beginning to penetrate the stone.

The children were nearly frantic as his wife screamed.

Mahoney saw the glint of the steel drill pushing through the crack, breaking apart more of the plaster and stone. Then the man moved on to another area, perhaps the latch, which Mahoney had locked from the inside.

He prayed that it would hold.

Fifty-Two

Nathan was speeding along the isolated back road in a heavily wooded area outside East Hampton when he leaned hard into an oncoming bend. Suddenly, he felt the bike slide away from him as he careened across the road. He skidded through a fence and a hedge and slammed hard into some trees. He felt himself being catapulted through the air. Then he landed with a sickening thump in a marshy thicket just off the highway.

The smell of gasoline and oil surrounded him.

"Fuck!"

He extricated himself from the tangled thicket. He tried to get up and felt a stabbing sensation in his lower back.

"Motherfucker!" He gathered his thoughts. "How far to destination?" he asked via the Bluetooth helmet.

"Point-seven miles," came the answer.

Nathan took off the helmet and threw it into the marsh undergrowth beside the smoking metal of the bike. He pulled himself up and felt a shooting pain in his hip. "Fuck." He got up and limped back to the highway twenty or so yards away. He tried to run. But it was too painful.

He ran anyway, pain erupting every step of the way. But he sucked it up, ignoring the passing cars, jogging the final few hundred yards as he headed to Mahoney's location.

Fifty-Three

The drilling stopped for a few minutes as Mahoney and his family huddled tight, wondering what was going to come next. The hairline crack had developed into a quarter-inch fracture. The glint of metal appeared again. A chisel trying to gouge out the stone. But it snapped, clanking onto the stone cellar floor.

The children jumped and began crying again as his wife moaned, trying to suppress the gunshot pain.

"I can't stand this, Mark!" she hissed.

Mahoney held her hand. "He's not going to beat us, do you hear me?"

The man began to laugh. "Hey, tough guy. *He's not going to beat us, do you hear me?*" he mimicked.

Mahoney felt an adrenaline surge and gripped the skewer tighter.

"Back in a minute, guys," the man said, laughing.

Mahoney and his family were at their wits' end. Clinging on to the final shreds of hope. But Mark feared that eventually the man would break through and kill them all.

He crawled over to the far end of the basement and pulled an old table, storage boxes, and wooden chairs in front of them to protect them from bullets or ricochets.

"Daddy, don't leave us!" his youngest daughter cried.

Mahoney huddled close to her again. "Daddy's here. And so is Mommy. Let's be brave and strong. Can you do that?"

"I don't know, Daddy. I'm scared."

"We have to overcome our fear. Can you try and do that for me, darling?"

"I'll try, Daddy."

A steel hammer, smashing at the stone hatch with a fearsome sound, spilled dust and fear into the basement. Mahoney and his family covered their ears.

"Make it stop, Daddy!" his daughter shouted.

Mahoney held her even closer.

The hammering continued as the dust fell, covering their hair, ears, and eyes. Coughing and spluttering. On and on the relentless noise assaulted their senses.

Mahoney thought his head was going to explode. He felt powerless, at the mercy of a man who was determined to smash his way in one way or another and kill them.

Eventually, a few minutes later, the banging stopped and the dust began to subside.

The tiny fissure in the stone was all the man had managed to open up. A strip of light came in, enough for Mahoney to see his family covered in dust, the dark blood congealing around his wife's legs, and the fear in his children's eyes.

The man lay down on the kitchen floor above and pressed his eyes to the gap. "I'm still here, kiddies! Just getting warmed up, don't you worry." He blinked, and then he laughed.

Mahoney pushed a chair upright.

"Hey, what's the plan now, Mr. Family Guy?" the man said.

Mahoney jumped up on the chair, reached up, and stabbed the barbecue skewer through the crack in the stone, right into the flesh under the man's eye. Blood dripped down onto Mahoney's face as the man pulled himself away, screaming like a banshee for what seemed like minutes.

"You motherfucker! You're dead! You're dead! You're all dead! Motherfuckers!"

Mahoney got down from the chair and went back to comfort his family, wiping the man's blood off his face.

"Daddy," his youngest daughter said, "he's going to kill us!"

"Not if I can help it."

The man's screaming had turned to violent animalistic groaning and snarling.

"I'm bleeding, you motherfuckers! I can't fucking see!"

The family held each other tight.

A few minutes later, the growling, cursing man was above them, separated by the stone cover.

"Fucking dead! All of you. I'm gonna kill you all!"

They heard the sound of material being ripped up and smelled gasoline.

"Mark," his wife said, "what's that?"

Mahoney was about to respond when he saw burning rags being pushed through the tiny crack. The flaming cloth ignited the gas, and the basement boxes caught fire.

"Mark!" his wife shouted.

Mahoney picked up a rag, wrapped it around his right hand, and beat the flames out. "Goddamn!" he shouted as his hands were singed through the burned rags.

Another burning rag dropped through from above. Mark darted across the basement and stamped it out. Then lit matches fell down, igniting more gas pools, which set fire to his clothes.

He dropped to the floor and rolled over as his eldest daughter beat out the flames with her sweater.

The man above them was pacing the kitchen floor. Through the crack in the stone cover, Mahoney saw him pouring gas all over the kitchen.

The man was trying to burn them to death.

"Getting the picture, you fuckers?" he shouted. "Am I making myself clear?"

Glass shattered overhead as a makeshift bomb ignited, starting a fire, quickly engulfing the kitchen.

"We're going to have quite a party!" the man laughed. "Quite a fucking party! Who doesn't like a party? Me? I love a party!"

Black smoke was filling the kitchen and seeping into the basement through the crack in the stone cover.

The children began to choke and his wife began to cry as Mahoney flung himself on top of them. Burning rags and thick smoke filled the dead air around them.

Fifty-Four

Nathan was sweating hard as he ran in agony the last few hundred yards to the isolated home. In the driveway, he saw a station wagon. He wondered if it belonged to the operative from the facility. He considered disabling the car. But he might need it himself in an emergency.

He ran up the driveway, smelled the gasoline, and saw pools of it around another car, most likely the family's.

Fuck.

Nathan headed down a path along the side of the house. He found a small frosted window, perhaps a downstairs bathroom. He pulled out a knife, pried open the window, and was immediately knocked back by the smell of smoke and gasoline.

He pulled himself up and wrapped an arm around the partially open window, yanking back the handle to open it wide. Climbing in, he heard the sounds of screaming children and shouts for help.

Thick, black smoke blasted his way.

Nathan began to choke and hit the ground. He pushed open the bathroom door. Through the smoke he saw a man holding a gas can. He didn't hesitate. He shot once at the can and then twice at the man's chest. Then a double tap to the head.

The man was engulfed in flames as he collapsed in a fireball, burning up in the choking room.

Nathan moved through the dense, sickening smoke and shot the man three more times in the head. He was still surrounded by flames. But he was dead. Nathan turned on the cold water, grabbed a large jug to fill up, and put out most of the flames engulfing the other assassin. Then he reached into the man's smoldering jacket and pulled out his cell phone. Nathan put it in his back pocket. He would check its contents later.

He picked up a dish towel from the floor and soaked it in cold water, keeping the water running. Nathan tried to put out the fire that was engulfing the kitchen, but it was getting worse.

He got another dish towel, soaked it, and wrapped it around his face as a mask.

The sound of screaming came from below.

What the fuck?

Nathan put his hands and hair under the tap, soaking his clothes and body. Then he crawled to the far side of the kitchen. Out of the corner of his eye he saw the dusty debris around a crack in a stone hatch.

Wailing and weeping continued from below his feet.

"Who's down there?" he shouted through the damp mask. "Who's down there?"

No answer returned as billowing black smoke continued to fill the space. He would've opened a window, but he knew the fresh air would only fan the flames.

Nathan pulled off his soaking mask and began coughing. He managed to blurt out, "Are you down there, Mark? Is that you?"

No answer.

Nathan saw the hatch handle and tried to open it, but there was no give. He used the Glock and shot off the rest of his magazine into the lock. He tried again. But it wasn't giving.

He bent down to the crack in the floor.

"Answer me! Is Mark Mahoney down here?"

A girl's voice answered, "Please don't hurt us."

"The bad man is dead. I'm here to help."

"No, you're not! Go away!"

"Is your daddy down there?"

The sound of coughing. "Daddy isn't waking up!"

"You need to wake him up!"

The sound of more coughing. "Mommy! Wake up!"

"What's wrong with your mom?"

"She's not waking up."

Nathan began to cough, nearly blind from the smoke. "Wake up your father! Right now. Slap him on the face. And start screaming. Right in his ear. Do it! Now!"

He heard the girl crying underneath him. Then a long silence. Followed by high-pitched screaming.

"Daddy! Wake up! Mommy!"

The sound of groaning and retching.

"Daddy, there's another man in the kitchen."

There was a sound of boxes and things being knocked over.

"Open up!" Nathan shouted.

A man's voice below shouted, "Who is it?"

"It's Nathan!"

"How do I know it's you?"

"It's me! Open up, you stupid fuck!"

"Prove you're Nathan Stone!"

"How?"

"Where were you brought up?"

"The Bowery."

Hacking coughs from below. "How did your father die?"

"My sister killed him with scissors. Satisfied?"

Suddenly, the hatch clicked open.

Nathan pulled it back. Inside, Mahoney was collapsed, face blackened, with two kids huddled in the corner and a mother covered in blood. Nathan jumped down into the basement and took out the children first, one under each arm, through a patio door and into the back garden, then turned a hose on them. The youngsters were spluttering and crying and shaking.

"Where's Mommy? Where's my daddy?" the youngest girl screamed.

Nathan was breathing hard and still coughing. "Wait here."

He headed back into the smoke-filled kitchen, crawled along the floor, and jumped into the dark basement. He picked up Mahoney's unconscious wife and slung her over his shoulder, climbed out, and carried her out to the back garden. Blood was dripping from his hands from the gunshot wound to her leg.

"Call 911 now!" he shouted to the kids.

The eldest daughter pulled out a phone. "My battery's dead!"

"Fuck!"

He laid Mahoney's wife on the lawn and the children doused her leg with water.

Nathan jumped back down into the basement and dragged out Mahoney. He pulled him outside, and his kids hosed his face for a few seconds. He spluttered to life.

Mahoney stared up at Nathan as he gasped for air. Tears filled his eyes as he held his wife.

Nathan handed Mahoney the dead operative's cell phone. "Find out what's on that. This guy was sent from the Canadian facility."

Mahoney took the phone, blinking away tears.

Nathan took one long, final look at the Mahoneys.

"You saved us," Mahoney said. "Why?"

Nathan didn't answer. He just turned away. Headed down the path at the side of the house as smoke billowed out of the rear. He jumped in the operative's station wagon and started up the engine.

He drove into the night, not turning around or glancing in the mirror, back along dark, deserted Montauk Highway.

Fifty-Five

Berenger was ushered through the warren of tunnels underneath the Toronto facility by two security personnel. He was shown into a windowless room. Inside, sitting behind a desk, was a withered man with rheumy eyes.

The man indicated the chair opposite, and Berenger sat down.

Berenger stared at the man opposite. He wondered if this was Fisk. He was maybe in his eighties, possibly older. His skin was sun scarred and mahogany brown. But his suit hung limply on him.

The man sighed. "He killed them all."

Berenger said nothing.

"Does that surprise you?"

"Of course it surprises me. I mean . . . everyone?"

"Everyone . . . apart from you." The man's gaze settled on him, letting the words sink in. "Why do you think that is?"

"Why do I think what is?"

"Why do you think you're the only one left?"

"I have no idea."

"The only one . . . Do you know how the others died?"

"Yes, I've just been told. Terrible."

"Nathan Stone is out of control."

"His behavior patterns the last time, the way it all went to shit, should have been a warning."

"What do you mean?"

"I mean, his handler on this job contacted me shortly before he went missing to say he'd conveyed his doubts to Clayton as to Nathan's suitability, or more to the point, his lack of suitability."

"Hang on, the handler on this job, McKeevit, spoke to you about this?"

"Yeah, and apparently Clayton didn't listen to his concerns."

The man leaned back in his seat, stroking his chin. "The five original members of the Commission have all been neutralized by that fuck."

Berenger nodded.

"By that one man. I say *man* . . . I don't know if I can call him that."

"Do we know where he is?"

"No. But his sister's back in the nuthouse in Florida."

"Psychiatric hospital would be more accurate."

"Whatever."

"So there are no plans to take her again to punish him?"

The man shook his head. "Look where that got us. To the verge of extinction."

"Fair point."

"The question is, Where do we go from here? I mean, we have several highly skilled operatives within this facility, but none of them have the experience of working at the highest levels. It might take the better part of a year to get a new team in place to restart this operation."

Berenger wondered where the man was going with this.

"Which leaves us with a major headache. Well, actually, it leaves us with several headaches. First, Mahoney is still alive. He knows too much. And that's not good. Because we needed that fuck out of the way to clear the ground ahead of the forthcoming spectacular. But Nathan dragged it out, stalling, trying to figure out how to extricate himself from it. And he succeeded. Against all odds. So that's a problem."

Berenger nodded.

"Second, we have no executive in place, no command and control structure if you will. They've all been taken out. Third, we still have Nathan unaccounted for. I believe—at least, this is what I'm hearing through the cops—that Nathan neutralized one of our best operatives in the Hamptons."

"Listen, I'm a psychologist. This command-and-control thing isn't my area of expertise, as you know."

The man was quiet for a few moments. "True. That said, we had an unbelievably qualified team in place, and Nathan Stone single-handedly laid waste to them. To the whole fucking thing. I mean . . . there has to be retribution."

Berenger allowed the man to say what he had to say.

"Are you psychoanalyzing me? Is that what this is?"

"Not at all. Just taking stock of what you're saying. It is without question a huge fuck-up."

The man pointed at Berenger. "I like that kind of talk. That's the sort of straight talking I like."

"Look, I'm not exactly sure what you called me in here for."

"The operation, which is imminent now—we don't have a lead for it. I want you, Mark, to see this through until its conclusion."

Berenger was stunned as he tried to come to terms with what the man had said.

"You're former CIA, you've operated in this world, you're aware of the sensitivities, and you're scrupulously fair. Sharp. But you adhere to one of our central tenets."

"What's that?"

"You believe in American hegemony. You believe passionately that we have to intervene, mold, and sculpt events for the greater good. You believe our country needs to do what is necessary in the shadows to keep us at the forefront of this world. And for that we need access to resources. Consider if we weren't intervening around the world. China and Russia and Iran would smell blood. They smelled blood in Syria. They intervened. And we were caught unawares."

Berenger sighed. "I don't know what to say."

"All you need is to be locked in here until this is over, overseeing the events."

"I had planned to head back home."

"We want you to assume overall responsibility. And we're well placed to offer you whatever it takes."

Berenger was already being paid a high six-figure sum for the three-month contract. "I don't know."

"What don't you know?"

"This isn't what I do."

"I get that. But the plans are all in place. We have people here. We just need someone to oversee everything. Clayton *was* the overseer. And I want you to be my overseer on this, to make decisions you feel are best for the operation."

Berenger shrugged. "Why not you?"

"I'm too busy dealing with the fallout, liaising with various intelligence agencies, to become the operation head. So that leaves you, Mark."

Berenger took a few moments to consider his situation. "And the plans are in place? Time scales, objectives?"

"Every hour is planned. You just need to sit, listen, and watch. Chances are it will work without any input from you at all."

"My wife and kids will be expecting me tomorrow night."

"You'll be with them, all things being equal, in a week. We have two patsies we're going to drop on the Canadians. Islamist sympathizers in Toronto. Misdirection afterward, confusion, fog of war, all that stuff."

"What if the Canadians want to find out what's inside this place?"

"We have a cover story just in case."

"I'm not fond of the idea of being in here if it all goes to shit."

"This facility has been designed in compartments. We could invite them in and show them what we want them to see. Two-thirds of the facility is underground."

Berenger's mind was racing. He felt obligated to step in. He was a patriot. He believed in American hegemony. The security of the West relied on American might, power, and reach. He couldn't abide the doctrine of nonintervention, isolationism, advocated by some. Including the late Senator Crichton. It was dangerous to America, its interests, and those of its allies. But perhaps more than anything, the position would give him a chance to be privy to any decisions about how to neutralize Nathan. His mind raced as he began to imagine how it would work. He began to imagine having such power over Nathan. A man he was fascinated with. Even obsessed with. Since the first meeting, Berenger had kept a private diary of every meeting he'd had with Nathan. How he looked, spoke, behaved. His mannerisms. The lingering icy stare. This role would be a unique opportunity to be part of the inner circle at a crucial time. His private diary would become a momentous record of their extraordinary relationship, which had spanned years.

The more he thought about the chance to influence actions to bring Nathan down, the more excited he got.

It now seemed as if everything that had happened was for a reason. So he could be the one to decide if Nathan would live or die. And how he would die. That in itself was intriguing. They had always sought his opinion. But he never had the last word. He wanted the last word. To know that he was the one who would decide how to neutralize Nathan.

He began to fantasize. He needed experts who would guide him. What would they recommend? Would he lay a trap for Nathan? Would it be a simple fall? The kind that Nathan understood.

"I want to make you an offer," the man said.

"What kind of offer?"

"It's a one-time, one-week offer, and it means you have to oversee this operation, including the days ahead."

Berenger pondered on this.

"Now I understand you might have misgivings. But I have faith that you are the right man for this. I have faith in you. And you've been integral to several of our operations."

"Nathan's inclusion has brought us to the edge of the precipice," Berenger said. "My specialty is the mind, the motivations driving men, but what we're facing is not just this oncoming operation. It's the outstanding matter of Mahoney still loose, the neutralizing of this facility's operative, and Nathan Stone himself as a wild card. This is not good. Look, my contract is for three months. I knew my responsibilities."

"I haven't mentioned money. You have a young family. Commitments. College tuition."

"I'm comfortable."

"I want you to feel very comfortable. Ten million dollars tax-free. Cayman special account."

Berenger whistled. "Just for a week?"

The man nodded. "I have to warn you, there can be no contact between you and your family, or anyone else for that matter, over the next week. Am I clear?"

"That's not a problem."

"Good. We'll get a message to your wife."

Berenger felt his heart beginning to race. "OK, I'm in."

The man smiled. "You've had an inkling about the forthcoming parallel operation I'm assuming."

"I knew something was afoot. Is it someone on the list?"

"The list was updated two months ago. This man is an addition. We began to assess our capability in the light of the damage done by Nathan. And we realized the glaring omission of this target, who has been advocating something very similar to Senator Brad Crichton— protectionism, withdrawing from NATO, becoming friends with Russia."

Berenger nodded.

"We have devised a very elegant plan for this man. We looked at his medical records, and something caught our eye. A condition of his. We believe it is imperative that the target, a very high-profile Canadian, is silenced. And that's why we were relying on Nathan Stone. Ideally, we wanted Mahoney out of the way first. Get him out of the way before the main event. Clear the ground. So Mahoney wouldn't get suspicious and think to link the death with our other dealings in Canada and around the world. Sadly, it's not turning out that way. But we'll deal with that. We'll get to him. Sooner rather than later."

"This Canadian is the next hit?"

"He's a big fish. We had considered suspending our operations. But we decided to go forward. What you need to know now is that the Commission will never die. It will continue no matter what. We have tentacles across the military, intelligence, and political spheres. And we will go on. We have plans. Big plans. Long-term goals."

"Killing Clayton and the others wasn't the end of it?"

The man shook his head. "Absolutely not. Everyone can be replaced. We have some top-notch operatives that we can deploy on any continent at twenty-four hours' notice. Nathan can be replaced. And yes, even Clayton. That's why we're reaching out to you, Berenger. You will chair the Commission."

Berenger sighed as he contemplated the magnitude of what he was being asked.

"You need to get up to speed."

Berenger felt a surge of adrenaline through his body. "I have the final say?"

"Of course."

"Have I got the power to pull the plug if I feel it's necessary?"

"Absolutely. You are the overseer."

"Where do I sign?"

"Nothing to sign. I'll transfer two million dollars to the Caymans within the hour. And eight million more on successful completion."

"Who's the target?"

The man smiled. "You'll find out."

"When?"

The man leaned over and shook his hand. "Soon. In the meantime, come with me."

Berenger got up from his seat and followed the man down a narrow corridor, past security guards, then into a further biometric screening zone. He wondered if they were headed into an operations room. But instead he was shown into a huge windowless room with a one-way mirror.

He walked up to the mirror and stood beside the man. On the other side of the glass was a woman doing sit-ups and squat thrusts in what looked like a glorified boxing gym.

The man turned and smiled. "This is Deshi."

"Who is she?"

"She's an assassin. From Chechnya."

Fifty-Six

It was midafternoon amid bright sunshine when Nathan pulled up at a diner outside Pittsburgh. He'd stopped off at a motel in New Jersey and grabbed a few hours' sleep. Ditched the car he'd taken from the dead operative he killed in the Hamptons and stole another, a Honda SUV, from a hotel parking lot in downtown Trenton. Now he was feeling refreshed but in dire need of sustenance.

He pulled up a stool at the counter and ordered a gigantic late breakfast. Pancakes, eggs, home fries, toast, hash, waffles, washed down with Coke. He wolfed it all down. Then he had apple pie and ice cream and two black coffees.

The waitress was fiddling with the TV remote and switched it to Fox News. A female reporter was standing outside a house in East Hampton, police tape flapping in the wind.

Nathan leaned in close to the waitress. "Can you turn that up, honey?"

The waitress turned up the volume.

The reporter said, "Police sources believe a home invasion at this colonial house not far from beautiful East Hampton was the cause of this horrific incident. The family, believed to be that of a journalist from the *New York Times*, whose identity is being withheld at this time, were enjoying a vacation when their lives were cruelly violated.

It's thought they hid in a cellar basement as the attacker tried to burn them out of their hiding place. Thankfully, the family managed to fight back, wounding the unnamed attacker in the eye, allowing the family to escape. The attacker is believed to have perished in the blaze, his charred remains found in the vicinity of the kitchen by horrified cops who rushed to the scene."

Nathan listened intently. It was clear that Mahoney and his wife hadn't told the police the full story. And the cops had assumed it was just a violent home invasion.

The more he thought about it, the more he began to question his actions. First, killing the men who had sought to control him. The consequences were obvious for him. He was facing the possibility they would kill his sister whether or not he assassinated Mahoney. That, for him, had been the deciding factor. He'd come to the realization that it would be in their interests to disappear him and his sister permanently once Mahoney was out of the way. They had left him no choice.

Nathan's mind flashed back to the killing of Stanton. It was a cold-blooded way to end the guy's life. Did he feel bad about it? On reflection he felt Stanton, like Clayton Wilson and the three other men he'd blown up on the Upper East Side, had gotten what was coming to him. Live by the sword, die by the sword.

"You want more coffee, honey?" the waitress behind the counter asked.

"I'm good, thanks." He paid the check and left a ten-dollar tip, then left.

Nathan got into the SUV and headed off. He made a call to the psychiatric facility on the edge of the Everglades.

A man answered. "Everglades Psychiatric Hospital."

"Looking to speak to the director."

"Who's calling?"

Nathan said, "I'm calling about my sister, Helen Stone, who was taken out of the facility a few days back. This is urgent."

"Hold on, sir. I'll see if she's available."

Mantovani strings played for a few moments. Eventually, a woman's voice came on the line. "Good evening, sir, my name is Patricia Hyatt, director of the hospital. How can I help?"

Nathan introduced himself. "I'm calling to check my sister is back in the hospital."

"I've just come from her room. She's fine. And in good spirits. Do you want to talk to her?"

"Not right now. Let her relax. I'm glad she's back. But I'm wondering what the hell happened."

"Mr. Stone, I can only apologize. Our initial finding from our internal investigation is that false papers were presented to my staff giving the go-ahead for a transfer to another hospital in Florida. We have no idea what the purpose of this was."

"I want assurance that this will never happen again."

"I can give you my personal assurance. I've overhauled all our systems, and this will not happen again. There would, in the future, be a series of checks and balances to make sure there has been express permission for a transfer. For example, the hospital would call a senior member of staff to ensure that the transfer is going ahead. But as a secondary check, no transfer can go ahead without my written permission. And I can assure you your sister will not be leaving here again without your verbal and written permission."

"Excellent. I want her to stay there. She likes it there."

"I appreciate that, thank you. We do our best. But on this occasion it was our internal systems that were at fault. We are just grateful she was returned unharmed."

"Were the police informed of this?"

"Yes, they were, as is protocol."

"So I can rest assured that this will never, ever happen again."

"You have my word."

"That's good enough for me."

"Are you planning to visit your sister, Mr. Stone?"

"I'm out of the country on business, but I hope to be back within the next week. I appreciate the update and the reassurance. Pass on my love to her."

"Will do, Mr. Stone."

Nathan ended the call, drove off, and got onto the nearest highway. He headed northwest to Cleveland and left the car in a downtown parking garage. Then he walked half a mile to the bus station. Panhandlers and homeless men milled around. He used the filthy bathroom, charged his phone, and then caught the last Greyhound to Buffalo.

He sat near the back as the bus pulled away.

Half an hour later, as he dozed, his cell phone vibrated in his pocket. He didn't recognize the caller ID.

"Who's this?" he asked.

"Nathan, it's Mark."

Nathan sat up in his seat. He kept his voice low. "Yeah."

"Is it OK to talk?"

"Sure."

"I just want to say thank you."

Nathan felt uncomfortable with the praise. He cleared his throat. "How's your family?"

"They're alive. We all needed oxygen and some observation at the hospital."

"Where are you calling from?"

"I'm in New York."

"And your family?"

"They're in protective custody."

"Smart. Why not you?"

"My first priority is to make sure they're safe."

"Mark, you need to know that what happened changes nothing. They will still be looking for you. Do you understand?"

"I do. But I need to get this story out."

"Is that wise?"

"It's too important not to write. Besides . . ."

Nathan's voice was a whisper. "Besides what?"

"I got a guy I know, a computer forensics expert, and he's analyzed the data on the cell phone you handed me from the . . . guy from, you know, the facility."

"What did it contain?"

"One piece of information."

"What's that?"

"Encrypted messages that were sent between the guy who died and an unidentified person."

Nathan closed his eyes, wishing Mahoney would get to the point.

"We're still trying to decipher some of the messages. But one thing's clear. There's something going on."

"Something going on? . . . What kind of something?"

"We don't know. The forensics guy is still looking into it."

"So why are you calling me?"

"They say they're going to kill you. No matter what."

Fifty-Seven

It was just after one in the morning, and Mark Mahoney, having been discharged from the hospital the day before, was sitting at his desk in the *New York Times*'s newsroom on the West Side of Manhattan. He had a bizarrely early meeting at six with the executive editor, who wanted to see the "fundamentals" of the story. He was three-quarters of the way through completing the narrative of what he knew so far.

It would take several more weeks of double- and triple-checking what he'd gathered before it would be ready for publication. But for the first time in a long time, after days of gut-wrenching terror for him and his family, he was excited by what he'd learned.

Mahoney sipped the rest of the cold coffee and washed it down with a bottle of water as he scanned the last couple of pages. The details of his own life being put at risk, and how he'd only been able to survive through the intervention of the man who had first been sent to kill him, not only unsettled him but put the fear of God into him.

His mind flashed back to that night.

The smell of the smoke, being trapped in the choking basement as the assassin tried to break in—it had left his sanity hanging by a thread. And following so soon after Nathan had entered his life, he felt lucky not only that he'd escaped unscathed—physically at least—and his family were alive, safe, and well, but that the trauma had slightly abated in the last few hours.

He could function. The decision not to hide and instead to commit to writing the story was something both he and his wife thought was the right call. It was hard to believe it had all begun with the assassination by Nathan Stone of Senator Brad Crichton and the revelation of the secret black site in the Outer Hebrides in Scotland. It was shocking and had taken up all his time for the last few months.

His wife agreed he had to write the story. They both knew he couldn't conceal what he knew. It was in the public interest. And besides, he was an investigative journalist. He was aware the job wasn't all sunshine and roses. The fact that his family was in FBI protective custody was all he needed to know. He missed them. He felt slightly conflicted, if he was being honest. He didn't know if the Feds had been compromised in some way by the Commission. He wondered if their tentacles extended to those at the very top of the Hoover Building. He had, after all, reached out to the FBI just a few months back, not long after Stone first sent him the list. But they hadn't gotten back to him. That gave him pause.

Mahoney pushed any negative thoughts to one side. This was the only thing he could do. He would continue to miss his family. But if he had to do the story properly, he needed to be on the ground, so to speak, and not hidden away in a safe house.

He needed to communicate, talk, and be here, in the building, with his fellow journalists, talking about the story. There would be tough meetings, grillings, and discussions as they went over the story with a fine-tooth comb before it was published.

It would first go to what they called the backfielder, who would go over the story and do the most significant edit, reviewing sources, identifying holes. Then it would go to a copyeditor to check grammar, punctuation, spelling. And then to the head of the copy desk. But that would only be the start of the story's journey. Senior editors would be getting involved in this story for sure. And the executive editor had a personal hand from the outset, and he would want to have his input.

The more Mark thought about what he'd uncovered, the more excited he got about the story, the ramifications, the fallout.

Mahoney was going to tell this story without fear or favor. He wanted the world to know about this cabal. Men who operated in the shadows. Outside the law.

He leaned back in his seat and stretched his arms up in the air.

The business section's night editor, Ron McEvoy, walked up to him and smiled. "Sorry to hear about what happened out in the Hamptons," he said. "You sure you're OK to be back here?"

"Yeah, I'm fine."

McEvoy glanced over his shoulder. "What you working on?"

"Not able to talk about it just yet. When I can, I'll let you know, don't worry."

McEvoy patted him on the back. "Take it easy, Mark. And I look forward to reading your story."

"Sure thing."

Mahoney watched McEvoy get himself a cup of water and head back to his desk, glancing up at the Bloomberg channel on one of the TVs. He knew there would be a lot more inquisitive journalists asking what he was up to first thing in the morning. But he couldn't say anything until the story was ready. As it was, it was a work in progress. He couldn't risk any leaks. The story was too important. Even the slightest bit of information in a competing paper would be bad news.

It might be that the Feds themselves would leak part of what they knew after speaking to Mahoney before taking his family to a safe location. He thought of them now. His wife and kids, safe and sound somewhere in America. He hadn't been told where. He thought of his children being reassured and cuddled by their mother before bed. The stories. The bedtime routine she'd instilled in them.

He thought of them all gasping for air down in the fetid, smoke-filled basement, terror in their teary eyes, his wife screaming after being hit by the ricocheted bullet.

The doctors had thankfully gotten the fragments of the bullet out of her thigh; apparently, it had narrowly missed a major artery.

His cell phone rang, startling him. The FBI had told him not to answer with his name when he spoke on the phone.

"Yeah," he said.

"I got something." The voice of the computer forensics expert.

"Sure thing."

"I'll put this information into a full report and send it to you later today. But the cell phone you sent me that we've been decrypting—well, we finally deciphered the messages."

"Did you have to call in the Israelis?"

"A guy who works for us was trained by them. He was one of the team that unlocked the messages."

"So what've we got?"

"You've got a problem, that's what you've got."

"What do you mean?"

"The guy whose phone this was . . ."

"Yeah."

"He was communicating with a woman."

"I'm listening."

"The woman had a cell phone moniker—Crazy Chick."

"Crazy Chick?"

"Right. And the messages contain information that appears to indicate—and I stress the word *appears*—that there is indeed something big about to go down."

Mahoney scribbled everything down in shorthand. "When? Where?"

"Later today."

Mahoney took a few moments to process the information. "Are you kidding me? Where?"

"The messages indicate that it's—and this is their words—'going down imminent in 416.'"

"416? What the hell?"

"We've thought about it. And we think we've got it. It's pretty cute. Even though they were encrypted, they still wanted to conceal the name. The number 416 refers to the original telephone area code for Toronto. I'm ninety-nine percent certain of an impending terrorist attack or assassination in that city."

Fifty-Eight

Nathan's bus pulled up in the dead of night in downtown Buffalo. He saw a cop car parked nearby. When he filed out along with the other passengers, two cops stopped him.

"Got any ID, buddy?" one of the cops asked.

Nathan nodded. "Sure, Officer." He handed over the fake ID. "Everything OK?"

The cop looked over it for a few moments, then handed it back to Nathan. "Thank you. So, you mind explaining why you're in Buffalo?"

"Don't mind at all, Officer. Hoping to find some work. Construction. I do general labor, almost anything."

The cop showed him a photo of a young Latino boy, late teens. "You ever seen this boy before?"

Nathan looked at the photo and shook his head. "No, I haven't. Why?"

"Name's Charles Gomez. The kid's a runaway. Last seen getting off this bus a week ago. We're wondering if any passengers recognize this face or have seen the boy."

"Sorry, Officer, no idea. Hope you find him, though."

The cop nodded.

Nathan forced a smile.

"And best of luck with the job hunting," the cop said.

Nathan watched as the cops got back in their car and drove off. He headed inside the bus station and got himself a coffee from a vending machine. A handful of homeless were hanging around. One of the guys, an old man with a burst lip, was eyeing Nathan with suspicion.

"What you looking at, son?" the man asked.

Nathan ignored the man and drank his coffee as he looked at the timetables.

"You want some weed. Is that what it is? You think I've got weed? Well, let me tell you, I ain't got no fucking weed. Because if I had, I wouldn't be walking around here, do you understand? Fucking people always wanting stuff. Shit."

Nathan saw there was a Megabus to Toronto at 4:10 a.m. He brushed past the homeless man and bought his ticket, showing the fake ID again. He got himself a hot dog from a vendor and a Coke. He felt a tap on his shoulder and turned around.

The old man was pointing a knife at him. "Not so tough now, huh? How you like this? Gimme your money. Wallet."

Nathan stared at the man for a few moments. He was aware there were people in his peripheral vision who were watching the whole scene. He dropped the drink and hot dog and quickly parried the man's knife hand away. Then he smashed the old man's jaw hard with his other fist. The old man crumpled in a heap and fell backward, blood spilling out of his mouth. The knife was still in his hand.

Nathan stood on the man's arm until he released his grip, screaming. He picked up the knife and tossed it in a trash can.

"Motherfucker!" the man snarled.

Nathan looked down at him. "You need to watch that temper, old man. It's gonna get you into trouble someday."

He stepped over him and headed for his bus, which had just pulled up. A few passengers looked rattled at the scene. But they all climbed on board. He followed close behind, showing his fake ID and bus ticket. The driver nodded, and Nathan headed to the back of the bus.

A few minutes later, the bus pulled away, negotiating the near-deserted streets of downtown Buffalo. He was now on his way back to Toronto. He wondered why he hadn't just disappeared somewhere in America. Iowa was nice. Texas was so huge it could hide anything and anybody. It was easy. He'd done it many times before.

The more he thought about it, critically analyzing why he was doing what he was doing, the more he couldn't see that it made much sense. He'd gotten his sister back. He'd destroyed the Commission. Single-handed. And he'd even wound up taking out another one of their operatives.

Nathan wondered how it had gotten so crazy. His usual way was to get in, get the job done, and get the hell out. He'd gotten out and now he was actually going *back* to Toronto.

His mind flashed a succession of searing images. The dead intelligence operative lying in the kitchen. The drunk girl lying on Mahoney's sofa, covered in cocaine. The Mahoney family cowering in the basement. More than anything he remembered the look of fear in Mark Mahoney's eyes. He didn't feel anything anymore. Had he zoned out so much there was no feeling left in his soul? The excitement and thrill of the kill were still there. But he felt something in him, deep within his being, that he had learned to switch off many years ago.

Nathan thought of what Mahoney had said. The message on the dead operative's phone said Nathan was going to be killed. Was it being organized from within the facility? It was as if he was being drawn back to Toronto without even thinking. Like he needed to be there.

Nathan knew he had benefited from the element of surprise when he assaulted the Scottish facility. But they would be looking for him at the Canadian facility. They wouldn't make the same mistake again.

He wondered if Berenger was the weak link in the organization. Away from the facility, but almost certainly connected to it in some capacity.

Nathan stared out of the window, realizing he was going to have to kill again, come what may.

Fifty-Nine

Just after six in the morning, Mahoney was called into the office of the executive editor, Mort Weiss. An hour earlier, he had emailed Weiss a summary of what he knew with the "fundamentals" of the story.

"Take a load off, Mark," he said.

Mahoney slumped in the chair and stifled a yawn.

"You look like shit," Weiss said.

Mahoney smiled. "Yeah, morning to you too, Mort."

"Nice to have you back in the city."

"Good to be back. Early start for you?"

"Heading out of town on business for a couple of days. So needed to get a few bits and pieces out of the way first. And I thought it was important we touched base."

"Sure."

"So, hell of a business out in the Hamptons."

Mahoney sighed. "This whole investigation is so monumentally fucked up it's unreal."

Weiss leafed through the pages of what Mahoney had sent him an hour earlier. "Mark, I'm gonna level with you, and you're not going to like this."

Mahoney shrugged, wondering what he was going to say.

"I'm going to play devil's advocate on this."

"Sure, whatever."

Weiss took a few moments before he spoke. "I can see these original documents Nathan sent you from Scotland got this whole ball rolling."

"Yeah, that's right."

"And just to check, if these documents, allegedly showing some assassination list, which you're telling me were recovered from previously deleted files on an NSA server, amount to espionage or treason . . . We just need to look at the Snowden case. The theft of government property."

"Mort, listen, I'm not disputing these things. But this goes way beyond what the government says. I'm talking public interest. This needs to be out there. We're talking a cabal who had eight people killed, made to look like accidents, including Senator Crichton in Scotland."

"Mark, I'm not disputing that. I love your work. This is what we aspire to at this paper. But you've got to realize they're going to come after not only you but the *New York Times*. We'd be taking on the might of the American government, including the intelligence agencies."

"I'm well aware of that."

"The unauthorized removal and retention of classified materials— and they won't be too picky about how they came into your hands— would carry eleven years in a federal jail. I'm talking the combined maximum sentence. But you can guarantee, absolutely guarantee, the Justice Department wouldn't rest there."

Mahoney sighed, knowing the hurdles he would now face to get the story published.

"You know what I'm talking about, don't you? The Espionage Act, additional charges, and potentially far more severe penalties if you were convicted. This is classified. And I can see, from what you've sent me, it included a top-secret email chain."

Mahoney was disappointed at Weiss's tone. He'd been expecting far greater positivity from his editor. More support. But as it was, it appeared the paper was very wary about getting embroiled in the whole shitstorm of a story. "We need to publish this. Publish and be damned."

Weiss leaned back in his seat. "I don't know. This has got so many legal pitfalls in it, it'll take weeks to get through it."

"Fine, weeks it is. I'm prepared to do this. And remember, I've been the one at the sharp end of this. An assassin, two assassins actually, were tasked with taking me out."

Weiss nodded. "Absolutely. Look, I'm not denying it's a story."

"A story? It's explosive stuff. This alleges that retired members of the intelligence community formed an organization to extinguish anyone who rails against global wars or globalization or wants our whole post-9/11 strategy reset. They don't like dissent from opinion formers, influential people like Crichton."

"There are other aspects of the story that I find very troubling."

Mahoney shrugged. "Yeah, like what?"

"Like accompanying this assassin, this Nathan Stone, back to New York before he went out into the city, was possibly responsible for killing Clayton Wilson, perhaps using a drug to induce a heart attack, then set up a gas explosion to take out three members of the so-called Commission on the East Side, met up with you and your family in Chelsea for a cozy dinner and a drink with you, and then headed off and shot Richard Stanton in cold blood in an abandoned hotel. I mean, Mark, I'm as open-minded as the next man, but this is not right."

Mahoney showed his palms, as if not disputing what was being said. "Sure. I get that."

"You're too close to the story. That's a problem for me. What's that old saying? Once you become the story, you've crossed the line, or something like that."

"Listen to me, I didn't have a fucking choice. Nathan Stone would've killed me."

Weiss shrugged. "Like I said, I'm playing devil's advocate, and I can see all sorts of ethical issues you've got yourself embroiled in."

"The fucker was sent to kill me."

"Which is part of the problem. There are a lot of questions. An operative you believe was from the Canadian facility tracked you down to the Hamptons. And then Stone kills this operative? I mean, why would an assassin sent to kill you come and save you? It's almost like— and remember, I'm playing devil's advocate—collusion."

Mahoney rubbed his face. "Like I said, the whole thing is fucked up."

"OK, I don't mean to be too hard on you. I know what you've been through."

"Do you, Mort? Do you really? I'm not so sure. My wife and kids, my family, were nearly burned to death."

Weiss cleared his throat. "I'm sorry, that's terrible. Inexcusable."

"Thankfully they're now safe and out of harm's way."

"That's another thing. If what you're saying is correct, this might very well result in any remaining associates of this 'Commission,' perhaps in the intelligence community, coming after you."

"I've thought about that. A lot. And you know what, Mort? I'm not going to bury this story."

"Problem is, they might bury you."

"I know. But that's a risk I'm prepared to take."

Weiss was quiet, staring down at the papers on his desk. "Tell me about this call from the computer forensic analyst in LA."

Mahoney cleared his throat. "High-end encryption and decryption specialists."

Weiss flicked through the papers. "And it says the bill for their services amounts to twenty-three thousand dollars. Not an insignificant amount."

"It's not. But their work has produced what I think is another even more worrying aspect of this whole thing."

Weiss stared long and hard at him.

"The possibility of an imminent terrorist attack in Toronto. That's what they've uncovered from the decryption and the analysis.

Remember, this firm works with, among others, Homeland Security. They know their stuff."

"And this is in code, you're saying."

"Toronto is referred to as 416. And their analysis—and this company has ex-FBI, CIA, and NSA on their books—is saying this is a red flag."

"Did they have any recommendations for a course of action?"

"None at all. We're a private client. And they've passed on their thoughts and findings."

Weiss was silent for what seemed like an eternity as he pondered what he had been told. "First, we need to get our lawyers involved."

"Agreed."

"I'll give Olivia Bernard, our new general counsel, a call. But assuming she has no objections, we really need to pass on this particular case to the Feds. What're your thoughts on that, Mark?"

"Couldn't agree more. If this is for real, we need to let people know. The legal stuff aside, I want this story out there."

Weiss nodded as a smile crossed his face. "You're crazy. Do you know that, Mark?"

"Tell me about it."

"Leave this to me. But in the meantime, I love this story, warts and all. Write it up how you see it. Tell the story. Be true to the story. And then we'll get the ball rolling."

"Good to hear."

"One final thing: if the Feds get involved, there may be no hiding place for you. We absolutely stand by your right to write this story, just as it's our right to scrutinize it to the nth degree. But I have to warn you, Mark, I've got a bad feeling about this."

"What do you mean?"

"From what I've read and what you've told me, there are powers at work that we don't yet fully understand."

Sixty

Just before dawn, Nathan handed the driver one hundred Canadian dollars and was dropped off a couple blocks from the downtown bus terminal in Toronto. He had no reason to believe anyone knew he'd be in town. But his instincts after everything that had happened were to take sensible precautions. He didn't know if they'd tapped into the bus terminal computer system and were running face-recognition software.

He caught a cab to a sketchy area, the Garden District, and checked into a cheap, divey hotel under his fake name.

"You know, there's a gentlemen's club on the first floor," the man behind the counter said.

"What do you mean, a gentlemen's club?"

"You know, a place for guys to watch girls dance, if you like that sort of thing."

Nathan handed over his deposit and the price of one night and was given a card for his room. He peered out the windows over the morning street scene. A crackhead longhair was walking in the middle of the road, stoned out of his head. It wasn't even seven o'clock.

He watched as the man began yelling at oncoming traffic before taking his top off, despite the cold. The crazed addict was spewing obscenities at passersby. A cyclist had to swerve to miss him. Nathan stared transfixed at the man, who had lost his mind to drugs. His life. He'd abandoned hope. One of the forgotten, the hopeless, the left behind, who were usually hidden from plain sight in the city. Invariably, they came out at night if they were homeless, headed to hostels, park benches, under freeways or subways: panhandlers, druggies, alcoholics, the mentally ill. But this guy, who could have been any of those things, was out there, in the harsh early-morning light, railing against everything and everyone, his grievances, real and imagined, shouted to no one and everyone.

Eventually, a cop car pulled up. Two burly cops stepped out and slammed the poor fucker to the ground. He was cuffed and thrown unceremoniously in the back of the cop car.

Nathan couldn't help thinking of his fuckwit of a father. He had seen his father meandering through the streets of the Lower East Side, drunk, cursing, and threatening onlookers in the same uninhibited way. He remembered crying the first time he saw his father like that. But years later, he didn't cry when his father was taken. He cried when he came back.

He remembered his sister's quiet voice as she tried to reassure him. But nothing could assuage his deep fear of his father. The belt buckle across the face or back, or the leather strap across the back of his neck. Sometimes he just stood and took it. Other times he cowered in the corner, protecting himself with his hands and arms. But it was always to no avail.

His cell phone rang and Nathan checked the caller ID. He didn't recognize it. "Who's this?"

"Nathan." It was Mahoney. "Are you there?"

"Yeah."

"I'm real frazzled."

"What is it?"

"I wanna tell you a few things."

"What kind of things?"

"I'm writing the story. And I've just spoken to the executive editor."

"What are you telling me this for?"

"The cell phone . . . You know the one?"

"What about it?"

"Remember I said the cell phone contained several messages that mentioned killing you."

"Go on."

"We found more. Coded messages."

"Why are you telling me this?"

Mahoney said nothing.

Nathan shut the blinds in his room. "You know something. What else was on the phone?"

"I'm telling you . . . I'm telling you because we've informed the FBI of the contents."

"So why are you telling me?"

"I'm not sure I should be."

"But you are."

"Yes, I am."

"Do you think the Feds will come looking for me?"

"Nathan Stone doesn't exist, does he?" he said.

"Good point."

"No, I don't think they'll come for you. But I wanted you to know there's something planned for Toronto. A hit. Maybe an attack. Today maybe. I don't know when exactly, but it's imminent."

Nathan took a few moments to process the information. "A hit organized from within the facility?"

Mahoney said nothing.

"I get it. The instructions will still stand, no matter what. No matter if the Commission is destroyed, if there's one man left standing, the hit will still be on."

"I'm trying to understand what this is all about. You know what I also don't get?"

"What?"

"Why you came back for me. For us. For my family. Why did you do that?"

Nathan closed his eyes and sat down on the edge of the bed.

"You didn't have to do that. But you did. Why?"

"You've got a family. A beautiful family. I don't want to talk about that, if you don't mind."

"I do mind. What you did was amazing. You came back for us. You . . . you can't deny that."

Nathan said nothing. Mahoney's emotional outburst was making him feel awkward.

Mahoney snuffled down the phone, as if tearful. "I just wanted to say that whatever crazy shit went down there, I'm grateful to you for sparing my family."

Nathan felt his throat tighten.

"When I write this story, I want to mention you. I want to mention your name. Your real name."

"Why do you want to do that?"

"The story is authentic or it's nothing. Besides, Nathan Stone doesn't exist anymore."

Nathan thought long and hard about what Mahoney was asking. "OK."

"You're fine with that?"

"Sure. On one condition."

"What's that?"

"Do not mention my sister's name, or the facility she's in."

"Can I say she lives under an assumed name somewhere in the United States?"

"Sure."

266

"Nathan, you're back in Toronto, aren't you?"

"Maybe."

"Jeez."

A pause. "Want a final bit of advice, Mark?"

"Sure, why not?"

"I'll say it one last time. They'll come for you. And they will kill you."

Sixty-One

Berenger was in the main situation room within the Canadian facility, huge screens on the wall in front of him. Standing to his left was the operations director, with whom he had worked before. His name was Malcolm Strutt, ex-CIA senior operative. A dozen men and women sat at desks around the room running the operation, checking live news feeds. "I want to see the feed from outside the hospital," Strutt said.

Instantaneously, the main screen showed three split-screen images of members of staff and the public entering and leaving Toronto General Hospital.

Berenger turned to Strutt. "What time do we expect the barriers to go up?"

"We're hearing late afternoon," he said.

"And the crowds we expect to turn up?"

"It's all very choreographed, as you'd expect. We've been led to believe he'll be talking to two handpicked nurses."

"So there'll definitely be people, members of the public, allowed behind these metal barriers?"

Strutt nodded. "We believe forty or fifty will be allowed."

"I want to talk about our options. These were devised when Clayton was in charge."

"Absolutely. This was the agreed plan of action."

"And these are the three best scenarios?"

Strutt nodded. "We worked the problem, as we usually do, and came up with what would do the job. Namely, take out the target."

Berenger cocked his head, and Strutt followed him out of the situation room to a meeting room fifty yards down the hall. He pressed his index finger against the fingerprint scanner, face against the retina scanner, and the door clicked open. They went inside.

He sat down and poured himself a cool glass of water from a jug on the table. He took a couple of gulps and put down his glass. "Tell me about scenario one, the first choice for the operation, which was unanimously agreed on by Clayton and his guys."

Strutt opened a folder on the desk and flicked through the pages, scanning the information. He sighed. "Sniper from nearby roof. That was deemed most likely to succeed. We know for a fact there will be no security detail or police on roofs. It is viewed as a soft win-win, this appearance by the target."

Berenger had been up half the night considering the scenarios. He understood the rationale of the direct hit. The fact that it would be carried out by the Chechen woman was perfect. She would be taken out as she escaped, under orders to fire at anyone who tried to stop her. And the false flag trail had already been laid down. An Islamic terrorist. It was an outrage. But no one would see the real motivation for taking down the target. "Tell me about scenario two."

"We considered a suicide vest. But the thinking was that it might not be practical in the short time frame we have. We needed far longer to get specialists working on the vest, and there just wasn't time."

Berenger was quiet a moment before continuing. "Scenario three—I'm intrigued. To me, this appears to be the most elegant. And the most convincing. The target won't expect it. No one will."

Strutt nodded. "Scenario three, if I remember correctly, provoked a lot of debate."

"And what did you conclude? What were the chances of success? Since I wasn't involved in the discussions."

"There were no guarantees it would work."

"I've looked over the target's medical records. And there are three times in the last eighteen months when his illness has been triggered. Once he nearly swallowed his tongue, once he blacked out, and another time he lost consciousness. Have we done a probability study?"

"We believe there's a sixty-eight percent chance it will succeed. That wasn't considered high enough—by Clayton and Stanton in particular."

"What about the others?"

"The other two liked it, but Clayton thought it was a bit out there."

Berenger contemplated scenario three for the umpteenth time. "What about you, Malcolm?"

"My thoughts?"

"Yeah. What are your thoughts on scenario three?"

Strutt arched his eyebrows. "I'll talk about scenario three in a moment, if I may."

"Sure."

"The beauty of the sniper scenario is the finality. My problem is and was how our operative accesses and then gets out of the building. What if she's discovered, either by design or chance? What if we are wrong? What if there are police snipers on the roof?"

"You were against that?"

"Yes, I was, but it wasn't up to me."

"I appreciate your honesty. What about scenario two?"

"No problem with it at all. Islamist, posing as a doctor in a white coat. I actually like this scenario. I think it'll work."

"It's not ideal, I'd imagine, to change things last minute."

"It's far from ideal. But our operative will do whatever is required of her."

"I read in her file that she fantasized about being a martyr."

"Yeah."

"I share your concerns about scenario one. While there might not be a police presence on those rooftops, according to our intel anyway, have we considered news choppers inadvertently spotting our operative?"

"That had been considered, but Clayton was sure the cameras in place were all at ground level for such a small visit. He thought the possibility was small."

"I want to talk about scenario three. What do you think about it?"

"I think it's interesting," Strutt said. "What I liked about it was that it would allow the operative to get in close. The scenario said the female operative, wearing a white doctor's coat and fake hospital lanyard with a real doctor's name, would evade basic security quite easily. And then—well, it's interesting."

"But you're not convinced?"

"I'm not convinced," Strutt said.

"So you could be persuaded?"

"I think the scenario could have been tightened, giving it a far higher probability of success," Strutt said.

"How would you do that?"

"Stage one, the female operative takes her action. I believe it will spark a reaction in the target. Our analysis shows he is, and I'm quoting, 'highly susceptible' and will very likely be triggered. Stage two, when he goes down, she will kneel down—she's a doctor after all—and summon a doctor standing beside her, another one of our operatives, who will jab him surreptitiously on the back of his neck. Dead within seconds."

"So . . . walk me through this. The operatives—male and female?"

"Yes. They're brother and sister. Chechen. You saw the woman yesterday, I believe."

Berenger sighed. "The operatives would both be in plain sight, perhaps for thirty minutes, maybe more."

"It's a risk."

"An acceptable risk?"

"Ideally, we want zero risk. But this is real life. The rationale for scenario three is it would look like the target is collapsing, perhaps having a heart attack. But then, when he starts to seize, to have two doctors there right by his side would look convincing. They're in there. And the target would be dead before he's in the ambulance, which would be parked, with a doctor and two nurses, just over a hundred yards away."

"This wouldn't be on live television?"

"No. But there will be cameras there."

Berenger began to contemplate his favored scenario. It felt strange that instead of evaluations of an individual's psychology he was assessing the best assassination strategy. But his years at the CIA and his knowledge of international security, terrorism issues, and the psychology of terrorism left him well placed to offer rational arguments in this arena.

"The operatives, just to be clear, are capable of carrying this out. They would be inserted into the location by an ambulance. They aren't on any watch lists. We've made sure of that. They're clean skins."

Berenger reflected on that. "Are you sure? These are Chechens, and there's no trace of terrorism?"

"We've already made up some great IDs, lanyards, as a backup. My first rule is always have a backup in place."

"Do they speak English?"

"Both fluent. She can speak four languages fluently."

"So face recognition wouldn't pull them out of the crowd."

"Even better than that. We can update the hospital's database remotely to have the photograph changed to match the IDs we gave them. And we have an operation green-lighted."

Berenger was quiet for a few moments. "And the medical records of the target. These are genuine?"

"We hacked them. We have full access to his medical records."

"I see he had a fondness for cannabis as a student."

"Still does by all accounts. Very liberal. A mistress too. But his health details also reveal a rare condition that makes him susceptible."

"Tell me, does the media know about his medical condition?"

Strutt shook his head. "Absolutely not. The target's people have kept it quiet."

"Why do you think that is?"

"Doesn't fit into his healthy, sporty image."

"So this condition, this is good from our point of view."

"It is."

Berenger nodded. "OK, I like scenario three, but in two stages, not as you originally indicated. I want the Chechen girl, doctor's coat on, getting a selfie with him. He's not going to refuse, right?"

"The guy's a social media nut," Strutt said. "Preoccupied with how he looks, how he comes across. There are literally thousands of photographs of him posing with people across Canada, America, Europe. He's a narcissist. And a pretty girl wanting to get her picture taken with him? He'll want that, trust me."

Berenger smiled. "Stage two, I want her brother, also in a doctor's coat, alongside another operative dressed in hospital garb, in the back of the ambulance, which will reverse up within seconds of this happening. The target will be moved into the ambulance, and we assume how many security personnel would accompany him?"

"Two. One in the passenger seat, another in the rear. Operative two begins to work on the target, and when he administers a drug to counteract the effects of his ailment, he will die."

Berenger leaned back in his seat and smiled. "Now that I like."

"There are no guarantees it will work."

"We're not in the business of guarantees. However, this works in two ways. First, there will be TV footage of him collapsing, perhaps foaming at the mouth. Then him being transferred to the ambulance. His clean-cut, healthy image will be shot. Then the lethal dose inside the ambulance takes him out of the game for good. The cool thing is it's made to look like a medical condition that has become fatal. By the time they realize what actually happened, if they even realize, we'll all be long gone."

Sixty-Two

Deshi Umarov was lying on her bed in a room deep within the bowels of the facility. She was thinking back to what her mother had told her. About how Deshi had been born in a freezing basement in Grozny as Russian artillery shells rained down. Amid the dust and dark, civilians huddled for warmth and comfort, reciting passages from the Koran as children cried. Her father was killed when he went outside to scavenge for food. And it was left to her mother to keep Deshi and her older brother alive, giving them whatever milk she had. The days turned into weeks. Then months.

Deshi's mother had told her these tales when she was a child. Stories of men and women she had seen drowning in sewage tunnels under the city. When she had emerged out into the streets, it was rubble, destruction.

Deshi had grown to hate the Russians. Her great-grandfather, her mother said, had been one of the thousands of Chechens who had sided with the Nazis. Anything but the Russians. And when the war was over, Stalin had expelled thousands of Chechens, including her great-grandfather, sending them to Kazakhstan. They only returned in 1957, after Khrushchev allowed them back. But the simmering hatred for Russia remained.

She closed her eyes. Her mind flashed back to when she was ten. The vigil for her mother as she lay dying. Her mother motioned her to come closer. And she whispered in Deshi's ear.

Commit yourself to jihad.
Commit yourself to the Koran.
Commit yourself to Islam.
Commit yourself to die, my darling Deshi.

At that moment, Deshi set aside any hopes and dreams she might have possessed. She had wanted to be a journalist. But from the day her mother died, she only wanted jihad. She wanted to commit herself to fight the enemies of Islam.

It had begun when she was a teenager, with the fight against the Russians in Grozny. Ambushes on Russian troops. At sixteen, she was encouraged by Chechen fighters her age to move to Moscow. She worked in a factory. She was living in a Soviet-era apartment. She was part of a jihadist Chechen cell.

Deshi had vowed that she would avenge the blood of the Chechens. She passed on intelligence about a man she suspected was in the FSB, the Russian secret police. She watched as he was killed in front of his family. She had been part of countless operations that had targeted the Moscow Metro. Explosions. Shootings. On and on, the rage against Mother Russia.

Then one day, in Moscow, her brother introduced her to a soft-spoken American. He called himself Mike. A short while later, she was smuggled out of the country with her brother. Jordan became their home. They were trained by the CIA in bomb making. Sniping. Martial arts. Survival skills. Tradecraft used by spies. She learned about poisons. She learned languages. She became fluent in English. She learned all about assassination techniques. She learned how to kill with her bare hands. She learned how to use a knife. And guns.

Deshi became proficient. She fought in Syria. In Iraq. She fought wherever she could. But now, this day, was something else.

Today was the day she was going to die. Her blood would be spilled. It would be spilled on foreign soil. She did not care. This was not about her. It would spill for all the jihadists over the years, the centuries, who had sworn to fight those who disbelieved in the religion of Islam. The *kafir*.

Sixty-Three

Nathan was laying spread-eagle in a field, staring through high-powered binoculars at a remote house nearly a thousand yards away, fifteen miles outside Toronto. He watched as the security man leaned against the trunk of a car. The man wore a suit and was smoking a cigarette, talking into a cell phone. The man was one of those he'd seen inside the house Berenger was staying in. He scanned the windows of the rest of the house. The window of the room on the first floor where he'd had his meetings with Berenger, no lights on.

The man ended his call.

A few minutes later, a huge white moving van reversed down the gravel driveway and pulled up beside the car. The driver and two other guys jumped out and opened up the back of the truck.

The double doors were wedged open and they traipsed in. Over the next twenty minutes, they removed everything. Desks, carpets, computers, laptops, a printer, large-screen TVs, wooden tables, three water coolers, paintings, filing cabinets, phones, trash cans, plastic trash bags bursting at the seams. Then a younger guy went up a ladder and removed security cameras from the front of the building.

Nathan turned around and crawled back into the nearby woods. Then he doubled back and approached the house from the rear. Through fields, hedgerows, dirt paths, dirt roads. He was within one hundred yards and closing.

The man's voice could be heard talking into the phone. "They've taken everything. I watched them. The phone extensions all drilled out, removed. All the wiring, cameras, you name it, your guys have stripped it to the bone." He laughed.

Nathan waited until the guy ended the call. He waited until the man went inside to have one last look around. He headed down a gravel path, past the car, and then slipped into the lobby of the house.

The man was upstairs by the sounds of it.

Nathan tiptoed up the stone stairs in his rubber-soled sneakers. His senses were fully switched on. He crouched behind a pillar as footsteps came down the hall.

Nathan waited and held his breath. He turned and pointed the gun. The man froze. "Hands in the air!"

The man slowly raised his hands.

"On your knees!"

The man didn't move.

Nathan pulled back the slide and shot the guy's right knee. The man screamed and the sound echoed around the walls of the old house. Then he crumpled in a heap, writhing in pain, as blood spilled onto the stone floor.

"That's better. I seem to have your attention now." Nathan edged closer and stood over the man. He pressed his foot down hard onto the man's bleeding knee. "Who are you?"

The man grimaced in pain. "Motherfucker!"

Nathan smiled, pressing his foot down hard again. "I don't think that's your name, is it? Now, let's try again . . . Last time I'm gonna ask. Who are you?"

"What does it matter?"

"I did give you a warning, didn't I?" Nathan aimed the gun down at the man's face. "Did I or did I not give you a warning?"

The man closed his eyes tight, teeth clenched. "Yes. I'm security for this project."

"What project is that? Just for this house?"

The man screwed up his eyes. "No!"

"I'm going to count backward from three, and if you haven't given me a satisfactory and correct answer, I will blow your head off. How does that sound?"

The man began to moan. "You're Nathan?"

"Three . . . Two . . ."

"Hang on! Yes, I oversaw security for this house."

"The house that Berenger worked out of, right?"

The man closed his eyes tightly and nodded. "Yes."

"Tell me about the facility."

"I worked there until a month ago. And then I was moved down here to look after Berenger."

"Did you know anything about my handler?"

The man shook his head. "Nothing."

"Tell me more about the facility."

The man shrugged, tears spilling down his cheeks. "I'm just low-level security."

"How much do they pay you?"

"Three hundred thousand US dollars. Tax-free."

"Who did you used to work for?"

The man moaned. "I'm bleeding out here, man."

"Who did you used to work for?"

"I'm a contractor. Private security. Iraq. You know the drill."

"Been there. Who else?"

"The firm I worked for was contracted by the Agency from time to time."

"So you worked within the facility. What do you know?"

"I know this place had to be clear by midafternoon. Not a trace."

"Why?"

"Berenger's in the facility now. He's not here. So they decided to shut it down."

"Why is Berenger inside the facility?"

"I heard he took over. He's a cold bastard."

"Berenger's in charge?"

The man nodded.

"What else?"

"Everyone is on lockdown there."

"Why?"

"I don't know for sure. But I heard—"

"Don't fuck with me!"

"It's going down tonight."

"Here in Toronto?" Nathan pressed the gun tight to the man's forehead. "Who're they going to kill?"

The man grimaced. "Goddamn it. I want to show you something."

Nathan smiled. "Don't fuck around, my friend."

"My cell phone. Pocket."

Nathan reached into the guy's inside jacket pocket and pulled out his cell phone. "Fingerprint recognition. Press your thumb on it."

The guy did as he was told.

Nathan began to scroll through the messages. "So what am I looking for?"

"Two months ago, I was sent a photo of a woman. The message was sent from my boss, Larry Campbell."

Nathan looked back and opened the message. It showed a grainy black-and-white picture of a young woman and a young man. "Who are they?"

"I escorted them from a private plane that landed at the facility's airfield to private quarters."

Nathan stared at the ghostly features of both.

"They're assassins. Jihadists. From Chechnya."

"And who's the target?"

"I don't know. But they've been brought in as a false flag."

Sixty-Four

Nathan dragged the man out of the house as he screamed in pain. He slammed the door shut and it clicked as its mechanism locked in place.

"You can't just leave me here!"

Nathan pointed the gun at the man as he lay facedown on the gravel driveway. He pulled the man's wallet out of his back pocket and scanned his details. "Is this real?"

"It's fake."

"Do you want to live?"

"Of course I do, man!"

Nathan sighed. "What are you supposed to do now?"

"Disappear."

Nathan took a couple of steps back and turned around. He saw the keys were in the car. He popped open the trunk. Inside was a large empty backpack.

The man was still moaning.

Nathan examined the carpeted trunk. He pulled back the carpet, revealing a sealed metal compartment. Inside was a long-range Barrett scope rifle. It used .50 cal incendiary ammo, already locked and loaded. He took it out and pointed it at the man's head. "What the fuck is this for?"

"If I ran into trouble."

Nathan knew the power of the weapon and the ammo. It was an anti-matériel weapon. It could take out a car. Truck. An armored truck even. It was also very useful for nighttime, with the tracer fire to see the target. "This is a serious weapon. What about a car search at the border?"

"They've taken care of that."

"Is that right? Get up."

"Where are you taking me?"

Nathan cocked his head. "Get in the fucking trunk."

"Man, don't do this."

Nathan stepped forward and smashed the man on the side of the head, splitting his lip, spilling more blood.

"Motherfucker!" the man said.

"In the trunk."

The man clambered in, whimpering. He adjusted himself into the space in the trunk. He looked up at Nathan, eyes pleading. "Don't kill me, man."

Nathan took out the backpack. "Head down. Not a word."

"Don't kill me."

Nathan slammed the trunk shut. He disassembled the rifle and put the parts, including the magazine and the tracer ammo, inside the backpack, zipped it up, and placed it at his feet. He started up the engine and drove off toward downtown Toronto.

His actions made no sense. He was doing everything he'd been trained not to.

The decision to go rogue and tear down the Commission had now fully engulfed him. He wasn't thinking straight. But by this point he didn't give a damn about the consequences. Devoid of reason, all he had was a visceral rage propelling him on. But to what end?

Half an hour later, he was in the parking garage of a hospital. He picked up the backpack and disappeared down a stairwell.

Nathan called 911, gave the license plate number. "Level Four, Toyota Prius. The guy's in the trunk. He's lost some blood."

He ended the call.

Nathan went into a coffee shop on Queen Street East. He got a large latte, a muesli bar, and a chocolate muffin for energy and some water. He sat down, back to the brick wall, backpack at his feet. He looked around. The café was filled with a sprinkling of young men and women chatting, drinking coffee, laughing, some working on laptops, some gazing at their phones. His natural habitat was a bar. A dive bar, Stones on, some people playing pool. Cold beers. That was his thing.

He enjoyed the caffeine hit, ate the snacks, guzzled the water, and felt a million percent better.

He pulled out the security guard's cell phone and surreptitiously looked again at the images of the Chechens.

Nathan wondered exactly what he should do. He'd gotten his sister back. He didn't have a dog in this fight, not anymore. But the tidal wave of anger Clayton Wilson and the rest had sparked in him was threatening to drown him. He thought back to Richard Stanton's final words. This wouldn't end with the death of these five men. It would go on.

He didn't have a reason to be back in Toronto. He should have just disappeared and been glad he had his sister back. But the sequence of events he'd initiated—forcing the handler in Toronto to flee, then heading to New York to kill all members of the Commission—had emboldened him.

But he wasn't doing it for money. So what did it matter to him if a hit was planned in Toronto that night, or the next day, or whenever?

Was it simply that he wanted retribution, in whatever form, to weaken, undermine, and ultimately destroy the organization that had made him? He was destroying his creator. Was that it? Anything they wanted to do, he had to stop. Was that really why he'd saved Mahoney and his family?

The more he thought about it, the more he wondered if there was something else at work. Maybe he wasn't irredeemably damaged. Maybe deep within him, within his soul, within his very being, he was beginning to sense more human qualities. He wasn't wired the same way as everyone else. He knew that. But was it possible there was a small part of him that had feelings?

It was as if he was being pulled toward his fate by mysterious forces. Maybe to his doom. Nathan looked again at the photos on the phone. He thought of Mahoney trying to piece together the whole story. His mind flashed to images of the journalist and his family gasping for breath after he'd dragged them out of the smoke-filled basement of the house in East Hampton.

What did it matter to him? Mahoney's life was his own. Then he began to consider other questions.

What if Mahoney had this information about the Chechens? What would he do with it? Apart from giving him a potentially great lead in the story, maybe another piece of the jigsaw, it would also result in the images being forwarded to the Feds. The cops in Toronto. Homeland Security.

And they could then take action, perhaps thwarting the assassination attempt that was almost certainly under way in the city at that moment.

Nathan checked the GPS location where the photos had been taken. Sixty miles north of Toronto. He made a mental note. Then he sent the photos to his iPhone. From there he sent them to Mahoney. Then he got up, dropping a ten-dollar tip on the table, and headed out onto the street.

Sixty-Five

Mahoney was sitting at his desk in the *Times* office, staring at the images Nathan had just sent. He saved them to Dropbox so there was a backup.

A few moments later, his cell phone rang.

"Did you get the photos?" Nathan asked.

Mahoney's heart skipped a beat. "I'm looking at them now. Who are they?"

"I've been told they're Chechens. They get the blame. So this is a false flag."

Mahoney looked at the faces. "How do you know?"

"That's what I was told by a guy in Toronto."

"How do I know this is for real?"

"You don't."

"Why are you sending me these pictures?"

"I'm assuming journalists have a moral responsibility to alert the authorities if they believe a terrorist operation might be under way."

"Do you have names?"

"No. And you need to get into protective custody. Now. Since I didn't neutralize you, I think someone else will."

"These two?"

"I don't think so. The operation today in Toronto, these two have been picked for it."

Mahoney wondered why Nathan was telling him all this. "You want me to disrupt this operation? Stop it?"

Nathan said nothing.

"Are you fucking with me?"

"What do you think?"

Mahoney leaned back in his seat and sighed. "No, I don't think you're fucking with me. Let's assume what you're saying is true. Remember that list you sent me?"

"Sure."

"There were no Canadians on the list."

"Maybe someone on the list is visiting Canada."

Mahoney said, "Then again, what if there's an updated list?"

"Perhaps."

"I still don't understand why you're doing this. You were hired to kill me."

"That's what *they* wanted me to do. But then they would've killed my sister too. And then ultimately me. The moment I killed you, they would have killed my sister."

Mahoney cleared his throat.

"You writing the story?"

"Working on it now."

"Do it. And then get safe. They're going to come for you, Mark."

Sixty-Six

Across the newsroom, Mahoney saw Caroline Ovitz, managing editor of news, the most senior person there with the executive editor out of the office. He picked up his iPad, approached her, and smiled.

"Hey, Mark," she said, catching his eye. "You look terrible."

"Thanks. If sleep deprivation were an Olympic sport, I'd win gold, trust me."

She laughed.

"Caroline, do you have a few minutes?"

"Now?"

"Yeah . . . Something pretty urgent has come up."

Ovitz nodded. "OK. Wasn't Mort overseeing something you were working on? An investigation?"

"Yes, he was. Spoke to him first thing. I'm working on it now."

Ovitz smiled. "Mort gave me an indication of what it was."

"He did? OK, that's fine."

Ovitz cocked her head and he followed her through the newsroom and into her huge office. He pulled up a seat as she sat down behind her desk. "Mort's been following this story with interest. And he confided in me a little while back. So it's him, me, and the publisher that know."

"Not another soul?"

Ovitz nodded. "Not another soul."

Mahoney sighed.

"Talk to me. What's going on?"

"I just got a call. From a guy in Toronto."

Ovitz leaned back in her seat.

"It was the guy who sent me the list. The original list."

"The assassin?"

"Yeah."

"Fuck."

"I had a drink with him in New York."

"Are you kidding me?" she said. "Mort didn't tell me that."

"There are so many things, it's hard to keep up. Anyway, he sent me some photos."

Ovitz arched her eyebrows. "The guy everyone thought was dead? Nathan Stone, right?"

"Right." Mahoney opened up the message with the photographs. He handed the iPad to Ovitz.

"What is this?"

"According to my assassin friend, these are two Chechens. And he says they've been tasked with some kind of terrorist act in Toronto later today."

Ovitz stared at the photos. "On whose orders?"

"I don't know the ins and outs. He passed these on hoping I'll alert the authorities."

"What if it's fake?"

"What if it's not?"

Ovitz sighed. "Yeah."

"I think this is linked to the facility. The Canadian facility."

"The secret facility?"

"Yeah, that one."

"And this comes from Nathan Stone?"

Mahoney nodded. "Yeah, he used the words *false flag*."

"Meaning throwing the blame at someone else during a war?"

"Pretty much. So, in this case, having these Chechens carry out the operation, or just being blamed for it. And the finger would be pointed at Islamists. But the people pulling the strings aren't Islamists. They want to neutralize someone who doesn't fit in with their worldview."

"We're talking about Clayton Wilson and his gang?"

Mahoney nodded.

"But they're dead."

"Yeah. But Nathan believes that's not the end of it. Not by a long shot."

"We'll have to call it in."

Mahoney cleared his throat as a wave of anxiety washed over him. "That's what I was thinking."

Ovitz picked up the phone.

"Who're you calling?"

"Mort. Then the Feds."

Sixty-Seven

Nathan stole a car with a modified keyless fob the security guy had packed in the backpack. He drove away from the parking garage and entered the GPS coordinates of the spot where the photos of the Chechens had been taken. It was sixty miles north of Toronto.

Just over an hour later, he pulled up. He could see it in the distance.

Out on the lake was a massive island covered in trees, shrubs, and bushes. Was this the place he'd been brought to?

Nathan trained his binoculars on it. Just over eight hundred yards away, a jetty, a few boats. He saw cameras.

He rechecked the GPS from the security guy's phone. This was it.

Nathan stared through the binoculars at the facility. Steel-and-concrete modernist structures were visible amid the forest and woodland. He moved the field of view and saw a sign for an electric fence. He focused and refocused and saw the ten-foot-high steel barrier virtually overgrown with ferns, trees.

He scanned the rest of the island, back to the jetty and beyond. He saw gas tanks to fuel the boats. But twenty yards from that, he also spotted what looked like a huge generator, enclosed by another electric fence.

A few minutes later, a small plane emerged and flew out and above the treetops on the island. It looked like a Gulfstream. He watched it disappear high through the clouds.

Nathan put down the binoculars and dialed Mahoney. The phone rang six times before it was picked up.

"Who's this?" The journalist sounded strained.

"You know who."

"Nathan . . . I was just talking about you."

"Taking about me to who?"

"My boss. About running the story. But also about what you were telling me about Toronto. The Chechens."

"What are you doing about it?"

"My boss spoke to the Feds and we've sent the photos to them. They've sent them to the Canadians."

"Excellent. That's a start."

"Where are you? Still in Toronto?"

"I'm watching the facility."

"You found it?"

"It's an island in the middle of a goddamn lake. Covered in trees and God knows what. That's where they must have taken me when they flew me in, I'm convinced."

"How do you know for sure?"

"I just saw a plane take off. I can't see the airfield. But it's there somewhere."

"Where exactly is this?"

Nathan gave him the GPS coordinates. "Listen, pass on the coordinates too. Very important. Lake Simcoe. North of Toronto."

A heavy sigh down the line.

"You sound stressed."

"Yeah . . . a bit."

"You're running out of time. You need to get the Feds to pick you up and get you to safety. It won't end well, if I know these people."

"I should be done soon."

"No further information about possible targets?"

"We're trying to find out if there are any high-profile public events in Toronto, but there's nothing of note."

"I don't think it's necessarily a high-profile event. But it would have to be in public."

"So maybe a routine engagement for a high-profile person."

"Maybe."

"I'll make a few inquiries."

"Get the GPS coordinates to the Feds to pass on. This is the second facility, I have no doubt."

Mahoney went quiet.

"What are you thinking?" Nathan asked.

"I'm just wondering if we could get a chopper up there, get some aerial footage of the facility."

Nathan looked toward the island.

"What are you going to do, Nathan?"

"I'll see you around."

Nathan ended the call. He pulled out the parts of the Barrett, locked and loaded the magazine. Flicked off the safety. Then he watched and waited for the right moment.

Sixty-Eight

Berenger was staring at the big screens of live feeds from outside the Toronto hospital. He checked his watch and the "official" clock up on the wall. "We're three and counting down, folks," he said. "Two hours and fifty-six minutes from now!"

Operation director Malcolm Strutt was standing, arms crossed, watching the feeds. He adjusted the Bluetooth microphone in his ear. "OK, Melissa, can you pan around three-sixty degrees so we get a full idea of what we've got?"

The screens showed TV news crews setting up. Cables being unfurled, laptops being checked, journalists drinking coffee in the backs of TV vans. "That's great," he said. "So you're in prime position?"

"Right up in front with my Canadian friends."

"OK, let's keep the chat to the bare minimum," Strutt said.

"Got it."

"So let's keep this live. Satellite feed coming through perfect."

"Good to hear."

Strutt took off his headset.

"How are we looking?" Berenger asked.

"Toronto? We're set. The two Chechens are now en route. Be touching down in a matter of minutes."

"What about New York? What about Mahoney?"

Strutt nodded and put his headset back on. "Pull up the feed from Chelsea, guys."

A few moments later, on the main screen they saw the line-of-sight view of Mark Mahoney's apartment from a nearby surveillance vehicle. The camera zoomed in on the front door of the elegant townhouse.

Strutt cleared his throat. "Thanks. Stay focused."

The screen returned to the live feed in Toronto. Journalists laughing, drinking coffee, some TV reporters adjusting their shirts, jackets.

Berenger smiled. "So we're good for Toronto and New York."

"Damn straight."

Berenger's gaze was drawn to the live feed from Toronto. "Malcolm, the guy who just entered the shot, short black hair, mauve tie."

"Yeah?"

"He looks familiar."

"Caleb McNeill. Well-known spin doctor for the Canadian prime minister."

Berenger felt his stomach knot.

Strutt looked at him. "How you feeling?"

"Counting down the minutes."

Strutt grinned. "Let's get this done. And let's get it over the line."

Sixty-Nine

Nathan was lying on his belly in the woods adjacent to the lake, the butt of the rifle pressed hard against the soft part of his right shoulder. His gaze was drawn to a speck on the horizon. The familiar sound of the Gulfstream's engines. Closer and closer it flew. It banked sharply over the lake as it came in low for its final approach.

He held his breath. He wondered if this was the same plane that had taken off thirty minutes earlier. It would be a short journey to and from Toronto.

Nathan took aim. He felt his finger on the cold metal trigger. Then he squeezed. The red tracer ammo exploded out of the rifle and headed straight for the Gulfstream. The smell of cordite. A split second later, a deafening noise from the shot.

He watched as the red tracer ripped into the plane as if in slow motion. The plane banked heavily, as if about to crash into the lake. But it spun as it caught fire, a gaping hole in the fuselage, before crashing straight into the huge gas tanks adjacent to the facility.

A massive fireball erupted and the flames licked the sky, setting off multiple explosions as other tanks caught, tearing into the ashen Canadian sky. The firestorm quickly spread to the trees covering the huge island.

Nathan once again pressed the butt of the rifle hard against his right shoulder. He lined up the sights, the steel monstrosity of the facility glinting in the pale sun, peeking through the clouds.

He took aim. And squeezed.

Seventy

The building rocked and the security screens showed the flames devouring the screen of trees shielding the facility as Berenger watched, aghast. The sound of security alarms rang out, and red emergency lights flashed.

"What the fuck is this, Malcolm? Where the hell did this come from?"

Strutt had his hands on his hips, face flushed, eyes fixed on the screen. "Talk to me, Aaron!" he shouted into his Bluetooth headset.

The head of security came on the line. "Tracer fire, direct hit on upper Level Four. Plane is down. I repeat, the plane is obliterated."

"Fuck!" Strutt said. "Where is this coming from?"

"We have a chopper about to take off, but we believe it came from due east, directly across from the headland. Incendiary tracer."

Berenger stood up and shook his head. "This is not what we need right now! Fix it, Aaron! Now!"

The screens showed live footage on the shore.

"Go right in as tight as you can!" Strutt bellowed.

A few taps on a laptop and the footage was magnified one hundred times. It showed a man crouched in the woods, aiming a rifle at them. Suddenly, a tracer came tearing toward them on the screen, followed by another explosion outside.

Berenger shouted, "Close-up of the face!"

The footage zoomed in.

"Crop it tight!"

The grainy footage was frozen. The reconfigured face of the Plastic Man, as they had dubbed him.

Strutt took a step toward the screen. "Stone!" He turned to face Berenger. "Tell me that's not Nathan Stone!"

Berenger stared, transfixed. The killer he knew so well was staring back at him. He felt a rage within him ready to explode. "Fuck!"

Strutt shouted, "Aaron, has the chopper taken off?"

"Just taking off," the voice boomed over the speakers. "What's the order? I need authorization."

Berenger said, "Kill Nathan Stone! I repeat, kill Nathan Stone! This is a Code Four. I repeat, this is a Code Four."

"Copy that," Aaron said.

Up on the screens, the chopper's onboard cameras showed it headed for the headland.

"We got a fix," the pilot said. "Preparing to engage."

A second later, two red tracers streaked across the sky. The chopper was destroyed in a terrible inferno as Berenger and the rest of the team could only look on in horror.

Seventy-One

Nathan watched as the chopper caught fire and crashed into the icy waters of the lake. He thought he saw a survivor in the water. He clipped in a new magazine and stared through the sights at the wooded areas on the island not yet alight. He fired four separate shots. Flames erupted as the other forested sections caught fire, winds fanning the flames, setting off blazes across the whole island.

He scanned the area. Focused on the boats moored on the jetty. Then he fired three more shots. The boats exploded as the fuel tanks ignited.

Nathan took one long last look, snapped some cell phone photos, and sent them over to Mahoney.

A few seconds later, his phone rang.

"Nathan?"

"Yeah?"

"Is this . . . is this the facility?"

"I believe so."

"Are you kidding me? How did you do that? Nathan . . . you can't be doing shit like this."

"It is what it is."

"How did you do all that? What the hell is happening?"

"I'm taking the fight to them. This wasn't my fight. But it is now."

"So is it over?"

"I have no idea."

"Nathan, I'm looking at pictures of fires across an island in a lake. How did this happen?"

"Incendiary ammo."

"What's that?"

"Tracer. Heavy-duty stuff in the wrong hands. Brought down a chopper they sent out and a Gulfstream that was trying to land."

Mahoney was silent as he processed everything Nathan was telling him. "Jesus . . . that's . . . a lot to take in. Are you there now?"

"I'm on the move very soon."

"Nathan, I've passed on the GPS location you gave me earlier."

"Pass on the photos too. The Canadians need to get their asses up here and ask what exactly is on that island."

"I've just sent the photos to the Feds."

Nathan's gaze was on the facility.

"Are you still there, Nathan?"

"Yeah."

"Nathan, what the hell? I'm . . . I don't know . . . I'm sort of struggling to wrap my head around everything, there's so much going on."

Nathan sensed Mahoney was slightly more hesitant, as if not wanting to reveal exactly what he knew. "You know something, don't you? Something else. You're not telling me everything."

Mahoney said nothing.

"OK, so let's work this back. I sent you photos of the facility. I've identified its location. I've seriously disrupted this facility. And probably pissed them off more than a little bit. And I've shared all of this with you, Mark. Is that correct?"

"Nathan, I know what you're getting at. But can I be honest? It scares me to even talk to you."

Nathan didn't answer.

"This is unsettling stuff. I feel like I'm going nuts."

Nathan could see Mahoney was changing the direction of the conversation again. "Let's get back to my original point. I've shared what I know. And I'm sensing that you're not being quite so forthcoming."

A brief pause. "I passed on everything to the Feds."

Nathan detected a slightly colder tone in Mahoney's voice.

"They'll deal with this. And I'm told the Canadian intelligence service have been alerted as well."

Nathan allowed a silence to stretch between them.

"The information on the Chechens has been passed on too."

"What did the Feds say about that?" Nathan asked.

A sigh. "I don't want this to turn into a running commentary, Nathan. I think I've said enough."

"Why so reticent, Mark? Are the Feds listening in on this?"

"That's not how I operate, Nathan."

"So . . . we know something's going down in Toronto today. And the identities of the two Chechens. Incidentally, before I took the heavy-duty ammo to the facility, the Gulfstream took off and returned about half an hour later. That would give it more than enough time to head down to Toronto, drop off the operatives, and get back here. These people are in place or on their way."

"What about you, Nathan?"

"What about me?"

"What are *you* going to do? Is this over for you?"

"I'll find out soon enough."

Nathan ended the call. It was time to move.

Seventy-Two

Mahoney headed across the newsroom and was shown into Caroline Ovitz's office, where he was greeted by two men in suits. They identified themselves as FBI.

The younger of the two Feds was scrolling through the photos Mahoney had messaged to him a few minutes earlier. "Pull up a seat, Mark."

Mahoney did what he was told, his mind virtually in free fall at the new developments.

"Just so you know, we've alerted Ottawa, and they've sent several teams to locations across Toronto."

Mahoney nodded. "You know where this is going to happen, don't you?"

The young Fed said, "There are several scenarios we are exploring with our friends in Canadian intelligence. This is a fluid situation. I can't say any more than that at this stage."

"I know this will be far more than cross-border cooperation," Mahoney said. "We all know for a fact the FBI is allowed to operate in Canada."

"I can't get into too much detail, as I said. We are tasked with investigating and preventing acts of domestic and international terrorism. So within that remit, there is clearly scope for having agents on the ground working with international intelligence agencies and law enforcement."

"You get the pictures?"

The young Fed said, "Yeah. You seem to have gotten very friendly with this Nathan Stone character."

"I'm a journalist. You have to take the time to get to know people. Cultivate sources."

"He's an assassin. A trained killer. And he's responsible, we believe, for the deaths of at least five men in New York during a recent trip home."

Mahoney sighed. "Is this a formal FBI interrogation?"

"Mark, we have reason to believe you are at risk. We believe protective custody would be for the best."

"Do you think I'm at risk from Nathan?"

"I can't say . . . What I can say is that this investigation you're conducting, and the strands of criminality that are being revealed in it, coupled with the deaths of these five men in New York—very senior retired intelligence and military personnel—make it imperative that we take you to a place of safety."

"You believe I'm going to be killed?"

"Honestly?"

Mahoney nodded.

"It's a distinct possibility."

"By who?"

The young Fed didn't answer.

"Do you know what my investigation centers on?"

"We're aware of the broad-brush aspects of it."

"Let me be clear. I'm going to call it what it is. In front of you all. This is a deep-state operation. Plausible deniability. Meaning those within the military and intelligence structures are not linked. At least not formally."

"Mark, I can see how this whole thing, especially with the terrible incident involving your family, has taken its toll on you. And that's why we would strongly suggest you be taken to a secure location, with your family, to get you out of harm's way."

"I'll get out of harm's way. Eventually. But I need to finish this story. I need to see it through."

"Mark, if what you're telling us is true, then those behind this operation, if indeed it is an operation, might very well want to take you out of the picture."

"Do you have any evidence to confirm that?"

The older Fed leaned forward, his gaze fixed on Mahoney. "We don't have any specific evidence or information pointing at this. But from the sequence of events that has so far unfolded, and the fact that your own wife and children are now in protective custody, it makes sense for you to join them, at least until this is all over."

Mahoney sat silently as he thought over his decision.

"I think this will be your last chance to get out of harm's way," the older Fed said. "Your very last chance. And I hope you'll come with us."

Mahoney looked at Ovitz. "I've got to finish this story."

Ovitz nodded but didn't say anything.

The young Fed said, "Is that your final word?"

"Yeah . . . that's my final word."

Seventy-Three

Nathan drove south, heading back to Toronto, keen to put as many miles between him and the facility as possible. He stopped fifteen miles away, removed the SIM card and battery from his cell phone, and threw them into a trash can by the side of the road.

He got back in the car and didn't stop until he got to a parking garage in midtown Toronto. He left the car and headed to a nearby diner, where he sat in a booth in the corner and ordered a burger, fries, and a large Coke. He glanced over at the TV, showing an interview with a Toronto family raising funds for an orphanage in Africa. He ate his food quickly.

Doubts began to crowd his mind. Should he have just gone back to Florida and gotten on with his life? It would have been the rational thing to do. But he knew that, whatever he did, there was no way back for him now. He knew there would be consequences for his actions. He had laid waste to their operation and their infrastructure and exterminated the prime movers. And there would be a price to pay. A day of reckoning. Someday. Maybe not tomorrow. But somewhere down the line, when he least expected it, they would return. For vengeance. Payback. Retribution. Whatever you wanted to call it. Blood would be spilled. Of that he had no doubt.

The more he thought about it, the more he wondered why the fuck he hadn't just hightailed it down to Florida. Lain low. Checked into a new motel. Visited his sister. Money wasn't a problem. He had squirreled away significant sums of money he'd earned from the murky world he had inhabited for years.

He wondered if he'd ever be able to get back to where he was before he had gone rogue in Scotland. It had seemed at first that the new shadow world he inhabited would suit him well. But that hadn't turned out to be the case.

The more Nathan thought about it, the more he realized nothing would ever be the same again for him. He would be hunted until the day he died. Whether he liked it or not.

"You want a coffee, honey?" a waitress said.

"Yeah, black please."

The waitress poured him his fresh coffee as he gazed over her shoulder at the TV. She looked at the screen. "Oh, the goddamn traffic by the hospital was crazy because of that thing. Police and all sorts of delays. Nearly late for my shift."

Nathan stared at the screen, then fixed his gaze on the waitress. He checked out her name badge. "What's happening out by the hospital, Madge?"

"TV says it's a special visit."

"By?"

"The prime minister. Thanking the kids' hospital for looking after his daughter. She had heart problems."

Seventy-Four

Deshi Umarov was sitting in the back of a specially kitted-out ambulance nearing downtown Toronto, wearing a white doctor's coat, chewing on high-strength Captagon capsules. She felt her heart rate hiking up. The amphetamines were rousing her system. She was clenching her fist repeatedly. She was wired. She'd used the psychostimulant drug when she'd fought the Russians in Grozny years earlier. The jihadist drug of choice, they called it. And it was. They could stay awake, fight, focus, for days. It gave them even more courage.

She looked across at her brother. He wore scrubs and his eyes were closed. Reciting a verse from the Koran.

Deshi crunched into the drugs, swallowed two more capsules. Then she handed two to her brother, who knocked them back with a glass of water.

The closer they got, the more excited she became. Her heart fluttered for a few moments before adrenaline began to surge through her.

The drugs were already kicking in. She felt invincible. Euphoric even.

In her mind's eye, she saw the man she was going to kill. The method was brilliant. They'd thoroughly researched the target's medical history. And they'd found the chink in his armor.

He suffered from fits. Epilepsy. But this had never been shared with the public.

The people who'd hired her were mere infidels. But they had a shared interest in killing the man. Her interest was that he had talked about the threat of Wahhabism. About Islamic terrorism. And how he wanted to reset Canadian foreign policy. But he was also a major Western politician. All that made him a perfect choice for her and her brother. They despised the West.

And if an organization in the West was going to facilitate this jihad, they would work with them to achieve their mutual goals.

The money she was getting paid would allow her cousins to buy food and clothes and move to a bigger house in Chechnya. It would also allow money to be funneled back into the jihad against Russia. More attacks on Moscow. It was guaranteed.

Today, though, was her day. Her brother's day. They would finally be martyrs.

Her earpiece buzzed. "How're you feeling, Deshi?"

"I am at peace. I feel very honored to get the chance to slay this heretic."

"Cell phone in your pocket?"

Deshi checked her jacket pocket. "Yes. I have the phone."

"How did the practice go this morning?"

"It worked perfectly on the woman you provided. How is she?"

"Not too good."

Deshi smiled. "In what way is she not too good?"

"She's been hospitalized. She's giving cause for concern."

Deshi closed her eyes.

"It was a very good trial run. Tell me, do you have your black doctor's bag?"

"At my feet."

"Don't disappoint us, Deshi."

Deshi looked over at her brother, who was deep in prayer. "Trust me, he will die today."

Seventy-Five

Nathan pulled up at the second-highest level of a parking garage in downtown Toronto in a stolen RV. He reversed into the perfect position, switched off the engine, and drew all the curtains, giving him privacy. He picked up the backpack and climbed over the seats and into the back, crammed with camping gear. He unzipped the backpack and assembled the rifle, locked it, and loaded a fresh magazine. Then he fixed the telescopic sight he'd bought from a hunting shop, along with a tripod for accuracy.

He leaned forward and cracked open the rear window of the RV. He looked through the crosshairs. He had a line of sight to the back entrance of the Hospital for Sick Children, on Elizabeth Avenue, just over a block away.

A small crowd had assembled, cameras and TV crews waiting. A few cops, some in plain clothes, were milling around.

Nathan lay down flat, got himself comfortable using cushions and pillows and a duvet. He scanned the crowds. Good-natured faces. A few nurses. Some doctors. A few kids in wheelchairs.

He'd been told by the woman in the diner that the visit was imminent. Traffic was down to a crawl, since the cops had blocked off the road to allow easier access for the VIP.

The minutes dragged.

Nathan's nerves were twitching. He pressed his eye tighter to the sight, trying to identify anyone suspicious in the crowd. He wished he had face-recognition software in his armory. A few more people drifted into the crosshairs. The crowds were being held behind steel barriers.

It always amazed him how lax the security often was for major politicians. The only person who had that wraparound protection was the US president. The Secret Service invariably covered all the bases and then some. He wouldn't be allowed anywhere near. Layers of security. Layers of Secret Service personnel.

But this was different. Wide open.

The more he thought about it, the more he was tempted to call it in and say the PM was going to be killed on live TV.

But how would they do it?

He'd seen the sallow faces of the Chechens. But where were they at this moment? Were they mingling among these crowds? Were they waiting nearby? The decision to allow the Canadian PM so close to crowds of people who hadn't been vetted, searched, and checked was inexcusable.

He wondered if it was a feel-good PR opportunity, if it wasn't deemed to be a high-risk appearance. If so, it was foolish and complacent in the extreme.

Nathan spotted a bodyguard touching his earpiece. He scanned the periphery of the crowds.

A familiar face.

Nathan had the man in his crosshairs. "What the fuck?"

It was Mark Mahoney.

Seventy-Six

The ambulance dropped off Deshi two blocks from the hospital. Her heart rate was hiking up a notch every step she took toward her goal. She gripped the handle of the black leather medical bag as she strode toward the hospital. As she got nearer, she saw the crowd. Her brother had been dropped off a few minutes earlier a mile away. His job was to head to the hospital and await instructions.

Her earpiece crackled into life. "Deshi, an update on your brother." The voice of her handler. "He has ditched the white coat so he can blend in among the crowds. We now have a second target."

"Copy that," she said into the name badge on the lapel of her doctor's coat.

"We have someone he needs to take care of. So you will now handle stage one and stage two."

"Copy that."

"Do you understand what that entails?"

"Absolutely. Affirmative."

"Good."

"So, stage one. Are you clear?"

"Yes."

"Then on to stage two immediately."

"I've got this."

"Make sure you do."

Seventy-Seven

The crowds outside the hospital were beginning to swell. Nathan felt more agitated as he stared at Mahoney through the crosshairs. He was talking into his cell phone. Standing beside him was a photographer, probably from the *New York Times*, and flanking them were two Fed types.

Fuck.

Nathan began to scan the rest of the crowd. A few kids in wheelchairs near the front. He wondered what the hell Mahoney was doing there. It was dumb. After all that had happened. What was he thinking? Shit.

The more he thought about it, the more he wondered why the Feds hadn't dissuaded Mahoney from coming here. Why the hell hadn't they just taken him into protective custody, out of sight? As it was, Mahoney was putting himself directly in harm's way.

Nathan knew better than anyone that the operatives might very well discover he was there. He knew there'd be extra eyes and ears, electronic surveillance, in and around the hospital. They'd be scanning police channels.

Fuck.

Nathan observed the crowds dotted around. A lot of happy kids and parents and staff.

Slowly, in his peripheral vision, a trio of black SUVs turned into the road outside the hospital.

A terrible sense of foreboding washed over him.

Seventy-Eight

Deshi pulled out her cell phone as the prime minister's car approached. Her heart was now racing. The adrenaline rushed through her body. She felt wild. Focused. Suddenly clear of thought.

The sight of his expensive black leather shoes as he stepped out of the middle car. Bodyguards flanking him. The prime minister was only yards away, shaking hands. She watched as he kneeled down and spoke to a girl in a wheelchair. A girl not unlike his own daughter, who had been saved in the same hospital.

Her lines had been rehearsed. He was shaking hands with a nurse.

Deshi leaned forward. "Prime Minister, a photo for my daughter?"

The prime minister smiled, instinctive and natural. "Not a problem, Doctor."

Deshi held up her cell phone, and he put his arm around her as he smiled at the camera. She pressed the home button hard.

Blinding strobe lights flashed on the screen.

He loosened his grip and fell backward, hitting his head. Then he broke into a violent epileptic fit.

Screams erupted as his handlers moved in.

"I've got this," she said.

Deshi kneeled down and jabbed the EpiPen into the prime minister's neck. His eyes were shut as he began to foam at the mouth. Then he stopped breathing.

Seventy-Nine

Nathan recognized the woman in the white coat through the crosshairs. It was the Chechen. She was surrounded. She appeared to be helping the fallen PM. But he knew that was bullshit.

For a split second, the Chechen woman was isolated as pandemonium and chaos gripped the crowds, people running in all directions.

He felt the cold metal trigger. He squeezed. A shot rang out. The Chechen woman collapsed, bullet in the neck.

Everyone turned and pointed in his direction.

Nathan stayed put. Panic reigned as people ran in all directions. Then he saw the second Chechen on the periphery, walking calmly toward Mahoney. The journalist was on his phone, finger in ear.

Police were running in Nathan's direction.

Nathan ignored them. He blocked it all out. He focused on the second Chechen. But there were people in the way of his shot, running in terror.

Fuck.

He waited for a split second. Then a gap appeared.

Suddenly, the Chechen was within ten yards of Mahoney.

Nathan watched as the man in the white coat pulled out a gun. Nathan aimed and pulled the trigger. The jihadist fell to the ground.

Other cops in the crowd threw themselves on top of Mahoney as mayhem escalated.

Nathan quickly dismantled the rifle. He threw the parts into the backpack and drove off, dropping it in a trash can fifty yards away. He headed down the winding parking garage and aimed for street level just as some cops and plainclothes security headed up the stairwell.

A short while later, Nathan was on the freeway. He drove south. He ditched the RV in a small town near the border. Hitched a ride on a truck to the border crossing.

His fake ID and passport were inspected.

He was waved through and was soon on his way to Buffalo.

There, Nathan abandoned his ride and headed to the bus station. Caught a Greyhound to New York, where he got a room at a seedy motel, locked his door, lay down on the bed, and closed his eyes.

Eighty

Forty-eight hours later, Nathan arrived at the psychiatric hospital near the Everglades. He was shown to a special visitors' room, where his sister was patiently waiting for him, smiling, hands folded.

"Oh my God, thank you so much for coming, Nathan," she said.

"I promised, didn't I?"

Her eyes were sparkling. She was loaded on lithium and all manner of antipsychotic medication.

Nathan hugged her tight. "I told you I'd be back. I'll never leave you. You know that."

She sat down and stared at him, arms folded.

"I'm sorry I couldn't tell you in advance about my friends looking after you for a while."

"They were really sweet. And you know the great thing? They must've known how much I like ice cream, because they made sure there was plenty!"

Nathan looked at his sister. "Did they give you your medication there?"

"They did, so my mood was super."

"Do you know where my friends took you to look after you?"

"It was pretty cold, I know that."

Nathan took a few moments to contemplate that. "And my friends, they were all American, right?"

"Yes."

"Yeah, I especially liked the doctor."

"You met a doctor. Did the doctor talk to you a lot?"

"Oh yeah, he was real nice. You must've known him real well because he knew all about how we grew up in New York, but he hadn't seen you for a while. And he was superinterested to know everything about you. Said he'd met you recently. But he also seemed to know a lot about me too."

"He did?"

His sister looked off into the distance, as if for inspiration. "Yeah, he knew what medication I was on, the dosage, and he said he'd met you the day before. Said you were a really interesting person. But he also said he'd like to get to know me better. Wasn't that nice?"

"You wanna go back a sentence or two? He said he'd met me the day before?"

His sister was smiling and singing an old show tune.

"Did he have a name?"

"His name was Mark. Dr. Mark."

"Did Dr. Mark have a last name?"

"I think it was Berenger . . . Yeah, Dr. Mark Berenger. How long have you known him, Nathan?"

So it was true. Berenger was now embedded within the facility. He had a greater role than Nathan had imagined in the operation. He wasn't just a psychologist talking face-to-face to determine whether Nathan was fit to carry out the job.

Berenger was aware of his sister. Had even spoken with her.

And that had to mean his sister had been held at the Canadian facility. It made sense. It was secure. A controlled environment. Out of sight. And out of mind.

As of now, Nathan was just glad his sister was safe and sound and back in the psychiatric hospital she called home. But how long would that last? Would she be disappeared for a second time? Maybe next time she wouldn't come back. She'd be neutralized as a punishment. His punishment.

Helen closed her eyes and began to rock back and forth. "Don't ever leave me, Nathan. Promise me."

"Trust me, I'll never leave you."

She opened her eyes, tears streaming down her face. "Will you always be here for me?"

Nathan reached over and touched the back of her hand. It was warm. Just as he remembered it all those years ago on the Bowery. "You were there for me. And I'm here for you. That's the way it works, right? Together. Always."

Epilogue

Three months later, as night fell, Nathan was driving on the Overseas Highway through the Florida Keys. His cell phone rang.

"Nathan, are you there?" It was his sister.

"Of course I'm here. I'm always here. Whenever you need me. Did you get the birthday cake I sent you?"

"Nathan, that was so nice."

"Don't eat too much, though, not at once. You don't want to get sick."

"Nathan, thank you so much for the cell phone. The nurses say I can use it with their permission."

"That's perfectly fine and reasonable. It means if you want to call me, or talk to me, I'll be here. So, you ready for bed?"

"Almost. I'm so lucky. I also got flowers."

Nathan wondered if he'd heard right. "Flowers? Who sent you flowers?"

"They didn't say. There's a note with it."

"What does it say?"

"It says . . . 'Happy birthday, Helen. Pass on my regards to Nathan. Tell him to give me a call.'"

Nathan felt his stomach tighten. He sensed something was wrong. No one other than Nathan cared about his sister or visited her. Ever.

"Did they give a number?"

"Sure." Helen repeated the number slowly.

Nathan made a mental note and repeated it back to her.

"Is that one of those friends of yours maybe, the ones I stayed with?"

"Yeah, maybe."

"They were so nice."

"Helen, why don't I call you tomorrow, maybe about ten o'clock? What do you say?"

"That would be great, Nathan. Tell your friend the flowers are beautiful."

"Will do, Helen," he said. "Night, night."

Nathan ended the call. He pondered whether to call there and then. Nearby, herons took flight in the near-black sky. He dialed the number. It rang five times before someone answered.

An electronically distorted voice said, "Check out Fox News, Stone."

Then the call disconnected.

Nathan's heart hammered in his chest. He pulled off the highway in the Lower Keys and went to a tiny bar. He bought a cold beer and asked them to turn on Fox News.

"And the breaking news tonight is that a man, thought to be *New York Times* journalist Mark Mahoney, has been found dead at his apartment in the Chelsea neighborhood of Manhattan. It is believed the award-winning writer had a heart attack. There are no suspicious circumstances. Friends close to the family say they are devastated at losing Mark at such a young age. The editor of the *New York Times* described him as an exemplary old-school journalist."

Nathan stared at the TV. It showed pictures of the Mahoney family smiling on a vacation to Disneyland.

Nathan drank the beer in one swig.

The bartender said, "When it's your time, it's your time."

Nathan nodded and paid for his beer, headed out to his car, got back on the highway, and headed south.

His cell phone rang.

The electronically distorted voice said, "Sad news."

Nathan said nothing.

"Did you think it was over, Stone?"

Nathan continued in silence.

"You see, Stone, this isn't personal for us. It's business."

"What do you want?"

"I just wanted you to know that you should've killed him when we asked you to."

Nathan felt a dark anger welling up in him.

"Oh, and we finally managed to access Mark's encrypted files. But apparently the Justice Department seized all records associated with three phone lines, including Mahoney's and those of two other senior members of the paper. The Feds and the NSA have also visited the paper three times in the last month. And they have court orders prohibiting the paper from publishing anything about what they know. Espionage Act, or so I'm told. If that's not enough, they accessed all the encrypted files on the *New York Times*'s cloud servers. They're citing national security. So no journalist will be able to access this information now or ever."

Nathan said nothing.

"I'm hearing that those encrypted files will be bleached pretty soon. Wiped clean. Accidental of course. So, just to let you know, we don't exist, none of this exists, everything that happened didn't happen . . . All that work has disappeared."

"So why are you telling me this?"

"We're coming for you next. We'll decide the time and place. Take care, Stone."

The line went dead.

Acknowledgments

I would like to thank my editor, Jack Butler, Jane Snelgrove, and everyone at Amazon Publishing for their enthusiasm, hard work, and belief in the new American Ghost thriller series. I would also like to thank my loyal readers. I'd also like to thank Faith Black Ross for her terrific work on this book. Special thanks to my agent, Mark Gottlieb, of Trident Media Group, in New York.

Last but by no means least, my family and friends for their encouragement and support. None more so than my wife, Susan.

About the Author

J. B. Turner is a former journalist and the author of the Jon Reznick series of conspiracy action thrillers (*Hard Road, Hard Kill, Hard Wired, Hard Way,* and *Hard Fall*), as well as the Deborah Jones political thrillers (*Miami Requiem* and *Dark Waters*). He loves music, from Beethoven to the Beatles, and watching good films, from *Manhattan* to *The Deer Hunter*. He has a keen interest in geopolitics. He lives in Scotland with his wife and two children.

37975263R00195

Printed in Great Britain
by Amazon